TILL DEATH DO US PURL

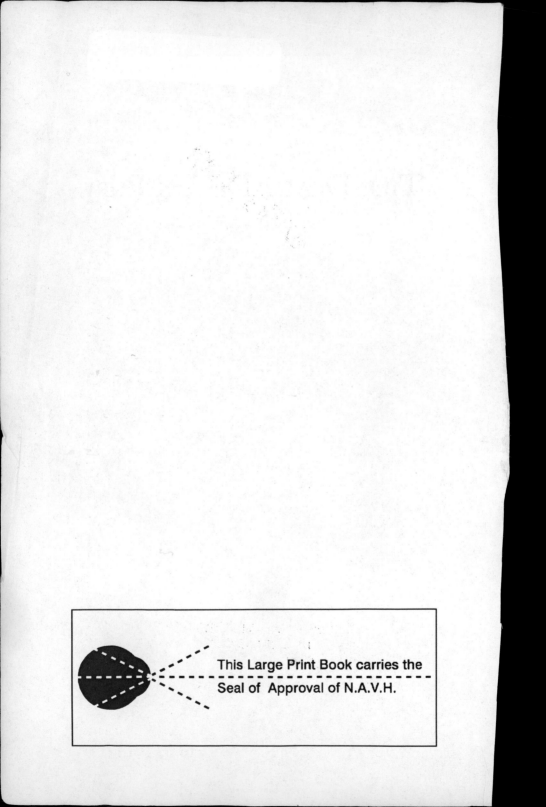

A BLACK SHEEP KNITTING MYSTERY

TILL DEATH DO US PURL

ANNE CANADEO

KENNEBEC LARGE PRINT
A part of Gale, Cengage Learning

GALE
CENGAGE Learning·

Detroit • New York • San Francisco • New Haven, Conn • Waterville, Maine • London

GALE
CENGAGE Learning®

LIBRARY OF CONGRESS CATALOGING-IN-PUBLICATION DATA

Canadeo, Anne, 1955–
    Till death do us purl / by Anne Canadeo.
      pages ; cm. — (Kennebec Large Print superior collection)
    (A black sheep knitting mystery)
    ISBN 978-1-4104-5040-1 (softcover) — ISBN 1-4104-5040-6 (softcover) 1. Knitters (Persons)—Fiction. 2. Large type books. I. Title.
    PS3553.A489115T55 2012b
    8137'.54—dc23   2012017085

Published in 2012 by arrangement with Gallery Books, a division of Simon & Schuster, Inc.

Printed in the United States of America
1 2 3 4 5   16 15 14 13 12

FD200

MEET THE BLACK SHEEP KNITTERS

Maggie Messina, owner of the Black Sheep Knitting Shop, is a retired high school art teacher who runs her little slice of knitters' paradise with the kind of vibrant energy that leaves her friends dazzled! From novice to pro, knitters come to Maggie as much for her up-to-the-minute offerings like organic wool as for her encouragement and friendship. And Maggie's got a deft touch when it comes to unraveling mysteries, too.

Lucy Binger left Boston when her marriage ended, and found herself shifting gears to run her graphic design business from the coastal cottage she and her sister inherited. After big-city living, she now finds contentment on a front porch in tiny Plum Harbor, knitting with her closest friends.

Dana Haeger is a psychologist with a busy

local practice. A polished professional with a quick wit, she slips out to Maggie's shop whenever her schedule allows — after all, knitting is the best form of therapy!

Suzanne Cavanaugh is a typical working supermom — a realtor with a million demands on her time, from coaching soccer to showing houses to attending the PTA. But she carves out a little "me" time with the Black Sheep Knitters.

Phoebe Meyers, a college student complete with magenta highlights and a nose stud, lives in the apartment above Maggie's shop. She's Maggie's indispensable helper (when she's not in class) — and part of the new generation of young knitters.

To my daughter, Katherine,
with all my love.
You are a wonder to me every day.

A mouse does not rely on just one hole.
— TITUS MACCIUS PLAUTUS

If love is the glue that holds the world together, guilt must be the staples.
— ANONYMOUS

CHAPTER ONE

"Now that you're all here, I have a confession to make." Maggie stood at the counter in the middle of the shop, sorting a pile of knitting needles by size order. She was carefully avoiding everyone's gaze, Lucy noticed.

Lucy and her friends were settled in their usual places at the long oak table nearby. They could always be found together on Thursday night and, most often, in the rear room of the Black Sheep Knitting Shop. Now all four of them — Lucy, Suzanne, Dana, and Phoebe — hit the pause button on their needles and conversations.

Suzanne looked alarmed. "Please don't tell us you didn't make dinner. I've been running all day on an expired yogurt and half a chocolate doughnut."

"I meant a small confession. That would be a major one. There's plenty to eat. I've invited Nora and Rebecca Bailey to join us. Nora called a little while ago to see if the shop was open late. She has a real emergency."

One that somehow involved needles and yarn, Lucy assumed. Maggie was the official EFT — emergency fiber technician — in town. She had even been known to make house calls.

"She sounded desperate, so I said they could just come over. I hope you don't mind." Maggie stored the needles and walked over to join them, though she didn't sit down.

"Very compassionate to see a patient after hours." Dana approved in teasing tone. With a PhD in psychology, Dana actually did hold the title of doctor, though she only used it for her practice. And when she wanted to pull social rank a bit.

Lucy had no objection, either. Nora Bailey and her daughter, Rebecca, were very familiar faces, always stopping by the shop to pick up yarn or take classes, or consult with Maggie about knitting issues. Nora and Maggie had grown up in Plum Harbor together and went way back.

"Rebecca's getting married soon, right? Isn't she knitting her own gown?" Lucy admired that kind of courage. The same way she admired people who went hang gliding or bungee jumping.

Not a project she'd ever attempt. Not that anyone was breaking a leg to propose to her. But that was another story.

"Yes, Rebecca's knitting her gown and Nora is making shrugs for the bridesmaids and a flower girl." Maggie had strolled over to the antique server and laid out some silverware next to a pile of linen napkins and a stack of plates.

"When I was about to get married, I was so insane, I couldn't have knit a coaster," Suzanne said, "no less an entire wedding dress."

"Maybe it's a distraction for her, a way to displace her anxiety," Dana offered. "Planning a wedding and launching off on a whole new stage in life just about tops the list of high-stress milestones."

"A distraction is having your nails done. Or trying out hairdos that work with your veil. Not making the dress you are going to wear on the biggest day of your life — when you should be looking your absolute, red-carpet best."

"Good point, Suzanne," Maggie agreed. "Which is why you all might feel some sympathy when I tell you that Rebecca's fiancé has suddenly announced they have to move up the wedding date. They were going to be married in May. But now the date is

13

two weeks away."

Dana had picked up her knitting again and examined her work. "Two weeks? Why is that?"

"I'm not sure. She didn't have time to explain. Something to do with his work. The bottom line seems to be, if they don't get married now, they'll have to put the wedding off for months. Neither of them wants to do that. They even talked about running off to a justice of the peace. But Nora knows Rebecca would be very unhappy with that plan."

"She's probably crushed at having that long white runner yanked out from under her at the last minute like this," Suzanne said, sympathizing. "She's probably frantic."

"Rebecca wasn't thrilled. But she does seem . . . resigned. She's a very levelheaded young woman." High praise, coming from Maggie, Lucy knew. "Very centered and even-tempered," Maggie continued. "She teaches grade school and is quite organized. But even with this major snag, she won't give up on making the gown. She's already put a lot of time into it. It would be an awful shame to see all that beautiful work go to waste."

"A terrible waste." Dana looked at Maggie over the edge of her stylish reading glasses. "So let me guess, Nora and Rebecca need some help finishing all these projects in time for the accelerated wedding date and you volunteered us?"

Maggie was trying hard not to look guilty as charged. But Dana had her cornered. "I merely said that they could come here tonight and I'd advise on the gown . . . and they could ask you. I didn't make any promises.

"But you had a pretty good feeling we'd agree, didn't you?" Lucy prodded.

Maggie couldn't help smiling for real now. "Does that mean you'll do it?"

Lucy and her friends exchanged glances.

Before anyone answered, Maggie added, "I thought maybe you could each make a bridesmaid's shrug. Phoebe could make one for the flower girl. It's a very simple pattern. I'm going to work with Rebecca on the gown."

It sounded as if Maggie had it all figured out and Lucy could see no reason to refuse. "Okay, I'm in. I'm sort of in the middle of three different projects, so what's the difference if I start one more?"

"Same here," Phoebe agreed. "Of course, I'd rather be making matching socks for the bridesmaids. That would look so cool. But I guess I can do a tragically ordinary shrug if

15

that's what Rebecca really wants."

Matching socks on bridesmaids? That would be a first. Unique, whimsical socks were Phoebe's specialty. Lucy should have guessed Phoebe would factor them into wedding party accessories. She could hardly imagine the little Goth girl's own nuptial. The concept was mind-boggling.

Phoebe had a steady boyfriend, but marriage seemed light-years away for her. She was slowly but surely finishing college and working part-time in Maggie's shop. Her boyfriend, Josh, was working on becoming a rock star, which was a slow, and not-so-sure process. Especially when one considered his music.

"You can count me in, too," Dana said. "I'm all for helping Nora and Rebecca navigate this trying time."

Dana was a human knitting machine, once she got started. Lucy had no doubt Dana would be the first to finish any assignment and would probably help the rest of them catch up.

"Who could resist helping with a wedding? Just saying the word makes me feel all . . . smiley and mushy." Suzanne pinned Maggie with a stare. "You knew that would get us, didn't you?"

"I couldn't say for sure. I will admit, I was

hoping." Before Maggie could confess any more of her manipulations — well intended as they were — the front door of the shop opened and Nora and Rebecca entered.

"Hello, ladies. We're back here," Maggie called out. "I'm just about to serve dinner. We've been waiting for you."

Right on cue, Lucy thought. As if Maggie had stashed the mother and daughter on the front porch until she'd finished negotiating.

Greetings were exchanged as Nora and Rebecca found seats at the table. Phoebe left to help Maggie bring in the dinner they had prepared. The shop was on the first floor of a Victorian-era house turned into commercial space. Some basic equipment remained in the former kitchen, which now served as a storeroom.

"I hope we're not interrupting anything." Nora smiled politely as she took a seat between Dana and Suzanne. "Maggie said you wouldn't mind us crashing the party. But I know this is your special meeting night."

"We're happy you could join us," Dana replied quickly. "We're amazingly free of rules around here."

"Totally. We're like free-range knitting chickens or something," Phoebe chimed in.

17

Free-range knitting chickens? Everyone paused a moment to process the image. Lucy suddenly saw herself in a barnyard, pecking at bits of corn, knitting needles tucked beneath a feathery wing.

But it was true. They didn't have any rules, just a few comfortable habits that seemed to work well for them over the years. Opening their circle to Nora and Rebecca tonight didn't feel odd at all, they were such regulars around the shop.

Nora was in her early fifties, at most. Her smooth brown hair was cut to chin-length with long sweeping bangs. She was always carefully made up and her taste in clothing and jewelry tended toward conservative style and good quality. Small and trim, she was attractive, in a quiet, classy way, Lucy thought. Her blue eyes were her best feature, a trait that Rebecca had inherited.

Otherwise, Rebecca didn't look at all like her mother. She had very fair skin, pale blond hair that went past her shoulders and fine, cameo-like features. She never wore makeup, but really didn't need any. Rebecca was quite a bit taller than Nora, and just plain bigger all over. Her figure, a softly rounded hourglass was the ideal of some bygone era. She even dressed a bit retro, Lucy noticed, with her long hair clipped back and a ruffle trim peeking out from the edge of her hand-knit cardigan.

While so many young women were starving themselves to match some bony body type, Rebecca seemed quite comfortable with her generous silhouette. The large diamond solitaire on her finger seemed to support a radical theory — real women had curves and some men really liked them that way.

Weddings could make people crazy under any circumstances. Lucy, who had been married and divorced, knew that for a fact. But she could see why the unexpected crash deadline had thrown the bride and her mother into a tizzy. Rebecca was not a little slip of a thing who could be covered with a few rows of lace here and there.

How long did it normally take to knit a wedding gown, anyway? Lucy had no idea. Longer than two weeks, she was certain of that.

No wonder they'd called in Maggie and her reserves. She only hoped her dear friend's nimble fingers were up to the challenge.

Maggie and Phoebe soon returned with the food. The smell was tantalizing and reminded Lucy that she had skipped lunch.

"Here we are. Everything's nice and hot.

Chicken with black beans and yellow rice."

Maggie and Phoebe set out the serving dishes, the entrée, and rice, along with a green salad and some trimmings — cheddar cheese, avocado bits, and sour cream. The women rose and fixed their dishes, returning to the table to eat.

"This is delicious, Maggie. I'd love to get the recipe," Rebecca said as she took another bite.

"Rebecca's already a good cook. Lucky Jeremy," Nora reported. "Miles ahead of me when I was a bride. These days most young women look at cooking as more of a hobby than some required skill they need to run a household. A sign of progress, don't you think?"

"I want to marry a man who can cook for me," Phoebe announced. "I think that's progress."

"You're always ahead of the curve, Phoebe," Lucy noted.

"Sometimes, right off the grid," Maggie agreed. "Does Josh cook for you?" she asked curiously. Phoebe's boyfriend played bass guitar and sang for a band called the Big Fat Whining Babies. With all that musical talent, Lucy wondered if he had any in the kitchen, too.

Phoebe shrugged. "He makes really good

coffee . . . and he made this quesadilla once. It had a scrambled egg in it. And some lunch meat."

Maggie's eyes widened. "Case closed."

"Kevin cooks every once in a while," Suzanne said of her husband. "But he makes such a big deal out of it. You'd think he'd just discovered fire. He's like, 'Look at me. I'm cooking food! Isn't this amazing?' I don't expect a standing ovation when I put dinner on the table every night, know what I mean?"

Dana smiled. "Jack's the same way. It might take a few more generations of sharing that gender-specific task before men stop expecting applause."

"In other words, not in our lifetimes, ladies," Suzanne translated with a laugh. "Anyway, getting back to the wedding," she quickly shifted gears. "We hear that your plans have been bumped up, Rebecca. Two weeks from now, is that right?" Suzanne posed the question in her best TV talk show hostess voice.

"March 24, not this weekend, the weekend after."

Rebecca seemed surprisingly resigned to this accelerated schedule, as Maggie had mentioned. But she did seem the type who took life's many speed bumps in stride.

A character trait that would come in handy during married life, Lucy knew well. Her marriage to her college boyfriend had lasted almost seven years and she'd been divorced now for three.

While Rebecca had sailed serenely through the change in plans, Nora obviously had not. "We'd booked the Harbor House. Settled the menu, the flowers, everything. They were going to be married at that pretty stone church on the green." Nora's voice held a shaky note of longing. "We had to cancel everything."

"But Jeremy's father offered to have the entire party, the ceremony and reception," Rebecca quickly explained.

"They have a huge estate . . . and a fabulous house," Nora added.

"And we managed to find a really good caterer. Even at the last minute. The rest of it, the music and flowers and all that, was rearranged somehow. Jeremy's family really saved the day," Rebecca said.

"It's only fair," her mother added. "The plans were changed because of some business situation at his father's company. Some big deal going on in the spring with a new product Jeremy is working on. His father told him that if they didn't get married now, they would have to wait until the summer.

Or maybe even the fall. Neither of them liked that at all. They want to have a reasonably sized reception and a honeymoon."

"I really want to be married with my family and friends around me." Rebecca smiled at her mother. "And we didn't want to wait. The wedding is just one day, no matter how nice the party. The important part is starting a new life with the person you love, for the rest of your life, right?"

"How true." Maggie nodded. "The way some young women plan their weddings these days, you'd think the priority was just the opposite."

"What does Jeremy do for a living?" Suzanne asked.

"He's a scientist. The senior chemist at At-Las Technologies. His family owns the firm." Rebecca sounded proud. Rightfully so, Lucy thought. She'd heard of that company, one of the largest in the area.

It all made sense now. The groom was the crown prince of At-Las Technologies, raised in a beautiful castle on the harbor, where the couple would soon be married. No wonder Rebecca seemed so serene. She was marrying into a fortune.

All the more impressive that she insisted on making her own gown, when her fiancé could have afforded to buy her any one in the world.

Nora seemed to sense what Lucy and the others must be thinking after pegging her affluent, soon-to-be in-laws. "I told Rebecca we should just go to Boston or even New York and buy a gown and all the trimmings. But she has her heart set on knitting her own — and the shrugs for the bridal party. She still wants the wedding to have a personal touch, to be meaningful to her and Jeremy."

"I'm going to do this just one time in my life," Rebecca insisted. "I want it to be special. Anyone can go out and buy a dress in some wedding boutique." She paused and glanced at her mother. "I'm sorry . . . does that seem really crazy or unreasonable?"

"Not at all," Maggie quickly assured her. "I understand. I made my own wedding gown, too."

Lucy and the rest of their group all turned to look at Maggie. Obviously, none of them had ever heard that before. "You did? I don't think you ever mentioned it." Lucy glanced at her friends, just to be sure.

"Oh, I must have." By the way Maggie shrugged, Lucy could tell Maggie knew she'd never told them.

"I definitely would have remembered." Dana pinned Maggie with a look.

"I wasn't a very proficient knitter back then. Ambitious, I will say. I'll show you pictures sometime," she added. "It was sort of a hippie-girl, granny-gown style." Maggie motioned on her figure as she described it. "Quite in keeping with the Golden Age of Granola. The first Golden Age, I mean. Anyway, Bill and I were married in a farm meadow. I dragged that gown through some nasty stuff on my way to say my vows and back. It wasn't very well made and didn't wash well, either," she finally admitted. "Maybe that's why I'm eager to try again to do it right. I promise you my skills have improved considerably."

"You're the best, Maggie," Rebecca replied quickly. "I appreciate any help you can give me. I really want to do this." She glanced over at her mother. "I just feel bad for my poor mom. She's been so great about all these sudden changes with the wedding. I know it's been harder on her than me."

"How sweet," Suzanne cooed. "I wish my daughter would say something like that. She's in that horrid teenage stage right now. She even hates the way I breathe," she added with a laugh.

"Rebecca went through all that. I promise it will pass," Nora said. She reached over and patted her daughter's hand. "It all passed much too quickly. Before you know it, they're all grown up and you're planning a wedding day."

"With a few unexpected glitches," Rebecca added.

"Hey, that's what we're here for," Dana said. "Maggie already signed us on to help you."

"Really?" Nora looked as if she didn't quite believe it. "All of you?" she asked, gazing around.

"Absolutely. One for all and all for one. We're like the musketeers," Suzanne said.

"With knitting needles," Dana added.

"We're your basic knitting dream team," Phoebe said.

"We'll each make a bridesmaid shrug. Phoebe is going to make one for the flower girl," Lucy noted.

"If you show us the patterns tonight, we'll get started." Maggie told Nora. Lucy could tell that their fearless leader was pleased the knitting circle had come to the rescue.

Nora glanced around at the circle of women, her smile wide and incredulous. "I thought we'd have to give up on the bridal party and just focus on the gown at this point. Honestly, we appreciate the offer, but you don't have to go to all this trouble —"

"No buts about it," Suzanne said, interrupting. "Where Maggie knits, we follow."

"There's not nearly as much chitchat once I get them pointed in the right direction," Maggie said. "Okay, ladies. Let's clear away these dishes and get to work."

Once the table was cleared, Nora and Rebecca took out the patterns and pictures of the gown and shrugs. Then they showed the group their progress, which was alarmingly little, Lucy noticed.

The shrug was fairly simple, as Maggie had promised. It was styled with a three-quarter-length raglan sleeve. The long V-shaped opening trailed off into two long sections that tied above the waist.

The style was very forgiving for a knitter and flattering to almost any figure. And it wouldn't need personalized fitting on the various bridesmaids, Maggie pointed out. Luckily, for there was no time for that step.

Nora had brought enough yarn to get them all started. Phoebe made copies of the pattern and picture, and Maggie handed out the correct size needles to everyone. They all cast on at the same time, Maggie acting as if the NASCAR of knitting was about to take place.

"Okay, ladies . . . on your mark. Get set. Knit!"

Lucy knew she was only kidding, but it

was hard to ignore the four sets of needles suddenly clicking all around her. She struggled to keep her own pace and focus on her own knitting without looking over at her friends to check their progress. It was the best way to run any race, she knew, and just another way that knitting imitated life.

Rebecca and Nora had chosen a silky, extrafine yarn in a dusty rose color that immediately brought to mind rustling gowns, rose petals, and the opening chords of the wedding march.

The bridesmaids' gowns were off the shoulder and fairly bare, they'd told the group. Since the gowns had been chosen for spring weather, the matching sweaters were needed now just for warmth.

Lucy liked the style, which she knew would make her knitting easier and faster. It was funny how that worked. She often knit items for her family — her two nieces mainly, who lived in Concord and sent in their orders by e-mail. She rarely refused to fulfill their requests. But when she didn't share their enthusiasm for some zany hat or miniskirt, it was slow going.

The wedding gown was another story. A long, complicated story, Lucy thought as she listened to Rebecca and Maggie discuss the pattern and formulate a plan of attack.

Like a general in a battle tent, Maggie didn't seem the least bit dismayed as she compared the completed sections to Rebecca's picture and tried to figure out ways they could speed along the process. The material for the gown was a fine ecru lace that draped over a lining of the same shade satin. A local seamstress had made that part of the dress, which now served as a basic outline for the rest.

Maggie brought out a dressmaker's form from the storeroom and they slipped the satin lining over it, then pinned on the pieces of knitted lace Rebecca had so far completed. It wasn't much, Lucy noticed . . . and didn't look like much, either.

But Maggie had an amazing ability to visualize. Not just imagining the blank spaces filled in, but also redesigning the entire style. She was amazingly artistic, using her needles and fiber the way a painter used a brush and pallet.

"— so I'm wondering if we could just add a few inches here, we might skip this other layer entirely," Maggie suggested, making a light sketch on the photo of Rebecca's gown. "That will save a lot of time and it will still drape smoothly. It might even look better."

"That's a great idea. I didn't even think of

it." Rebecca looked over the dressmaker's form again and nodded. "I was about to start that section tonight."

"Good, let's figure out the adjustments." Maggie found a pencil and paper, then set to work with her gauge tool and calculations.

"I honestly didn't expect you all to help out like this." Nora sounded so grateful, she almost looked teary-eyed. "I hope you didn't feel pressured. I'd feel so bad about that. I have the rest of the yarn at home, so please don't go out and buy anything."

"Oh, we rarely resort to that." Dana glanced over her shoulder at Maggie. "There are a lot of perks to hanging around here. Believe me."

Lucy couldn't deny it. Membership in their knitting circle definitely had its privileges.

Nora laughed. "I'll bet. But I absolutely forbid Maggie to supply the yarn, too. I'll drop everything off here tomorrow and you can each take what you need. I guess that's the best way to handle it."

It was a good plan, they all agreed. The knitting group was usually in and out of the shop all week long, bringing Maggie their knitting messes or just dropping in for a break from real life. Lucy worked at home, running a graphic design business. She needed to get out of the house at least once a day, and have a real conversation — with someone other than her dog — just to save her sanity.

Once Rebecca and Maggie were finished restyling the gown and dividing up the work, Nora and Rebecca packed up and said their good-byes.

"I just want to thank you all again," Rebecca said as she packed up her knitting tote. "I can't tell you how much better I feel about my wedding now."

"Aw . . ." Suzanne practically gushed. "We're happy to help you, Rebecca. You're going to be such a beautiful bride. A real knockout."

"You'll have to send us plenty of pictures, for Maggie's bulletin board," Dana added. "We'll definitely want to show off our contributions."

"Never mind the bulletin board, I'd like to borrow the gown and put it in my window." Maggie seemed to be inspired on the spot, having one of her visions. "I can make a gorgeous wedding display. I've been looking for something special to perk up business this spring."

"Pictures . . . window displays. For goodness' sake, you're all invited to the wed-

31

ding," Nora replied quickly. "After bailing us out this way, it's the least we can do. You must come . . . Please?"

Nora's tone was firm. She didn't want to hear any dissent. Lucy didn't think the mild-mannered mother of the bride had it in her.

Maggie answered for all of them. "That's very gracious of you, Nora. I think we'd all love to see Rebecca walk down the aisle. Perhaps we could come just for the ceremony?"

The rest of the group quickly agreed. Lucy felt relieved. She wanted to see the ceremony, but felt awkward about sitting through an entire wedding reception for a couple she hardly knew. It was hard enough sometimes when you were family, she reflected with a wry smile.

The others all agreed that the compromise would work well for them, and the Baileys seemed satisfied.

"We'll be checking in soon with a progress report," Nora said to Maggie. "It will still be a push, but I will say I might get a good night's sleep for the first time in weeks."

"Don't worry. I promise the wedding will be wonderful," Maggie said. "The gown will be finished in time and everything will work out fine."

Lucy didn't know how Maggie could be sure about all of this. But at times, her friend had a tone of such authority. When Maggie said something, it always sounded so convincing.

The front door of the shop had barely closed behind Nora and Rebecca when Suzanne gave out another dramatic sigh.

"Don't you just love weddings? No wonder all those reality shows about bridal gowns and wedding planners are so popular."

"You don't really watch that stuff, do you?" Phoebe stared at her, bug-eyed. "Those shows are so lame. *Bride of Frankenstein,* is that the one you like?"

"Bridezillas," Suzanne corrected her. "Actually, my favorite is *Dream Dress,* if you must know. The perfect mindless entertainment when I need to unwind after a hard day not selling any real estate." She picked up the start of her shrug again and made a face at Phoebe.

"Rebecca is no bridezilla, that's for sure. If they had a show called . . . *Cool, Calm, and Collected Bride,* she'd be a shoo-in." Lucy counted the stitches in her last row, careful not to mess up the shrug pattern. She found the start of a project was the easiest time to make mistakes. "I watch *Dream*

Dress once in a while, too, Suzanne," Lucy added, offering some support. "We all have our guilty TV pleasures."

"Oh, I don't have any of those." Maggie laughed. "Well, maybe one or two. But I'm surprised to hear you admit to that one, Lucy. Any special reason you're brushing up on bridal fashions? Is there some news you'd like to share?"

Lucy felt her face get a little warm and focused on her knitting. She blushed so easily, she hated it.

With all this wedding talk, she knew her friends would get around to her relationship sooner or later. "Just some junk food for the brain, that's all."

"Don't play dumb with us," Suzanne said. "I was wondering the same thing."

Lucy smiled nervously, but didn't know what to say.

"Look, she's smiling, but she won't answer," Suzanne said to the others.

"That's because I don't have anything to say . . . I don't even know what you're talking about," she insisted.

"Of course you know," Suzanne insisted. "How long have you and Matt been dating now? At least a year."

That calculation was correct. But why did Suzanne make it sound like a very long time and from Lucy's perspective, it wasn't long at all?

"That's right. *Only* a year, I'd say," Lucy corrected her.

"Is everything all right? I thought things were going well," Maggie said with concern.

"Everything is fine. We get along perfectly. But we're definitely not talking about marriage. For goodness' sake, we're not even living together," she reminded them.

"That's debatable," Dana added. "I mean, you spend most nights of the week together now. You have keys to each other's houses. And a space in each other's closets. His dog even sleeps over and has his own set of bowls on your kitchen floor. Practically speaking, you might as well be sharing the same address," she concluded. "You're both just a bit in denial about it."

Dana had a clear, unemotional way of pointing out the elephant in the room. Lucy couldn't argue with her assessment.

"Yes, that's all true. But we've both been married before and Matt has barely caught his breath from his divorce. And there's Dara to consider," she added, mentioning Matt's eight-year-old daughter. "It's very different for us than it is for Rebecca. We're comfortable moving a little slower."

"If you moved any slower you guys would

be going backwards," Suzanne noted, flipping her rows of rose-colored knitting to the opposite side.

"So you don't want to get married again, is that it?" Phoebe asked.

"I wouldn't go that far. I can see how great it could be, with the right person. But I'm not in any rush. And neither is Matt. And that's just fine with me. Honestly."

Lucy felt her friends looking at her while she stared down at her knitting. No one commented for a moment and she took a breath, thinking they had finally let it drop and would get on to some new subject.

"You don't hear your biological clock ticking?" Suzanne said suddenly.

Lucy hated that expression. All she could picture was the sneering crocodile from *Peter Pan,* which had swallowed an alarm clock and continually hovered just below the surface of the water, waiting to get another taste of Captain Hook.

Tick-tock. The biological croc, she called him.

But she didn't dare try to explain her ticking croc, even to her good friends.

"Suzanne, please. Let's just leave Lucy's poor ovaries out of this," Maggie said, rescuing Lucy just in time. "It's a whole different ball game the second time, especially when there are children involved. I know what she means."

Maggie had lost her husband, Bill, several years ago. She'd left her job as a high school art teacher soon after and opened the knitting shop. A decision she believed had rescued her from a deep well of grief. But so far, her new life did not include a satisfying, long-term relationship. Though she did date from time to time.

Lucy wondered if that was because she hadn't met the right person yet and wasn't the type to settle for a mediocre romance. Or because Maggie feared risking her heart again. Or maybe she was just content to be on her own. If Maggie felt a lack, she never mentioned it.

"I'm fine with talking about weddings," Lucy insisted. "And I'm not worrying about getting married again, or having babies . . . or any agendas about me and Matt. Right now, we're just happily rolling along."

Her friends looked at her and then at one another. She felt as if they weren't buying her story but were willing to let the matter drop. For now at least.

"If you say so, Lucy," Maggie finally said. "Just don't give us two weeks' notice if you decide to knit your own wedding gown. That's all we ask."

Lucy had to laugh. "Fair enough."

When Lucy got home she found Matt waiting for her, stretched out on the couch in the TV room, watching a basketball game. The Boston Celtics, of course.

Matt sipped a beer and had obviously shared a bowl of popcorn with the dogs; a trail of crumbs on the rug led directly to her golden retriever mix, Tink, and Matt's chocolate Lab, Walley. The two were now sleeping peacefully at Matt's feet, curled up back to back, like a pair of very large, fuzzy slippers.

Taking in the domestic scene, she couldn't help but recall the well-intentioned comments of her friends. But the happy equilibrium she and Matt shared didn't need discussing or dissection, Lucy reasoned. "If it ain't broke, don't fix it . . . And don't break it, either," had always been her motto.

Lucy carefully stepped over the dogs and dropped down onto the cushion beside Matt. He leaned toward her and gave her a long, deep kiss.

"How was the meeting? Any wild demonstration? Maybe Maggie spun a clipping from Bigfoot?"

He was teasing, of course. Though Maggie often showed them fiber findings from exotic creatures such as alpaca or angora rabbits, with fur as soft as clouds.

"It was even more thrilling than that," Lucy reported.

"Really? Tell all." He slipped his arm around her shoulder and Lucy leaned against him in a cuddling, comfortable pose.

"Maggie volunteered us to help a customer in distress. A bride-to-be, Rebecca Bailey."

Lucy quickly related Rebecca's crisis, then described the sweater she was going to knit for the bridesmaid.

"The pattern is easy. I just hope I can finish it in time. Maggie has the real challenge. Knitting a wedding gown is pretty intense."

Matt laughed. "That's a nice way to put it. I think it's sort of crazy. I'd worry if you ever started that project."

"No way. I'd skip the knitting shop and go straight to a bridal salon." She glanced at him, then back at the basketball game. "Not that I'm thinking about wedding gowns, or anything like that. I mean, if you're getting married a second time, most brides don't even wear a big fancy gown . . ."

She stopped herself. She was only making this worse. Now Matt was going to think that she had been daydreaming about weddings and gowns and all those combustible topics she was trying to avoid.

When she really was not thinking about any of this. Not until her friends had put the bug . . . or perhaps just a rose petal . . . in her ear.

He was suddenly so quiet. She felt his body tense up against her. Had all this wedding talk caused a problem already?

She snuck a glance to gauge his reaction. Then realized his eyes were glued to the action on the TV screen and he probably hadn't heard a single word of her rambling.

Matt sat up even straighter and held his breath as the Celtics' point guard brought the ball down the court and the players on both teams shifted and dodged.

He pulled his arm off her shoulder and yelled at the set, "Pass it to Pierce! He's wide open! Are you blind?"

The ball was passed, a shot taken, it bounced off the rim of the basket, and the guys in the red uniforms — not our team, Lucy knew that much — managed to snatch it.

Then a whistle blew — Lucy had no idea why — and Matt collapsed with a long, frustrated sigh.

"We're never going to make the play-offs. KG strained his groin muscle. He's out for two weeks . . ."

How did male athletes always seem to strain their groin muscles? Was that some macho thing? She didn't even know where her groin muscle was. She nodded, trying to commiserate.

"I'm sorry, honey . . . You were saying something?" Matt turned to her.

"Nothing important." She smiled and patted his knee. "I'm really beat. I'm going up to take a shower. When is this over?"

"One more quarter . . . I'll just set the DVR," he said quickly. He smiled as she picked up the empty bowl. "I'll clean this stuff up. Don't worry."

Music to her ears. That was one of the many things she appreciated about him, one trait that made it so easy to be not quite cohabitating. He never left a trail of beer bottles, shoes, socks, newspapers, half-opened mail, and dirty dishes in his wake. Well, rarely.

As Lucy climbed the stairs to her bedroom, she knew she'd dodged a bullet. She had to be careful not to let all this wedding talk rub off on her real life, like dog hair on a black sweater.

No matter what her friends thought. She didn't think she and Matt were ready for "the talk." Not even the living-together talk.

41

Sometimes, the less said the better. Most of the time, she thought.

CHAPTER TWO

Maggie sent a short e-mail around on Friday morning to let the knitting circle know Nora had dropped off the rest of the yarn for the bridesmaids' sweaters, just as she'd promised.

Please come pick up your yarn for the shrugs ASAP. You should all be finished with the sample by now and needing the rest. We have a deadline to meet. Let's not let dear Rebecca down.

Lucy cringed. She had hardly made a dent in the sample of dark pink yarn she'd taken home the night before. She'd planned to knit for a little while in bed before going to sleep. But once Matt came up, the needles had been tossed overboard without a second thought.

She decided to walk down to the shop to pick up her share of yarn that afternoon, whether she needed it or not. Right after she sent off a project she'd been working on all week.

It was a fairly simple brochure for a local jewelry store, promoting their top-selling spring items — mainly engagement rings and wedding bands. Lucy hadn't noticed the graphics very much. But she suddenly felt smothered this morning by photos of diamond solitaire rings and gold bands. It seemed like some sort of conspiracy.

The moment Lucy shut her computer and stood up, her dog, Tink — stretched out under her desk doing a perfect imitation of a yellow bath mat — jumped to her feet.

"Ready to go out?"

What a question. When was Tink ever not ready?

The dog picked up a sneaker and raced to the back door, her long tail swishing from side to side like a brush in a car wash.

The past winter had been brutal, even by New England's standards, with snow piles that often reached to Lucy's shoulder and frigid cold temperatures. It was a challenge to walk to the car without breaking a bone. No less walking a large, rambunctious dog down the street. Tink had definitely been deprived of exercise the past few months, but now that spring was almost here, Lucy vowed to do better.

She slipped on her jacket, then hooked up Tink's new harness. Lucy had adopted Tink about a year ago but had not progressed much with training, including walking properly on a leash. "Calm" was not a word in Tink's limited canine vocabulary. Though she did seem to understand multiple variations for the concept of dog treat.

"Just hold still now for a second." Lucy struggled to make the clasp meet under the dog's chest. "Suck it in a little, pal. And don't tell me that's just fur."

Did she talk out loud to the dog too much? Lucy sometimes wondered. Maybe that was a sign she should be more eager for Matt to move in.

With Tink leading the way at a relatively sedate pace, they headed down the winding streets that led to the village of Plum Harbor. Tucked into Boston's north shore, the town had once been a popular summer destination, but had since evolved into a place some might call an ex-urb. Not close enough to Boston to be a suburb, but not completely rural, either.

Lucy lived in an area of the village known as the Marshes, a neighborhood bordered by tracts of tall grasses and marshland that eventually led to the town beach.

The community of summer cottages had been winterized and expanded over the years, evolving into a distinct, year-round neighborhood. Small, cozy houses were the perfect fit for young families or seniors looking to downsize.

Lucy and her sister had inherited one such cottage from their aunt, who had died three years ago. They'd spent many summers with Aunt Laura and the place held special memories. Lucy had arrived intending to stay just for the summer and ended up making it her full-time address.

Somebody should have told the weatherman spring was coming, Lucy thought as she rounded the turn onto Main Street. There was no sign of it today and she pulled the zipper of her jacket up to her chin. A cold, sharp wind blew straight into her face, making her squint and making Tink squint, too, her ears blown flat against her head. The wind rose off the harbor and they were walking straight into it.

Lucy tugged Tink down the street toward Maggie's shop, then up the brick-lined path that led to the steps and covered porch. The shop looked stark this time of year, bare of flowers or even holiday decorations. But the bay window in front always held a creative display that rarely failed to amuse.

As Lucy tied one end of the dog's leash to the porch railing, she noticed Maggie had set up a new window today, showing different knitted pieces — a hat, a mitten, a baby sweater — floating against a blue sky, like airborne kites. Lucy had to look close to figure out how it was done. Very clever and original, she thought.

When she walked in, the shop was empty. Maggie was at the table in the back unpacking and sorting some new stock. The bright spring colors were enticing and put Lucy in the mind for warm-weather projects, like a halter top or felted summer bag.

"Hmm . . . this looks interesting," Lucy picked up a skein of sunny yellow yarn and touched it to her cheek. "Soft, too. What can I make with this?"

Maggie snatched it from her hand with a disapproving shake of her head. "Not so fast, my dear. First things first."

She picked up a plastic bag of yarn from the sideboard and handed it over. "Here's your share of the bridesmaid yarn. I think we need to have everything done by next Tuesday, so we can block the shrugs and they have time to dry."

"Next Tuesday? I thought you said Thursday."

"I had to rethink that plan. I'm concerned

that the sweaters might not dry in time for the ceremony. We're really cutting it close as it is.

"Tell me about it. I thought Thursday would be a tough date to make."

"Don't worry, Lucy, you'll make it. My mother used to say, 'A task will expand or shrink, according to the time you have to do it.' "

Which was probably true, Lucy thought, knowing how she could fiddle and procrastinate for weeks on a work project with a long, loose timeline.

Before she could reply, another voice chimed in, "I know just what you mean. It's the same about pocketbooks. Ever notice? If you carry a big clunky bag, you find all kinds of junk to fill it. Stuff you absolutely must have handy. Feels like you're carrying a ton of bricks. But if you grab a little bag, you can't fit half that stuff and never miss it."

"Oh, hello, Edie," Maggie said. Both Maggie and Lucy had turned to find Edie Steiber walking toward them. She'd obviously entered the shop without their noticing. Which was saying something, since Edie was not the type of woman who easily flew under the radar.

Edie ran the Schooner, the town's most

popular eaterie, though certainly not the fanciest. The diner was an unofficial historic landmark and Edie, sort of an unofficial landmark, as well. Edie worked at the diner from dawn until late at night, ruling her little fiefdom from a stool behind the cash register and filling her downtime by passing along town news — commonly known as gossip — and knitting.

She often trotted across the street to Maggie's shop to stock up on supplies, solicit a tip or two, or just to sit and chat. Lucy suspected that most of the time, the former reasons were just an excuse for the latter.

"Oh, that's a nice color. It would go with my coat." She picked up a bag of the bridesmaid yarn and held it up against her down coat, which reached to her ankles and puffed out around her body like a lavender thunder cloud.

"So what are you up to with all this pretty yarn? Did I miss a sign-up sheet for a class?"

"Nothing like that, Edie. The knitting group is just doing a good deed. Rebecca Bailey is getting married and she needed some help knitting shrugs for her bridesmaids and finishing her gown."

"Rebecca who . . . ? Oh sure, I know who you mean. She's making her own wedding gown, right?" Maggie simply nodded. "Well, good luck to her. Who's she marrying anyway?"

"Jeremy Lassiter. Do you know the Lassiters?" Maggie's tone was polite, though they both knew Edie was acquainted with everyone in town. If not personally, then by hearsay, which was just as good in her book.

"At-Las Technologies? Those Lassiters you mean?" She sat down at the table with a grunt and yanked open a few snaps on her coat. "Well, well. She reeled in a big fish. You wouldn't think she was the type to go after money. To look at her, I mean. She seems so homespun. So wholesome and whole foodie."

Lucy actually agreed with Edie's assessment. Though she would have phrased the impression in a more polite way.

"Edie, please. You make it sound like poor Rebecca is a gold digger. She's nothing like that. I'm sure it's a total love match," Maggie insisted.

Edie shrugged, unfazed by Maggie's scolding. "If you say so. Otherwise, she might be in for a little surprise. All mighty At-Las has hit some hard times, I hear. Her new in-laws might not be as loaded as she thinks."

Edie was still not conceding that Rebecca was not interested in Jeremy for his money, Lucy noticed. But her tidbit of gossip piqued Lucy's curiosity.

"What do you mean, Edie? Is the company having problems?"

"You might say that. Lassiter's partner, Lewis Atkins, up and left about a year or two ago. That was a nasty split. Nearly brought the whole place down around him. See it was Atkins and Lassiter from way back. At . . . Las, get it?" she asked the other women. "College roommates and close as brothers. They started that business fresh out of school with Lassiter's father's money. What, nearly forty years ago?"

"Why did they part company?" Maggie asked.

"Oh, the usual. Some fight over money or royalties from a patent. Something like that. Anyway, Atkins got a payout that drained the coffers. Not to mention the lawyers' fees. So now Lassiter is left beating the bushes for investors. He's definitely got a cash-flow problem since his BFF left. Mainly with the flow part," she added curtly.

"Investors? Is the family selling off shares of the company?" Maggie asked curiously.

"I wish. I would have bit on that carrot," Edie countered. "All my guy would tell me was that I could get in on the ground floor, on something big. But risky." Edie paused and pulled out her knitting. "I was tempted.

51

But I decided to pass."

Lucy had no idea of Edie's net worth, but guessed that their local queen of hash browns was one of the wealthiest people in town, if not all of Essex County. In addition to a thriving business, a prime chunk of Main Street real estate, and a grand Victorian showplace she called home, Edie had been the sole heir to her father's savings and investments, and spent almost as much time analyzing and manipulating her nest egg as she did knitting.

"Rebecca's future father-in-law is cooking up some hot new product and looking for R and D money," Edie continued. "Research and development," she translated.

"Yes. We get that." Maggie glanced at Lucy with a bland smile. "Nora Bailey did say that Jeremy's father insisted that the wedding date be changed because there was something very important going on at the firm. Perhaps it's all related."

"Sounds like. These things can be a boom or a bust. I need a safe bet at my age. It's almost time to cash in my chips. Or time for my kids to," she added with a laugh. "Hey, why did I come in here anyway? It sure wasn't to talk over my portfolio. Oh, right, Some buttons for this little sweater I just finished. Isn't it sweet?"

Edie had already taken the project out of her bag and now smoothed it on the table. A creamy white baby sweater with a pink border. Edie had done a nice job, Lucy thought. The sweater was totally sweet and Lucy had to admit, these knitted baby items could get her biological crocodile ticking without too much encouragement.

"That's for my new grandbaby. A little something for the spring. I have so many grandkids now, I can barely keep track of who I need to knit for next. I need to make a chart or something."

Edie suddenly rose, holding on to the table as she stood, then balanced on her big tan snow boots. The last flake had fallen some weeks ago, but Lucy knew Edie didn't like to take any chances, and would probably wear the boots until the temperature hit at least fifty-five or even sixty.

"Will you show me your famous button collection, Maggie?"

"Help yourself," Maggie said, though she only allowed her special customers that privilege. "Buttons for children's wear are in the top drawer."

Edie eagerly ambled over to the cabinet and Lucy saw her cue to depart.

"Well, I'd better get going. Tink must be restless. And I have to get cracking on the

53

shrug, of course," she added in a dutiful tone.

"Don't make me feel so guilty. I'm sure you'll manage to squeeze in a few hours with Matt here and there. Despite your dedication to the cause."

Lucy laughed and zipped up her jacket. "We'll get together tonight. But he has to pick up Dara tomorrow, and they have a busy schedule this weekend. A few birthday parties and some family events." Lucy often spent time with Matt and Dara. But she wasn't included this weekend, which was just as well, she thought. "Maybe I'll finish on time after all."

"Yes, please. No excuses now," Maggie warned as she walked Lucy to the door.

Just as Lucy was leaving, Dana walked in. "Ready for more yarn?" Maggie asked.

"Not a moment too soon. I whipped right through that first skein."

Dana reached into her knitting bag and pulled out her shrug, which was coming along with enviable progress, Lucy noticed. Dana was definitely teacher's pet today, wasn't she? "Dana . . . don't you have a life?"

"Two patients canceled on me this morning. I tried to use the time productively. Besides, it's not a race, Lucy," she reminded

54

her gently.

"Don't worry. You'll catch up," Maggie cut in, sounding very much like it was a race. "You have all weekend."

"That I do," Lucy replied glumly. "See you."

As usual, Tink was inappropriately happy to see her and eagerly licked Lucy's hands and face as she undid the leash from the post on the porch. "Thanks a bunch. I love you, too."

Tink answered with a wolfish smile and yanked Lucy down the steps to the street.

Just me and my dog, Lucy realized. Which was sometimes a great relief.

Lucy had the best intentions to focus on the shrug all weekend. But life and the usual chores — cleaning, grocery shopping, bringing Tink to get groomed — got in the way. She did make headway Saturday night, while watching a foreign film. But she realized too late that subtitles and knitting were not a recipe for speedy work. Sunday morning she took out the shrug before she'd even finished her coffee. But the newspaper and phone calls from her mother and sister were major speed bumps. After the gym, it was time to get ready to see Matt and she was not much further along with the shrug Sunday night than she had been on Friday.

On Monday morning, she found Maggie's gentle but nudging reminder in her e-mail box.

I trust that you're all making great progress. No one has called with any problems, so the pattern must be even easier than we thought. Rebecca and I are zooming along with the gown. Wait until you see it. She's coming to the shop tomorrow night for a final fitting, so please bring the shrugs over and we'll have a little "block party." :)

XO, Maggie

Block party? Lucy wasn't even half done. She swallowed a lump of panic and quickly scanned the other e-mails.

There was one or two about work. A message asking for some minor revisions in the brochure she'd sent on Friday. She dashed off a quick note, making some wild promise to return it by Tuesday night.

Then she ran to her knitting bag and pulled out the shrug.

Yes, paying the rent and keeping the lights on were important. But until she finished most of this stupid shrug, she wouldn't be able to focus on work anyway. There was clearly no choice but to settle down for some serious knitting.

Not in Maggie's shop, either, where she would usually take shelter at such trying times. She didn't want anyone to know she'd been such a slacker. Or perhaps in this case, a better term was a shrugger?

Lucy guessed that Suzanne, who was the slowest, most scattered knitter in their group, was in the same boat. In the late afternoon, Lucy checked in with a text and Suzanne's reply confirmed it. She was even further behind with the assignment. Lucy commiserated and invited her over for a secret knitting session.

"I feel a little guilty meeting like this," Suzanne admitted as she came in.

"I do, too." Lucy poured Suzanne a glass of wine and pulled out her shrug. "But misery loves company. We'll tell them tomorrow night. When we're done."

"If we're done." She took a sip of wine and looked down at her shrug. "Where's Matt tonight?"

"He wanted to come over but he heard that certain note of panic in my voice when we were on the phone today. He knows when to stay clear of the line of fire by now."

"You've trained him well. I think he's almost housebroken. I just say 'I have to go out after dinner tonight' in a certain way and Kevin knows better by now not to ask any questions. I tossed a few boxes of pizza in their direction and let them fend for themselves. Homework projects, last-minute laundry requests . . . lunches for tomorrow."

With three children, a full-time job, and a big house to take care of, Suzanne's to-do list was endless. Lucy had sympathy for her. If and when she ever had children, Lucy wondered if she'd be as skilled at all the juggling.

They eventually switched from wine, fruit, and cheese to tea and cookies, managing to knit steadily until midnight.

"Well, I'm not done, but I've made a good effort, don't you think?" Suzanne held up the nearly completed sweater.

"Absolutely. Don't worry about the rest. Dana or Maggie will love swooping in and coming to the rescue."

Lucy thought she would work a little more tonight and actually be finished by the meeting tomorrow. But she didn't want to tell Suzanne and make her feel bad.

When Tuesday night arrived, Lucy walked up the path to Maggie's shop, her fingers suffering a bit of knitting burnout as they gripped the handles of her tote bag. But her shrug was ready for blocking and a march down the aisle.

Her friends were in the back of the shop as usual, everyone showing off her handiwork. They had all finished on time, including Suzanne.

"You never fail to surprise me," Lucy whispered to Suzanne privately. "Did the fiber fairies take pity on you last night?"

"Not quite . . . I called in sick at the office this morning," she whispered back. "I needed a mental health day, anyway. It was the perfect excuse."

"The sweaters look wonderful." Nora walked around the table, admiring everyone's work. "The flower girl's is adorable . . . Did you add this trim?" she asked Phoebe, eyeing some tiny white daisies that were carefully sewn on along the collar.

"Yeah, well, I knew I was knitting outside the lines a little. But I thought it would be a nice touch. You know, flowers . . . flower girl?" Phoebe said.

"It's really lovely. I'm sure Rebecca will love it," her mother replied.

"Where is Rebecca? Is she here yet?" Lucy asked Nora.

"Oh, she's been here a while. She's in the storeroom with Maggie, getting ready to give us a sneak preview of the gown. I can hardly wait. Feel my hands, they're like ice,"

Nora confessed, reaching out to Lucy.

Lucy touched Nora's fingers. They were frigid, practically bloodless. Nora smiled nervously and Lucy forced herself to smile back. An odd feeling swept through her — a feeling totally out of synch with the bright, prenuptial mood.

Then they heard Maggie call out from the storeroom, "Here comes the bride, everyone."

Lucy heard Suzanne gasp. "Oh, my God! She looks gorgeous. . . ."

They all turned at once to watch Rebecca emerge with Maggie following close behind, holding up the hem of Rebecca's gown. Rebecca's handmaiden and personal fashion designer was beaming almost as much as the bride. And with good reason. The gown was really beautiful. Extraordinary. Lucy had no idea it would come out so well when she'd seen the scattered pieces pinned to the dressmaker's form last week. Or even when she looked at the pattern and photograph.

"Sweetheart, you look spectacular." Nora trotted toward her daughter. "I know I've been a pain about you making the dress yourself. But I understand now. I honestly do. It's just perfect for you."

"It is perfect, Rebecca," Lucy agreed.

"You look incredible. Absolutely beautiful."

"You should be very proud," Dana added. "What a masterpiece. What an accomplishment."

"Thanks but I couldn't have done it without Maggie . . . and my mom," Rebecca said modestly.

But she did look proud, Lucy noticed, as she should be. And greatly relieved. And a bit self-conscious as the center of so much attention. Good practice for her wedding day, which was coming up so quickly.

All eyes were on Rebecca as she reached the center of the room and stood up on a little step stool. The style complemented her figure perfectly, with a low, rounded neckline, form-fitting bodice, and nipped-in waistline, the finely knit ecru lace draping elegantly in the gored skirt.

The pieces were not completely sewn together yet, only basted, and she had to move carefully. Maggie and Nora helped her up on the stool and to balance on her brand-new silk high heels.

She was posed on the stool, her hand on Nora's shoulder, while Maggie checked the hemline, when Lucy heard the front door of the shop open and someone walk in.

"Jeremy . . . what are you doing here?" Rebecca gripped her mother's shoulder.

"You said to meet you here, remember?"

Rebecca's fiancé was handsome, Lucy thought, in a Clark Kent way, with short, thick brown hair, a strong jaw, and black glasses that framed his bright blue eyes. He wore a blue down parka with a thick, colorful striped scarf looped around his neck. It definitely looked hand knit and Lucy guessed it was one of Rebecca's creations.

Jeremy appeared to be in his midthirties, a few years older than Rebecca. But his nervous smile and intellectual air made him seem younger. He stared at them and waved awkwardly.

"Hello, ladies. I'm just the groom. Don't mind me."

The women laughed. All but Nora, who was trying to shield Rebecca from view. A fairly impossible feat, all things considered.

"Oh, dear . . . Jeremy. You shouldn't see the bride in her gown before the wedding. It's bad luck."

The groom laughed. "Sorry, Nora. I forgot."

Lucy sensed that even if he had remembered the traditional caution, like most scientists, he didn't put much stock in superstitions.

He walked toward her smiling, but Rebecca didn't smile back. "Jeremy . . . I said when we were done, after nine. It's not even half past eight."

He shrugged. "I actually forgot the time. I should have written it down."

"I should have . . . and taped it to your nose." But her scolding was delivered in a loving tone, Lucy had to say.

Nora still seemed upset about Jeremy seeing the gown and hovered around Rebecca. "Oh, don't worry about it, Mom. That's just an old wives' tale."

"Yes, of course," Nora said finally and made way for her future son-in-law.

"I'm glad I got to see you in the dress. A guy needs a little warning. You look so gorgeous. I would have fainted at the altar watching you walk down the aisle."

Rebecca shook her head, totally charmed out of any annoyance, Lucy was sure. Jeremy put his hands on Rebecca's waist and she leaned over to give him a kiss.

Everyone looked away, giving the couple some privacy. Lucy thought she heard Suzanne sigh again. Dana caught Lucy's gaze and rolled her eyes.

It was Maggie's voice that pulled them all back to the business at hand. "You're a lucky man, Jeremy," she said to him. "If you could just step back a moment, we'll finish pinning this hem and you can have her all to yourself again."

Jeremy did as he was told, his gaze finally drifting from Rebecca's as she was forced to turn, and then turn again.

He looked over at the knitting group and his future mother-in-law, as if noticing them all for the first time. Lucy got the impression that he was a super nice guy, but very awkward socially. She tried to think of some easy conversation starter, but Phoebe beat her to it.

"Cool scarf. Did Rebecca make that for you?"

Jeremy looked down at his scarf with pride. "Yes, she did. She does wonderful work. Fast, too."

"Wow, that is some wild self-striping yarn. I've never seen so many colors in one skein." Phoebe examined the stitch work closely. "This stuff would make awesome socks."

"Oh, it's not self-striping. I only wish it were." Rebecca looked over her shoulder as Maggie and Nora worked on the hem.

"Eyes front, Rebecca. You don't want this hem to be crooked do you?" Maggie used her firm, schoolteacher voice. Even Lucy looked forward suddenly.

Rebecca turned to face forward but kept talking. "He's very particular about his scarves and the colors he likes and the order of the stripes. He picks out the yarn himself and writes me long, detailed descriptions."

Jeremy looked embarrassed. He blushed like a teenager. "Oh, come on. I'm not that bad. You always tell me to choose. I just like certain colors. It's cheerful. It makes me happy when I wear it." He playfully flipped the end of his scarf over his shoulder. "We science geeks are all a little obsessive. You always knew that about me."

"Yes, I did." Rebecca smiled, risking Maggie's wrath as she turned her head for a second to meet his gaze. "And I wouldn't have you any other way."

Jeremy laughed. "Lucky me."

"So, Jeremy, the big day is almost here. The bride seems pretty calm. How do you feel?" Dana asked.

"I'm great," he replied with a quick nod. "I'm glad we moved the date up. I know it was annoying," he acknowledged, glancing at Nora. "But if Rebecca and I are married even sooner, all the better."

"How did you two meet? Rebecca didn't tell us." Suzanne's voice had that dreamy tone. She couldn't get enough of this romantic wedding stuff, could she? Little pink cupids were practically bobbing around her head.

"We met at the school where Rebecca teaches. Rebecca runs the after-school program and I came there last September as a volunteer to start a science club. I took one look and I knew she was the one."

"Chemistry, right?" Suzanne quipped, thrilled with the love-at-first-sight tale.

"What a sweet story," Dana agreed. "It's so nice that you met volunteering."

"Rebecca's students don't have many advantages," her mother said. "She gives a lot of extra time to help them. She may not be able to once she's married and has a family."

"Oh, Mom, please stop." Rebecca had come full circle on the stool and now looked down from her exalted height. "Let's just get through the wedding before you start worrying about grandchildren."

Nora laughed, taking no offense. "Fair enough," she conceded.

"And where are you going on your honeymoon?" Suzanne asked as if she had a checklist stashed someplace, Lucy thought — the top-ten questions to ask engaged couples. She'll be covering china patterns next.

Jeremy hesitated, as if he couldn't remember or perhaps wanted to keep the location a secret. "Thailand," he finally answered.

"Wow, that's exotic." Suzanne was definitely impressed.

Jeremy smiled at her but didn't reply. He suddenly seemed uncomfortable with all the attention.

Maggie stood upright and took a straight pin out of her mouth. "Hem's done. I can stitch it if you like."

"Would you? That would be a lifesaver. We still have so much to do before Saturday." Nora looked anxious again, though the sight of Rebecca in her gown had chased away her worries for a few minutes.

Jeremy helped Rebecca down from the stool, his arm around her waist. He seemed reluctant to let her go once her feet hit the ground. Her hand rested on his shoulder, displaying her large round diamond.

"Is that it?" he asked quietly.

"For now. I'll change and we can leave," she answered.

He nodded and she slipped away, heading for the storeroom. His gaze followed her, like a loyal pet, Lucy thought. Does Matt look at me that way? Boy, she hoped so.

Nora and Maggie talked about how the gown would be blocked and when it would be ready. Dana, Suzanne, and Phoebe had already begun blocking their shrugs and Lucy looked for a space to work on hers.

A few moments later, the happy couple said good night, Rebecca thanking everyone again for their help. With Jeremy's arm around her shoulder, she just about glowed.

"See you on Saturday," she said, finally sounding a tiny bit nervous.

"I can't wait!" Suzanne shouted, answering for all them.

Lucy could hardly wait, either. She'd forgotten how much fun preparing for a wedding could be. She really was looking forward to watching Rebecca walk down the aisle.

CHAPTER THREE

The Black Sheep Knitters decided to skip their usual Thursday night meeting since they had already gathered on Tuesday night to block the bridesmaids' shrugs and watch Rebecca model her gown. They did confer on driving arrangements for the wedding, deciding that they'd go together. Maggie was going to pick up everyone but Suzanne, who was coming straight from work.

Lucy was surprised that there were no e-mails flying around about who was wearing what. But when she went out to the driveway on Saturday afternoon and peered into Maggie's car, it seemed that they'd all consulted by telepathy, deciding on matching outfits of basic black and pearl accessories.

"We're all dressed the same, do you realize that?" she asked as she pulled out her seat belt.

Dana smiled and smoothed down the

neckline of her finely knit wrap dress, which she'd made for herself last fall, Lucy recalled.

"You'll never go wrong in a black dress and pearls when people like the Lassiters are throwing a party."

"Very true. Phoebe always wears black." Maggie glanced at her assistant, who sat in the passenger seat up front. "She must have the best taste of all of us."

Phoebe looked pleased with the compliment. "I did a pearl stud tonight. Did you guys notice? My mom gave it to me. I think she must have lost the other one and gave me the leftover."

She gently touched the edge of her left ear, which held a row of gothic-looking piercings and one lovely pink-hued pearl.

"We smell pretty good, too," Phoebe added.

"We clean up well, ladies. No question," Maggie said.

The Lassiter estate was located in the Landing, some distance from the village. There wasn't much to see en route, except for tall trees, privacy hedges, and high stone walls. Occasionally, a bit of palatial mansion or harbor became visible briefly, hinting at the hidden opulence.

The estate was not far from the Harbor

Club, which they passed on the way. Dana and Jack were members at the country club, mainly for Jack's law practice and because he was such an intense golfer. Dana was not at all the clubby type but she enjoyed playing tennis and acting out in subtly irreverent ways there.

Lucy wondered how long the ride would take, when Maggie suddenly slowed down for a traffic jam. Cars — most of them luxury models — sat bumper to bumper on the otherwise deserted road.

"The entrance to the estate must be up ahead. I guess we can just follow this line of cars inside," Maggie said.

Maggie merged her car with the line of Mercedes, Jaguars, and BMWs. Then turned through high, wrought-iron gates. Two bulky men, who must have been security guards, Lucy realized, peered into each vehicle. They wore orange traffic vests over tuxedos and waved large yellow flashlights.

Maggie's little green Subaru was waved right through and followed the procession down a woodsy road that twisted and turned and seemed to go on forever.

"My word . . ." Maggie said quietly. "Does anyone remember the opening scene to *Rebecca*?"

Lucy did remember it, but Phoebe spoke

71

up first. " 'Last night, I dreamt I was at Manderley,' " she offered in an eerie, uncanny Joan Fontaine voice.

"Bravo, Phoebe," Lucy leaned over and patted Phoebe's bony shoulder. "I was thinking the very same thing. I just didn't want to say it," Lucy admitted. "Didn't Laurence Olivier have a crazy wife locked up in the attic? And she sets the place on fire?"

"You're thinking of *Jane Eyre*," Dana recalled. "In *Rebecca,* the second wife thinks he's obsessed with the first wife's memory and still in love with her. But he actually murdered her . . . right?"

Before anyone could confirm that version, Maggie sighed out loud.

"Oh, dear . . . can we talk about something more cheerful? It is Rebecca's wedding day. I didn't mean to get you all started down that dark Gothic road . . ."

"There's something more cheerful. Look, it's Suzanne . . ." Dana turned and pointed out her window. "And she's not wearing black."

Suzanne was not wearing black — or anything close to it. Dressed to impress in a fuchsia silk suit and spiky, patent leather heels, she wiggled down from the driver's seat of her huge SUV and dropped to the ground like a Navy SEAL on cocktail party patrol.

"Wow, she looks hot . . . for a mother of three." Phoebe's mouth hung open.

"Phoebe . . . please." Maggie rolled her eyes.

"Well, she does," Phoebe said innocently.

She did indeed. And seemed to be enjoying every minute of it. The four women piled out of Maggie's car and joined her in the middle of the stone courtyard, beside a large fountain.

"Guess I didn't get the memo." Suzanne laughed, looking them over. "My little black dress is at the cleaner's anyway."

"You look like the lead singer of a girl group. And we look like the backup," Phoebe observed.

"Ladies, please . . . Let's go in and find a seat, shall we?" Maggie moved them along, like a border collie, nipping at their high heels.

They had driven into a large courtyard where valets collected cars and whisked them away . . . to who knew where, Lucy wondered. Water splashed down from a large round fountain and low lights in glass lanterns were just starting to glow.

The vast brick colonial manor house was built in the English style, complete with glossy black shutters, a slate roof, several chimneys, and long white columns. Thick ivy vines crept up the sun-faded brick facade.

At the stone entryway, two large black marble statues of mastiffs flanked the arching doorway. Phoebe reached out and patted one on the head. She was wearing a pair of black fingerless gloves she'd knit for herself.

"Nice doggie. Stay . . ."

Dana gently pulled her hand away. "Look but don't touch, remember?"

Another bulky, tuxedoed man who stood at the threshold cast a stern expression their way. Luckily the crowd pushed them along into a large foyer before he could remark.

Lucy quickly took in the black-and-white marble tile floor below and sparkling crystal chandelier above. Attendants took the guests' coats and directed them to the gallery where the ceremony would take place.

The gallery, just to the right of the foyer, was a vast room with long windows on one side, covered by swooping brocade drapes. A large fireplace and carved marble mantel was the focal point opposite. The walls were covered with oil paintings in heavy gilt frames and pedestals displayed sculptures in various styles.

"Look at all this art. I feel like one of the kids talked me into volunteering for a field trip," Suzanne whispered.

"Jeremy's mother, Patricia Moore, is a well-known collector and philanthropist," Maggie whispered back. "I guess when his parents divorced, they had to share custody of the masterpieces."

Lucy imagined that the room was normally filled with couches and armchairs and horrendously expensive little antique tables. But all the furniture had been cleared for rows and rows of white cushioned folding chairs that faced the far side of the room. An arch of beautiful tropical flowers and a speaker's podium had been set up on that end for the ceremony.

Suzanne squeezed Lucy's arm in excitement. "It's so beautiful. I'm going to cry."

"Suzanne . . . give me a break. We haven't even sat down," Phoebe said. Lucy smiled in disbelief.

"I know. I can't help it." She sniffed and shrugged.

They were lucky to find five seats together, in one of the rear rows. Suzanne angled for the aisle, pulling a camera out of her black satin clutch. "We need some photos, for Maggie's bulletin board."

It clearly meant so much to her to be closest to the bride when she walked by. No one dared deny her the pleasure. A trio of musicians — a violinist, cellist, and flutist — stood to one side of the flower arch and played a familiar classical piece.

Lucy sat back and glanced at the program she'd been handed as they walked in. The ceremony looked brief and to the point. Not much music, or miscellaneous readings by relatives on the schedule. Lucy was relieved. She did find it annoying when it seemed everyone in the family had to get up and say a few words.

The musicians paused, then suddenly they began a baroque piece that signaled the procession was about to begin. All the guests stood as Nora came down the aisle on the arm of one of the ushers. "Nora looks beautiful," Dana said quietly. They all nodded in agreement. With her hair and makeup professionally done, Nora looked surprisingly glamorous. Her long, flowing chiffon dress, in a dark plum hue, complemented the bridal party.

"Look, there's Jeremy's mother," Maggie whispered. A tall, elegant woman appeared next, escorted by the groom. Their resemblance was striking. She wore a dark blue satin gown that emphasized her blue eyes. Her thick glossy hair was worn in a smooth, upswept style, a lock of white in stark contrast to the dark brown shade she and her son shared.

After Patricia was seated, Jeremy took his place at the flower arch, tugging on his shirt cuffs. He looked quite nervous. Understandably, Lucy thought. Two groomsmen stood by, but Lucy couldn't tell which was the best man. The program did not indicate it, either.

Her friends suddenly turned to watch the next couple walking down the aisle. Lucy did, too.

"This has to be his father . . . and the trophy wife," Dana murmured.

"The second trophy wife, I understand," Maggie whispered back.

"It's hard to know the players without a scorecard. At least Nora gave you a briefing," Lucy whispered back.

"A few remarks here and there," Maggie conceded.

Philip Lassiter was a tall man, broad shouldered with a full head of unnaturally dark hair and artfully silver sideburns. He had thick eyebrows and a closely trimmed beard. He looked as if he was once very fit, but his tuxedo jacket tugged a bit against a round stomach, and his long arms and legs were rather thin.

He turned from side to side as he came down the aisle, acknowledging guests with a look or a smile like a politician strolling through a fund-raiser. The woman at his side, a shapely blonde in her midthirties, did the same. She wore a silvery, off-the-shoulder gown, a matching gauzy wrap, and large pieces of jewelry.

"Some dress," Dana whispered.

"Looks like she walked into a curtain," Suzanne whispered back. Lucy had to hold back a laugh. She did agree, now that Suzanne had mentioned it.

Poor taste or not, Philip Lassiter and his wife were clearly the celebrity couple, nearly upstaging the main act.

Once Jeremy's father and stepmother were seated, the music continued, but the aisle was clear. Suzanne checked her camera and peered down to the doorway. "Nothing yet. I think I see the flower girl. She looks sort of fidgety. She might be getting stage fright."

"Wait . . . who's that? Next to Jeremy?" Lucy squinted, wondering if she was seeing things. Another groomsman had taken a place at the flower arch. He must have snuck up a side aisle while all eyes were on the Lassiters, Lucy realized.

Jeremy was grinning and shaking hands

wildly, then he hugged the other man to his chest.

When they finally parted Lucy realized she hadn't imagined it. The two men were identical in every way. Mirror images of each other. Even more uncanny since they wore matching black tuxedos. Except for Jeremy's glasses, she was unable to tell them apart. Not at this distance, anyway.

"Jeremy has a twin? Why didn't anyone mention that?" Suzanne asked.

"Nora told me that Jeremy has a brother," Maggie replied. "I think his name is Alec. But there was a terrible falling-out with their father and he wasn't invited to the wedding. I guess he made it after all."

She'd barely finished the explanation when they heard a shout and Jeremy's father came to his feet. His regal manner and benevolent smile had melted, replaced by bulging eyes and an explosive expression.

Philip Lassiter's wife tugged on his sleeve, but he shook her off.

". . . I will not sit down," he roared. "Let me go."

He turned back to his sons and jabbed his finger in the air.

"You . . . you bastard . . . get out of here! Before I have you thrown out!" Then he spun around, looking for one of the many security guards, Lucy assumed.

Jeremy's twin, Alec, stood very still. He looked down at the floor, a small smile appeared on his face. Jeremy said something to him and touched his arm, then ran down to his father. He took his father aside and they talked behind a large floral arrangement, away from the guests.

A signal was given and the musicians began a lively interlude, playing almost in a frenzy.

When the two men returned, Philip Lassiter was still seething, but he dropped into his seat, ignoring his wife's attempts to comfort him. Jeremy returned to his post, squaring his shoulders as he took his place beside his brother.

Lucy had no idea of Alec's transgressions — real or imagined — but she thought Jeremy showed a lot of character to stand up for his brother and include him in the wedding. It was obviously very important to him. Philip Lassiter was clearly a strong patriarch . . . and perhaps even a bit of a bully. Hadn't all the wedding plans been changed to meet his demands?

But, what did she know? Nothing.

The musicians started the bridal march again, at a sedate pace, and everyone came to their feet once more, this time murmur-

80

ing about the little family drama that had just occurred.

An adorable flower girl, spreading rose pedals in her wake with tender care, quickly distracted them. "That's my sweater," Phoebe whispered. "Suzanne, get a picture . . . hurry!"

"Got it, don't worry," she whispered back, clicking away.

Three bridesmaids came next — two were close friends of Rebecca's and one was Jeremy's older sister, Claudia, Lucy read in the program. Once again she could easily tell the relationship. His sister unfortunately had not inherited their mother's looks, but very much resembled her father, her features heavy and severe.

The wraparound shrugs looked even better on the bridesmaids than they had blocked on Maggie's worktable. The knitters quietly admired their handiwork.

Finally, it was time for the bride. Lucy checked her program and learned that the older man escorting Rebecca down the aisle was her uncle. She remembered that Nora was a widow, Rebecca's father had died when she was in high school.

If Rebecca had looked beautiful in the dress in the shop last Tuesday, she looked ten times more so at that moment, making her grand entrance. All eyes in the room were on her. The subtle but effective makeup, her hairstyle, and her veil were the final touches that transformed Rebecca into a bona fide fairy-tale princess.

She would have made a stunning bride in any gown, Lucy realized. But her original creation drew gasps of surprise and amazement. Even in this haute couture environment, the handmade dress was garnering great reviews. The entire room buzzed with the news that the bride had knit it "all by herself!"

"Not quite," Maggie corrected under her breath. "But Rebecca must get all the glory today. I guess this is the first time I've ever been a ghost knitter," she whispered to her friends.

The bride finally reached the flower arch and was presented to her groom. Jeremy lifted her veil and gently kissed her cheek. Hand in hand they faced the minister and the real ceremony began.

Like most weddings, which took months or even years of preparation, it seemed the most important part — the ritual of words and blessing, and the exchange of "till death do us part" vows — passed much too quickly.

Before Suzanne could find her tissue pack,

the couple was pronounced husband and wife. As they smiled into each other's eyes and shared a long kiss, the sedate group of well-wishers broke into applause.

A spritely melody started up and the couple swooped down the aisle, beaming with happiness, smiling at their friends and family on either side of the aisle.

"Somebody grab this camera, will you? I can't have a good cry and take pictures at the same time." Suzanne waved the camera in the air with one hand, dabbing her eyes with the other.

Dana grabbed it just in time, and snapped away as the couple passed and the rest of the wedding party followed. Finally, the rows of guests began to file into the center aisle, heading for the receiving line.

Lucy and her friends took their place in line, chatting as it slowly moved along. "Short and sweet . . . and very tasteful," Dana said.

"Except for that outburst by Jeremy's father. What was that about?" Suzanne's voice was on low volume, for once.

"Serious issues there. No question," Dana noted. "But weddings will bring out all the buried tensions."

They came to Nora first and offered their congratulations.

"Thank you so much. Thank you all for everything. So glad you could come," she said, bubbling over with happiness.

Philip and Sonia Lassiter were next. No conversation was necessary. A quick, polite handshake — no eye contact, Lucy noticed — and they finally reached Rebecca and Jeremy.

The newlyweds couldn't have looked happier.

Not only were they beaming with joy but they both looked so relaxed and ready to enjoy their celebration. Lucy hadn't even realized how nervous and stressed they must have been on Tuesday night at the shop.

Before the line swept along, Rebecca paused to give Maggie a special embrace. "Thank you so much, Maggie. This is the happiest day of my life. You helped make it absolutely perfect."

"No need to thank me, dear," Maggie demurred. "It was an honor to play a small part in this fabulous wedding. Right ladies?" she asked her friends.

The Black Sheep Knitters had to agree.

While the rest of the wedding guests moved into another large room for the start of the reception, the knitters lingered in the foyer. They finally decided to skip the cocktail hour and head back to the village.

Each had her own plans for the evening and it was getting late.

There had been only a little time to dish about the wedding on the way back to town and Lucy was pleased to find an e-mail from Suzanne on Monday night with a photo of the bride and groom attached.

Got some great wedding shots! Printing them out right now. I'll drop them off at the shop on my way to the office tomorrow. Come by for coffee before you all start work? I'll be there.

XO, Suzanne

Lucy had worked hard all day and into the night, starting a new project. She woke up early Tuesday morning, ready for some exercise before sitting at the computer again. Tink was more than ready for a walk to town.

The weather had warmed a few degrees, though she still needed a down vest and heavy sweater. But the wind was gone and the sunlight streaming through the winter branches seemed stronger. Small green buds on the trees and bushes looked about to unfold.

When Lucy arrived at the shop, the rest of her friends were already there, coffee cups in hand. They sat in the small alcove near the front door, where Maggie had set aside a cozy work space for her customers and smaller classes.

"Sorry I'm late. Are those the photos?" Lucy noticed a pile of pictures on the marble-topped coffee table. She sat in an armchair and pulled open her vest.

Suzanne nodded, but Lucy suddenly noticed her friend was weeping again. This time, they were not tears of joy. Curled up in the rocking chair, Phoebe stared into space, her eye makeup smeared. She'd been crying, too, Lucy realized. Dana and Maggie, who sat together on the love seat, weren't crying, but wore blank, shocked expressions.

"Hey . . . what's up? What's going on?"

Maggie met her gaze. She silently shook her head and looked over at Dana. Dana cleared her throat and finally answered.

"We just heard some bad news, Lucy. There was an awful accident at At-Las. Very late last night. It started in Jeremy's lab . . ." Dana's low voice grew suddenly shaky and thin. "They don't know yet what caused it, but there was an explosion and fire. Jeremy was there and . . . he's dead."

CHAPTER FOUR

Lucy gasped. She felt as if someone had just punched her in the stomach. "Jeremy? Are you sure? That can't be true . . ."

"It's true, Lucy. I'm sorry," Dana said quietly. "Suzanne heard about it from Edie at the Schooner and I saw it on the local news this morning."

"But I thought they were going on a honeymoon. To Thailand," she suddenly recalled. "Why was he even in his laboratory last night?"

"They were scheduled to leave for their trip tonight. Jeremy had some work to clear up before he left town." Maggie reached over and squeezed her hand. "It's a horrible tragedy. Poor Rebecca. What a shock for the family . . ."

Her voice trailed off as if she couldn't say another word. The news was inexpressibly sorrowful.

Lucy took a deep breath. She felt as if she

might cry, but somehow the tears wouldn't come. "So, have you been in touch with Nora?"

"I called the house and spoke to Nora's brother, Gary. Remember him? He walked Rebecca down the aisle." As Lucy nodded Maggie continued. "He's going to let us know when the family has made funeral arrangements. It sounds like there's some tension between Rebecca and the Lassiters."

"Tension? What can they be arguing about at a time like this?"

"About who's in charge of planning Jeremy's memorial, that sort of thing. Philip Lassiter and Jeremy's mother both want to plan it and are forgetting all about Rebecca," Maggie explained. "You'd think they'd all take some pity and abide by her wishes. She was his wife, however briefly."

"I hate to judge people by appearances, but Philip Lassiter looks like the type who thinks he's entitled to running every show. Jeremy's mother doesn't look like any pushover, either," Suzanne said.

"The news report said the cause of the fire and explosion were being investigated," Dana said. "That will slow things down, as well."

"Do the police have some reason to think it wasn't an accident?" Suzanne sounded surprised.

"Gary told me that they assume it was," Maggie replied. "Jeremy's work involved dangerous chemicals. But Dana's right, the fire department and police need to determine exactly how it happened. The insurance companies will want to know, too," she added.

"Absolutely. They'll want to know most of all," Dana agreed. "Jeremy probably had life insurance and the company must be insured for the damage to the building. But I'm sure they'll be able to hold a funeral before all that's figured out."

Lucy nodded, feeling numb. Almost lightheaded. She was totally shocked by the news. Funeral arrangements? They'd just gone to the young man's wedding, what . . . two days ago? He had been beaming with joy.

"I'm sorry . . . I can't believe it." She shook her head and closed her eyes. "He was so young and they looked so happy on Saturday. Poor Rebecca. They were married only . . . two days?"

"It is unbelievable," Maggie agreed. "What are the chances of something like that happening? Probably ten million to one."

"Just goes to show you, you never know what's going to happen in life. Day to day.

Hour to hour," Suzanne offered between wiping her tears.

"But we rarely seem to remember, and live as if we have all the time in the world." Maggie sighed. "I just keep thinking of poor Rebecca. How radiant and joyful she looked on Saturday. She told me that it was the happiest day of her life. At least they had that much together."

"Rebecca is heartbroken. No question," Dana said. "But she's young. She'll get through this, eventually. In a way, I feel even worse for his parents. One never expects to outlive a child."

How true. It was impossible to say which perspective was more pitiable — Jeremy's newlywed bride, or his parents, Philip Lassiter and Patricia Moore.

"He was brilliant, wasn't he? A real genius," Suzanne said quietly.

"No question," Maggie agreed. "His death will be a blow to At-Las Technologies. He was their senior scientist and, Nora said, the real brains and talent of the operation."

Suzanne leaned over and scooped up the photos. "I'm going to put these away. For a long time, actually," she added.

A customer came in and Maggie sat up alertly and whisked a tissue under her eyes. "I look a wreck, don't I? I hope I don't scare the poor woman away."

"You look fine, Maggie." Dana soothed her.

The customer had made a beeline for a display of needles and other tools that stood just past the checkout counter.

"May I help you with something?" Maggie called out. The woman turned and nodded.

"I'll go." Phoebe got up and trotted over.

Maggie sat back and watched Phoebe for a moment. "It's not that I don't trust her, but I'd better get back to work."

"We understand." Dana stood up and slipped on her jacket. "I have to run, too. I have a patient in a little while."

Suzanne and Lucy said their good-byes as well, though Lucy knew it would be very difficult to focus on work this morning in her quiet cottage. That was the downside of working on your own. You were basically alone with your own thoughts and moods, for better or worse.

"I'll let you know when I hear more about the memorial plans," Maggie said as she left them.

"Yes, let us know." Dana's tone was somber. "I never imagined we'd be donning our black dresses again so soon. And for such a sad occasion."

No one replied. No one had to. Lucy knew Dana had just expressed what they were all thinking and feeling.

Lucy left the shop with Dana and Suzanne. Instead of turning up Main Street toward home, she and Tink walked with Dana to her office, which was in the center of town, not far from the harbor.

The two friends walked in silence for a while. Main Street was bustling with activity: young mothers pushing strollers, men and women in business dress hustling to their offices. Seniors were out for their daily exercise and window-shopping.

The sun shone brilliantly and Lucy could hear chirping in the bare branches all around. She sensed spring stirring, the earth waking up after a long winter sleep. It all seemed wrong today, out of synch.

She turned to Dana and shook her head. "How can everything look so busy and . . . happy today? How can life just go on, after what happened to Jeremy and Rebecca?"

Dana's expression was sympathetic. She reached out and touched Lucy's arm. "I know just what you mean. I feel the same. In a way, it's a comfort. Life does go on, Lucy. No matter what. Something larger lifts us up and carries us along, if we let it.

Lucy sighed. She understood what Dana

meant. She hadn't gotten there yet. She needed more time to process this sad news.

They reached Dana's building but she seemed in no hurry to rush upstairs. They stood together on the sidewalk and Tink leaned against Lucy's leg.

"Do you remember when Jeremy saw Rebecca in her gown last Tuesday night? He laughed when Nora said it was bad luck. But Nora and Rebecca were very upset."

"I do remember." Dana took a key chain from her purse. "It's an eerie coincidence. But I don't believe in that stuff . . . do you?"

"No . . . I don't, either." Lucy agreed. Though she did have a few quirks in that department. No one was going to catch her walking under a ladder anytime soon. Or crossing paths with felines of a certain hue.

Dana leaned over and gave her an impulsive hug. "See you soon . . . and call if you want to talk some more, okay?"

Lucy nodded. The news was so sad and shocking, Lucy had a feeling her entire circle of friends would get some free therapy from Dana this week, especially when they met for their knitting meeting.

Lucy started back up Main Street, intending to go home. But she found herself stopping at Matt's office, Harbor Animal Hospital, which was not far from the village green.

She rarely dropped in unexpectedly. She didn't like to bother him at work. The office was usually wildly busy with patients of all species, and their owners, trying to get along peacefully in the waiting room. Or Matt was in surgery and completely unavailable.

But today she had a yearning to see him. Just for a minute. To look into his eyes and connect with his warm, reassuring smile. Just long enough to recharge her battery.

Surprisingly, when she walked in, the waiting room was relatively quiet. A gray-haired woman waited, a cat carrier balanced on her lap. Tink immediately investigated, sniffing close enough to inspire a low growl from deep within the plastic box.

Lucy walked up to the receptionist's window and Tink jumped up, her paws on the edge of the counter.

After exchanging greetings Phyllis, the secretary, buzzed Matt and gave Tink a biscuit. "He said it's fine. Just go on back."

Matt's office was the last room on the corridor. Lucy opened the wooden door and walked in. Tink immediately jumped up on the small leather couch, opposite Matt's desk. She curled up in a ball with her head on her paws.

"Hey. What's up?" Matt looked up and smiled that amazing smile of his, the one that flipped all her switches. She tried to smile back, but this time, couldn't manage it. It felt as if the corners of her mouth had somehow been stapled down.

"I hope I'm not bothering you . . ."

"Not at all. I'm pretty bored. It's just about time for my beautiful-woman break." He smiled and walked toward her, then rested his hands on her shoulders. "Is everything okay?"

Lucy shook her head, losing her voice for a moment. "I have some bad news. Jeremy Lassiter died last night. There was an explosion and fire in his lab."

"That guy who just got married on Saturday to your friend?" Lucy nodded bleakly. "That's awful. His poor wife. How did you hear about it?"

"I went to Maggie's shop this morning, to see some pictures from the wedding. Ironic, right? Dana had heard a news report on TV."

He gazed down at her with a sad, sympathetic expression. Then pulled her close in a warm, strong hug. "I'm so sorry, honey. You must feel awful."

"I do." She didn't want to start crying, but thought she might. "They were such a sweet couple. So totally crazy about each other. When I saw them together last week they seemed so happy and connected. So . . . in sync. Know what I mean?"

He stroked her hair and kissed her forehead. "Like me and you, right?"

She couldn't tell if he was teasing her or not. If he was, it was in a good way, she decided.

"Exactly," she agreed. "An eccentric, reclusive, totally neurotic graphic artist obsessed with knitting and dogs. And an equally weird vet."

Matt laughed. "Don't forget nerdy. Me, I mean," he said.

"Didn't I say nerdy? I meant to."

He hugged her again and didn't say a thing for a while.

"I'm sorry we can't get together tonight," he said, and Lucy remembered Matt had to drive to Boston for some veterinarian association meeting. "Can this nerdy, neurotic guy make you dinner tomorrow?"

"Hey, who could resist an invitation like that?"

"Great." He pulled back a bit and looked down at her. "There's something I want to talk to you about." Lucy's expression must have immediately revealed her alarm. "Nothing bad," he promised.

"Okay, if you say so."

Lucy didn't exactly hate surprises. But she

sure hated it when people — like boyfriends, for instance — said they needed to have a talk. Then made you wait to find out what it was about.

But before she could ask any questions, both the phone and the intercom buzzed at once. "Sounds like my break is over."

"That's okay. I have a few other bored men on my list to visit today." She tried for a breezy tone and his alarmed expression was pleasing. Though they both knew she was only joking.

After an encouraging yank on Tink's leash, the big dog finally hopped off the couch.

Matt picked up the phone, then covered it with his hand. "I'll call you tonight. But I'm glad you came here today to talk to me."

"I'm glad, too," Lucy admitted.

She hadn't wanted to seem needy — the absolute kiss of death to relationships. She could see now there was no reason to worry. She and Matt really did seem to be in sync in all the ways that counted. That was saying a lot.

When Lucy got home she sat staring at her computer and forced herself to do deal with some mindless but necessary tasks. It was very hard to concentrate. Her thoughts kept drifting back to Jeremy and Rebecca. Lucy couldn't begin to imagine what the poor girl was feeling right now.

At the end of the day, she found an e-mail from Maggie, addressed to their whole group.

Just wanted to check in with everyone. It was hard to keep the shop open today but I managed. A little knitting helped. I'm sure you all feel the same. I've decided to visit the Baileys tonight. Rebecca is staying with her mother, and Nora's brother said he thought a few neighbors would stop by. Anyone interested in joining me? Let me know. Maybe we could ride together.

— XO, Maggie

Lucy wrote back right away.

I'll come with you. Call me and we'll figure out a good time.

XO, L.

Why not visit Rebecca and her family? She didn't have any plans and knew she'd just sit around tonight, feeling bleak about the whole thing. It would even be hard to knit. The shrug that she'd started for herself would remind her too much of the wedding.

No, it was far better to get out and do something — bring Rebecca and Nora flowers or some food. People could always use

98

something good to eat at a time like this, couldn't they?

Down in the kitchen Lucy checked the refrigerator and cupboards to see what she had on hand. Not too much. There was a chicken. Very promising. Never underestimate poultry, that was her cooking motto. One of them, anyway.

She grabbed an apron and got busy.

A few hours later, Lucy and Maggie arrived at the Bailey home, a wooden frame saltbox. The style was indigenous to New England and perennially popular. The neat, conservative-looking home, dark blue with white trim, was just the sort of place Lucy imagined Nora living. Though Rebecca had grown up here, she and Jeremy had their own apartment in the village, Maggie had mentioned. But Rebecca was staying with her mother now, at least until the funeral. Lucy had driven, picking Maggie up on her way.

"No other cars here yet," Maggie noted as Lucy parked her Jeep.

Lucy had noticed that, too. It was good in a way and bad. Good because she didn't know what to say to people she'd never met before, under these circumstances . . . after figuring out how they both knew the family and deceased. Bad because it would be hard to sit alone with Nora and Rebecca. Hard to know what to say to them about the tragedy, beyond the obvious.

Lucy took a breath as she retrieved the casserole dish from the backseat. These situations were never easy. This one in particular was uncommonly sorrowful.

Maggie had also whipped up something for the Baileys — a large date nut loaf that she'd wrapped in a basket.

"That smells good. What did you make?" Maggie asked, glancing at Lucy's dish.

"It turned out to be roast chicken with mushrooms, artichokes, and a few sun-dried tomatoes. Pretty much what I was able to scavenge in my kitchen."

"It sounds very tasty. I'm sure they'll appreciate it."

Lucy smiled but didn't answer. These acts of condolence cooking made the cooks feel a bit better. But she wasn't so sure that those on the receiving end noticed one way or the other what they were eating at such intense times of grief. If they were even able to eat.

Maggie rang the doorbell and Nora's brother, Gary, answered. He seemed to recognize them. "Hello, ladies. Come right in. Nice of you to stop by."

"We won't stay long. We just wanted to

see how Nora and Rebecca are holding up, and drop off some food."

"Rebecca is upstairs, resting. Nora's in the living room. Her next-door neighbors just left. Go right in," he told them.

Gary took their offerings to the kitchen while Lucy and Maggie made their way to the living room.

Nora sat in an armchair but stood up when the two women entered. "Maggie, Lucy . . . thank you for coming."

"No need to thank us," Maggie insisted. "I'm so very sorry." She gave Nora a hug and Lucy did the same.

"I don't know what to say. It's just so unbelievable."

Nora nodded sadly. "We still can't believe it. It's like a nightmare. You want to wake up and have everything be just the way it was. But you can't."

"Have they figured out how it happened?" Maggie sat down in an armchair and Lucy sat next to her.

"Not yet. It sounds to me like the fire department is in charge of sorting it out. They've called in special arson investigators. Jeremy worked with a lot of flammable chemicals. Even if he wasn't mixing them, there were many in his work space. A fire may have started and reached some explosive substance before he could put it out."

"What about sprinklers . . . that sort of thing?" Lucy asked. "Don't labs have all sorts of safety devices?"

Lucy remembered the lab in her high school and how their science teachers always demonstrated the special emergency shower to be used if anyone's clothing caught fire or if anyone suffered a chemical burn. There was always some kid who acted out every year by pulling the cord and flooding the room.

"Oh, there were plenty. But the sprinklers couldn't prevent the explosion. Once that occurred . . . it was . . . over." She swallowed hard and looked away. "The police officer I spoke to said poor Jeremy was . . . was blown to bits. There was no hope, even if someone had heard the alarm quickly." She took a deep, shaky breath and looked up at them again. "I know Jeremy was dedicated to his work and under a lot of pressure right now with his special project. But for goodness' sake, they'd just been married and about to leave for their honeymoon. Why did he have to go to that lab and work Monday night? If only he'd stayed with Rebecca."

If only . . . famous last words, Lucy thought. She sighed aloud. But there was nothing she could think of to say that would offer comfort.

"What is this project about, Nora? Do you know?" Maggie asked curiously.

Nora took a tissue from a box on the table and wiped her eyes again. "From what I can gather . . . it's just . . . glue. Some special miracle formula that's going to change the world. The world of glue, that is."

Maggie glanced at Lucy. No one could blame Nora for her sarcastic tone. It was obvious that she didn't think much of her son-in-law sacrificing himself to this questionable cause.

And her daughter suffering such a heartbreaking loss. One that would stay with her the rest of her life.

"A special type of glue?" Maggie also did not sound especially impressed.

"That's right." Nora glanced at the entrance to the living room, where they could see the foyer and staircase that led to the second floor.

"Rebecca doesn't like me to talk about it. That's why she's hardly told me anything about his work. Not that she knows that much. He had told her that it's some sort of amazing adhesive that could even be used by construction companies and to build cars, and for a lot of other industries. Supposedly, it will save companies millions of dollars in production costs."

Such a product would be extremely valuable and worth millions of dollars, Lucy thought.

"So it was important work, in that way," Maggie replied.

"Important to his father." Nora's mild tone took on a harsh note. So did her expression, Lucy noticed. "Philip Lassiter thinks he runs the world. He was nearly impossible about the wedding, and now he's totally impossible about the funeral arrangements. You would think he'd have some respect for my daughter's wishes."

"He doesn't?" Maggie asked.

"Oh, he starts off saying the right things. But if he doesn't get his way, he turns into an arrogant tyrant." Nora was incredulous. "Jeremy's mother, Patricia, has her own ideas about a memorial for her son. But she's much more considerate and concerned about Rebecca. I think Rebecca will just give in to both of them. She's so . . . bereft right now. She just wants to carry out Jeremy's wishes. He had some very specific ones," Nora added.

"He did? That's unusual for a young person," Maggie mused.

"Yes, it is," Nora agreed. "But he was very

detail minded. He wanted to be cremated, for one thing. He also added her name to all his bank accounts and investments before they were married, so that if anything happened to him, Rebecca would be taken care of. Maybe he was worried that his family wouldn't treat her fairly," Nora said in a hushed tone, glancing at the staircase again. "Cold comfort for my little girl, after all she's going through. Losing the love of her life."

Her voice faltered and she started crying again.

"Nora . . ." Maggie reached out and patted her friend's hand. Nora tried to compose herself, her head bowed for a moment.

"Is there anything we can do for you?" Lucy asked. "Or for Rebecca? Can we help you in any way?"

Nora finally looked up and shook her head. "Thank you but . . . I can't think of anything right now. I do appreciate you coming here tonight. Listening to me rattle on." She sighed. "It's been so hard since we heard the news. Thank goodness my brother was able to stay and help."

Gary seemed like a nice man, Lucy thought. Quiet and responsible. The type who would do what was needed in these situations.

As if on cue, he came in and glanced around the room. "Everyone okay in here? Would you like some coffee or tea? Some of that nice cake Maggie just brought? I'm sorry . . . I meant to ask you both before when you came in. I've just been cleaning up in the kitchen."

"I'm fine, thank you. In fact, I think we'd better go. We don't want to tire you out, Nora." Maggie glanced at Lucy.

Lucy stood up, relieved to end the visit. "I'm sorry we didn't get to see Rebecca. Please let her know we're thinking of her."

"I will," Nora promised. "We'll let you know about the memorial as soon as the plans are settled."

Lucy had just finished pulling on her pea-coat when the doorbell rang. "It's all right, Gary. I'll get it," Nora said to her brother.

Nora stepped forward and opened the door, then greeted the couple that stood in the front porch light. "Oh . . . Stewart. Pam . . ." Nora leaned forward and embraced them as they came in. "How good to see you. Come right in." She ushered the pair inside and the foyer suddenly felt a little crowded.

"Let me introduce my friends, Maggie Messina and Lucy Binger," Nora said. "This is Dr. Stewart Campbell, the principal at Rebecca's school."

The school principal seemed uncomfortable to be introduced that way and smiled nervously.

"Nora, you make me sound like a real boss or something. I'm an old friend of Rebecca's," he said, shaking hands. "This is my wife, Pam," he added, turning to his wife.

She smiled and nodded. "How are you guys doing? Hanging in there?"

"Just barely," Nora admitted. "Rebecca's upstairs sleeping. The doctor gave her something to calm her nerves."

"Yes, of course. That's probably the best thing now," Stewart said, sounding concerned.

"Poor thing. It's so unbelievable." A petite brunette with a shaggy haircut, Pam wore a dressy black coat with a fluffy fake fur collar. She glanced at her husband and squeezed his arm. Stewart responded with a sad expression looking lost for a moment in his thoughts.

He was not a very tall man, Lucy noticed, and the two seemed well matched physically. Lucy wondered if Pam was also a teacher. But she got the feeling that was not the case.

"Please don't disturb Rebecca," he said to

Nora. "We just wanted to drop off these flowers. Tell her that we're thinking of her. She's in our thoughts and our prayers. Me and Pam. And everyone at school. I don't want her to worry about a thing."

Stewart handed Nora a huge bouquet of pure white lilies, tied with a white satin ribbon. Very expensive . . . and dramatic, Lucy thought. Very thoughtful.

Maggie made her way toward the door, smiling politely. Lucy followed. "Nice to meet you," she said. "Good night now."

A few minutes later, Lucy and Maggie were seated side by side in Lucy's car, headed toward Maggie's house.

"I'm sorry we didn't get to see Rebecca . . . but in a way, it was a relief," Lucy admitted. "It will be so hard to face her. I'm afraid I'm going to just break down."

"I know what you mean." Maggie stared out the passenger-side window. "It won't be easy, no matter when we see her. Maybe it was just as well that Rebecca didn't come down. It seemed like Nora really needed to talk to someone about Rebecca's in-laws. She couldn't have vented like that in front of Rebecca, that's for sure."

"She has no great love for Philip Lassiter, does she? She makes him sound like he was cracking the whip over Jeremy. Nora didn't come right out and say it but, do you think Jeremy's father pressured him to finish up some work the night before his honeymoon?"

Maggie glanced at her. There was little light in the car, but Lucy could still see a certain glint in her friend's gray eyes. "I thought of that, too. That would be a heavy burden to bear. To think you may have played some part in your son's death. Even indirectly."

"That would be hard," Lucy agreed. Enough to haunt a person for the rest of his life. Enough to break some people altogether, she imagined.

Maggie had been watching out the passenger-side window, even though the road was dark and there was nothing much to see. She turned and looked at Lucy.

"This accident is more complicated than it sounded this morning, when we first heard the news. Don't you think?"

"I do." Lucy nodded, her gaze fixed on the empty road ahead.

It *was* more complicated. She had a feeling that there was more to come in this story. Much more.

Lucy was about to quit work early the next day, so she could do a bit of extra primping before she left for Matt's house, when she noticed an e-mail from Maggie. The subject line read: Jeremy's Memorial. She opened it quickly.

Dear Friends: I just heard from Nora's brother about the plans for Jeremy's memorial service. It will be held at Philip Lassiter's estate, on Thursday, eleven to one o'clock. I know this might be inconvenient for Suzanne and Dana, but Phoebe says she'll watch the shop so that I can go. If anyone else plans on going, just let me know. Perhaps we can drive over together. (This note sounds just like the one I sent around before the wedding!) Oh, that makes me so sad.

Hope we'll still have our meeting Thursday night.

Dana, it's your turn, right?

XO, Maggie

Lucy sent a quick note back to her friends, saying she wanted to go to the service and would check back tomorrow about who else was going.

Then she shut her computer and breathed a sigh of relief. For a minute there, she thought her turn to host the knitting meeting had come around. Not that she didn't like entertaining her group. But it did involve major house cleaning, shopping, and cooking dinner. A nice dinner. Which just didn't fit into her schedule this week.

As she dressed and blew out her hair, she wondered what Matt was making tonight. More important, what he wanted to talk about. Nothing too serious, she hoped. It felt like the end of a long difficult week. And it was only Wednesday.

She arrived at Matt's house right on time, for once. With a few overnight items packed in a knapsack for herself, and a few things for her dog. While Tink ran off to play with Walley, Lucy followed Matt into the kitchen.

She'd expected one of his usual manly "meat and potatoes" menus. But he surprised her with grilled salmon, one of her favorite dishes. Now she was really worried. When he cooked salmon, something was up. The side dishes looked equally tasty: string beans, roasted red potatoes with fresh herbs, and a salad of mixed baby greens and blue cheese and vinaigrette dressing.

The table had been set with brown woven place mats and candles. Lucy helped him bring the dishes to the table and they settled down to eat.

"This all looks delicious," she said.

"Help yourself. I'm starved. I didn't even

have a chance to stop for lunch today."

"Me, either." Lucy had been busy, and when she realized it was already three, she decided to skip lunch altogether and save her calories for dinner. She knew the way Matt cooked, without worrying about using butter or sugar, or any of the really good stuff.

They talked for a while about the usual things, trading stories about their day. Lucy told Matt about the new project she'd just started. Then the conversation came around to Jeremy again. When she described her visit to the Baileys', he didn't say much, but he didn't have to. She knew he sympathized with her.

Lucy looked over at him, ready to change the subject to something more cheerful . . . she hoped. "So . . . what's on your mind? You said you wanted to talk to me about something?"

He smiled, easily seeing through her Ms. Mellow act. "Yeah, I do. It's sort of important. It looks like I need to move out of this house by the end of the month."

Lucy was caught off guard by the news. Of all the serious talk topics that had bounced around her brain, this one had not been on the list

"Really? Why is that?" He had just moved

in when they'd met, so he'd only been here a year.

"My landlord told me he needs this house for his mother. She lives in Vermont and he wants to move her down to town. She's getting too old to live alone, but she won't move in with them. He lives around the corner, so this house is the next best thing."

"Oh . . . that's good of him. But bad for you," she added quickly. "When do you have to be out?"

"April 15," he said with a silly smile.

"That's just a little over two weeks. Didn't you get a month's notice in your lease?"

"Oh . . . he gave me about a month's notice. I guess I've been avoiding dealing with it."

Lucy was finished and put her fork aside. "I guess so. You didn't say a word. Any reason?"

He shrugged. Then sat back and took a long sip of wine. "So . . . what do you think?"

She squinted at him, not exactly smiling. She knew what he was asking, but wasn't he the one who had made the big dinner and asked her over to have a talk?

"About finding a new place to live? There aren't too many good rentals around here. Not as nice as this one."

"Nope, not at all . . . But I meant, maybe we should move in together. You must have thought about it . . . a little?"

"Not really . . . well, maybe a little," Lucy admitted. "Dana said she thinks we're already living together. Practically. We're just in denial about it. Something like that."

"So you have been thinking about it. You even talked to your friends."

"They brought it up. One night while we were knitting. They were practically interrogating me."

"Really? And what did you say?" he asked curiously.

She shrugged. "I don't know . . . I said we were perfectly happy and getting along great. And a year of going out isn't that long. But we're both divorced and it's a big step, especially for Dara and all that . . . don't you think?"

He shrugged. "It is a big step. But you know me. I think about things way too much. Maybe we should just go for it. Dana's right. What would be the big difference? Except sharing some bills and the shelves in the medicine chest?"

Lucy thought Matt could have the medicine chest in the half bath downstairs and she could get the big medicine chest in the upstairs bathroom. But she wasn't ready to

114

negotiate the fine print.

"Sounds pretty simple when you put it that way," she said.

"Isn't it? We're used to each other's habits, we know each other's tastes. I know what TV shows you like, how strong you like your coffee. Those silly pink foam earplugs you wear when you sleep. What else is there?"

Plenty, Lucy thought. She took a sip of her wine and eyed him over the glass. He sat perfectly still watching her, waiting for her answer.

"We are together almost every night. And when we're not, I miss you," he said finally.

"I miss you, too." She really did. Maybe that was enough of a reason, right there. . . .

"Can I think about this a little? It's come at me sort of suddenly," she said finally.

"Of course. I didn't mean we had decide right this minute."

He sounded sincere, though he would have probably liked it better if she'd just jumped into his arms and said, "Whoopee! Let's start packing your stuff right now."

"I know this is a big step, Lucy. I didn't mean to sound flip. Or make you feel pressured. I know how you feel about . . . your space."

He looked so serious and concerned. His eyes looked so blue.

She walked over to his side of the table and put her arm around his shoulder. "Thanks. You're being very understanding."

Lucy leaned over and put her cheek next to his. They stood like that for a moment or two. Then she stood up, her hands resting on his shoulders.

"Okay, I've thought about it. When do you want to move in?"

He laughed. "Are you sure? I don't want you to agree if you aren't a hundred percent positive. I can find another apartment, and my landlord will give me more time. I won't be upset. Honest. Why don't you take a day or two?"

"No need. I'm sure. One hundred and . . . a million percent. I want to be with you all the time. The first thing in the morning and the last thing at night. But I will be wearing my wacky foam earplugs," she warned him.

"Hopefully, not too much else." He grabbed her around the waist and pulled her onto his lap. "The dogs will be very disappointed if we don't go through with this. They've been listening to every word."

He glanced down at the dogs, resting together under the table. Lucy looked, too.

"Oh . . . in that case. I guess we have to."

CHAPTER FIVE

The memorial was held at the Lassiter estate. Maggie remembered the way. She was driving her friends there again, but this time, only Lucy and Dana. She was glad for any company. This type of event was difficult and she expected this one to be uncommonly so.

"I guess Jeremy's father got his way after all," Maggie murmured. They had just rounded the last turn and the tall gates of the estate came into view.

"Nora had a feeling he would," Lucy replied.

"Maybe they managed to reach some compromise," Dana suggested. She was sitting in the backseat and turned to look out the window. "The same long line of cars we saw at the wedding. Probably most of the same people inside."

"I'd imagine so. And even more coming to pay their respects to Jeremy. Nora said the family expected a big crowd. There have been so many calls and flowers sent already. Co-workers from At-Las Technologies and from the university. Jeremy taught a few chemistry courses there. He wasn't a tenured professor but he enjoyed it, Nora told me," Maggie said.

"I didn't know that," Dana remarked. "He did have an academic manner, now that you mention it," she added.

"I thought of that, too, when I first met him," Lucy said as they finally reached the stone-paved circle in front of the mansion.

From the sight of all the cars, it would seem that even a stadium would not accommodate the turnout. Once again, well-dressed valets and other household staff were on hand to park cars and then collect coats as the guests went inside.

The atmosphere was greatly subdued, compared to the wedding day, Maggie noticed. Not that the house decor had been altered in any way. It was just the somber, quiet mood of the guests as they moved through the foyer into the large gallery room again.

The room had been set up very much as it had been for the wedding, though this time, rows of black cushioned chairs filled the large space. The wooden podium stood in the same place. The beautiful flower arch that had sheltered the bride and groom as they'd exchange vows was gone. But there was a large ceramic urn filled with an arrangement of white roses next to the podium and a small, curved-legged table that displayed framed photographs of Jeremy at various stages of his life.

As the knitting friends walked in and looked for seats, Maggie noticed Nora and Rebecca sitting up front. She turned and waved to them.

"Look, there's Rebecca," she whispered to Lucy and Dana. "Oh, she looks awful. Poor girl."

Rebecca did look awful, it was no exaggeration. Her hair was pulled back in a tight ponytail, her face bare of makeup, her eyes puffy and red-rimmed. She wore a plain black dress with a black cardigan on top. Pearl earrings and her sparkling wedding band and engagement ring were her only adornments.

It was not only her bedraggled appearance but her entire aspect; she sagged in her seat, staring blankly at the floor, looking too weak and worn out to hold her head up.

Nora sat on one side of her daughter and Rebecca's uncle Gary sat on the other side of Nora.

119

Nora held her daughter's pale hand, their fingers entwined. She also looked tired and tested, but far more alert. Ready for the event to begin . . . and be done with, Maggie imagined.

"I'm going to visit with them a moment. Save me a seat, will you?" Maggie said to the others.

Dana nodded and walked off with Lucy to look for seats. Maggie continued up the aisle to the front row. She leaned over and kissed Nora's cheek and then Rebecca's.

"You poor thing. You're very brave. I feel for you," Maggie said sincerely as she hugged Rebecca close.

"Thank you for coming, Maggie. I appreciate it," Rebecca replied quietly.

"What a turnout," she said to Nora and Gary. "Jeremy was very loved and respected. That's for sure."

"Oh, he was. No question," Nora agreed. She glanced at her watch. "I think we should be starting any minute. We're just waiting for the rest of the family to arrive. You would think Philip Lassiter would be the first one here. It is his house," she said with a sigh.

Nora had a point, but they already knew how much Philip enjoyed making an entrance. But it was a mean thing, even to

120

think, Maggie scolded herself. The poor man had just lost his son.

She stood up and looked for her friends. "I'd better find my seat. We hope to see you later," she said, though she imagined there would be a crush of people around the Baileys, offering condolences. She'd been lucky to have a word with them.

Maggie finally spotted Lucy and Dana a few rows back on the other side of the aisle. But Dana shook her head, making a face at the woman next to her, who was just fitting herself into the seat Dana had tried to save.

No help for that. Maggie realized she was on her own and looked around for a single spot.

The row behind Nora with a black ribbon on the aisle side was reserved for family. She watched as Jeremy's twin brother, Alec, and his sister, Claudia, entered the row and sat behind Nora and Rebecca. Their mother, Patricia Moore, looking stunning in a black crepe wool suit and an upswept hairstyle, took a seat beside Rebecca and gently took the girl's soft white hand in her own.

Maggie noticed an empty seat in the row behind the Lassiter siblings and quickly claimed it. She felt a little awkward, sitting so close to the front when she wasn't even a family member. But there was no help for it now. She sat back in her seat, waiting for the proceedings to begin and took out her knitting — a new spring pattern she was making as a sample for a class she would teach at the shop.

As she began to stitch, it was hard not to overhear the conversation of Alec and Claudia, who sat directly in front of her and commented on everyone who walked in.

Maggie had once playfully listed one of her hobbies as eavesdropping on some singles match-up application. It was true. Just a little quirk she had. She couldn't help listening in on other people's conversations. It was usually very interesting.

"Look who's here, *Icky* Ferris," Claudia whispered to her brother. "We're lucky there's no open burial plot. Little Erica would be tempted to jump in."

"That would be a bad thing?" Alec said. "What a piece of work that woman is. The best thing my brother ever did for himself was to get untangled from her claws. Too bad he didn't live long enough to reap the benefits," he added sadly.

The barb was wicked and sharp. Maggie looked back, curious to see the intended target. A very attractive young woman had just found a seat on the opposite side of the aisle, a few rows down. Her dark looks were striking and exotic, Maggie thought. She was slender with high cheekbones and large brown eyes. Her shiny dark hair was pulled back and twisted at her nape, and she wore a straight charcoal gray skirt with a black twin set. Pure cashmere and high quality, Maggie could tell, even from a distance. The ensemble was quite conservative, even bland, yet she somehow looked sophisticated and subtly sensual.

The ex-girlfriend, Maggie surmised. The significant other in Jeremy's life before Rebecca had come along. The exact physical opposite of Rebecca, too, Maggie could not help but notice.

Jeremy's taste in women certainly ran the gamut. Was this sultry beauty mourning the death of long-lost love? Or simply paying her respects to the past and the family. Jeremy's siblings obviously hadn't been rooting for her as their future sister-in-law, that was for sure.

"Is she still at the lab?" Alec asked Claudia.

His sister sighed and nodded. "She transferred to another department. But we couldn't fire her. Jeremy didn't want us to. And we couldn't risk a lawsuit."

"She was probably just hanging around in case Rebecca didn't work out," Alec said.

"She's like a gorgeous spider."

"Speaking of insects," Claudia said, "look who else crawled out of the woodwork. Up front, making nice to Mother. I'm glad Dad isn't here yet. He'll have a stroke." Claudia practically gasped and Maggie saw her grip her brother's arm.

"One can only hope," Alec said spitefully. "But I always liked Uncle Louie. I hope he stops to say hello to me. He was never cowed by Dad. I'll give him that much."

"No, he never was. Jeremy liked him, too," Claudia recalled quietly. "He took Lewis's side in the split. Dad nearly banished him over that."

"But the family business needed Jeremy's brains too much. Unlike my own," he quipped with a self-deprecating laugh.

Maggie realized then that the man they were talking about, whom they called Uncle Louie, had to be Lewis Atkins, Philip Lassiter's former friend and business partner.

"Louie has a clear run at the goal now, with Jeremy gone. It's first down and two, I'd say. Personally, I wish the old guy luck." Alec sounded quite sincere.

"Bite your tongue," Claudia snapped. "Jeremy backed up all his notes. We just have to find everything and fit it together."

"Before Uncle Louie fills in the blanks,

you mean." Alec was needling her.

"If he had a clue, don't you think he would have gotten there already?" Claudia's tone was low and angry now. But underneath, she sounded scared, Maggie realized. Very scared. "We're there first, no question. I don't think you get it. A lot of people are depending on this, Alec. Not just our family."

"I get it, dear." Alec patted his sister's hand. "I'm just not part of the home team anymore. You forget."

Claudia turned and faced Alec, then shook her head regretfully. He had a truckload of anger toward his father, that was for sure. Enough to have sabotaged At-Las Technologies' big project himself, Maggie realized. Though somehow she doubted Alec would have harmed his brother. But maybe that part had been unintentional?

Maggie was surprised at the odd turn her thoughts had taken.

As far as anyone knew, the lab fire and explosion had been an accident. What in the world made her think otherwise?

But she was interested to hear what else the siblings had to say. She stitched away, the perfect cover for listening in on private conversations, she'd discovered. People think you must be concentrating on your

work when it's really going on quite auto-
matically.

She heard someone clear his throat nearby
and looked up to find a man waiting to
move into her row.

Not just any man . . . it was Lewis Atkins,
eyeing the empty seat right next to her.

"May I?" he asked politely.

"Oh, I'm sorry. Of course, just let me get
my things out of your way." She quickly
stood up and moved her purse and knitting
tote to allow Atkins to pass by. He was not
a tall man, just a few inches taller than her
and about her age, she'd guess. He had a
good head of hair, once fair and now white.
His dark eyes peered at her from under
bushy brows but he had a soft smile, and
looked vaguely amused at his surroundings.
He wore a dark tweed sports coat with a
white oxford cloth shirt and black satin bow
tie. She hardly ever saw men wear bow ties
anymore. It seemed to her a mark of character.

He glanced at her with a polite smile.
"Sorry to interrupt. I hope you didn't drop
any stitches." He looked over her knitting
project with interest. "Nice work."

"Thanks. Do you knit?" Maggie wasn't
trying to be facetious, though she may have
sounded that way. Male knitters came into

126

her shop all the time. It wasn't as uncommon as some thought. At one time, only men were allowed to knit, working in medieval guilds. But people had long since forgotten that.

"No, I don't. But I've often thought of learning. It's a wonderful, productive pastime."

"It is. But more than that for me. I own a knitting shop in town. The Black Sheep, on Main Street."

"I know that one. I've noticed your shop but have never gone in. Maybe I will now," he added. "My name is Lewis Atkins, by the way."

"Maggie Messina," she answered. And I already know all about you, Uncle Louie, she was tempted to add.

But didn't. Partly because she really didn't know anything about him, she realized. It was all hearsay, filtered through the lens of other people's experiences . . . and grievances.

It was awkward to make someone's acquaintance at a funeral. But he had excellent social skills, she noticed, and it didn't feel quite as odd as it could have.

"I hope you don't think it's disrespectful to be knitting here." She began to put her knitting away, realizing that some people might be offended.

"Not at all. I admire anyone who makes good use of their time. Life is short. None of us can afford to waste a minute. You can never get any of it back, you know," he said somberly.

"Very true. Unfairly brief for some. Like poor Jeremy." Maggie sighed and pushed a rubber tip on the needle that held her work, then stashed it all in her tote.

Atkins nodded. "I watched him grow up. He was always curious. Always asking questions, amazed by the natural world. That boy could sit and look at an ant hill for hours. Stare up at the clouds all afternoon. Collected things, rocks, seashells, dead bugs. He loved brain teasers and puzzles. He would make up secret codes and try to stump me." Atkins laughed at the memories. "A brilliant student. He made us all very proud. What a waste of talent." He paused and sighed, then looked over at her again. "Did you know him very well?"

Maggie was awed by the vivid picture Atkins had painted of Jeremy as a boy. How touching, she thought. It sounded as if Lewis Atkins truly did love Jeremy, as if he was his real blood relation.

"No . . . sorry to say I did not. We'd only met once or twice. I do know his wife, Rebecca, and her mother, Nora," Maggie replied.

"Rebecca, his beautiful bride." Lewis Atkins sighed again. "I just met her. I wasn't at the wedding. I heard it was wonderful," he said. "What a great loss. And she's so young."

"Oh, yes. They say time heals all wounds. I hope it's true for her."

"I do, too. Though all the time in the world won't heal some rifts."

It sounded as if he'd experienced the exception to that rule. Was he thinking of his break with Philip Lassiter and At-Las Technologies?

But before they could continue their discussion, Maggie noticed that a minister had come up to the front of the room and took his place behind the podium, arranging a pile of typewritten pages.

The room grew silent but he didn't begin. He kept glancing over his reading glasses, at the seated rows of guests. What were they all waiting for? Maggie wondered. Then she realized, when all heads turned, the delay had been caused by Philip Lassiter.

She turned, too, to watch as he slowly walked up the middle aisle. He used a cane today and his young wife walked on his other side, holding his arm for further support.

He looked very different from the wedding day. Hardly the lionlike patriarch. He was greatly diminished, as if he'd suffered a true body blow and had barely staggered back into the ring.

Even his fine clothes — a black suit, white shirt, and silvery tie — seemed to be wearing him today, Maggie thought. Large glasses with aviator frames and smoky lenses covered much of his face.

Maggie knew it was unfair, but she had to wonder if this pathos was indeed real, or simply a play for sympathy. Many here would find him culpable in his son's death. She didn't doubt that for one moment. Perhaps his infirmity was some sort of diversion? But it was not fair to even suspect such a thing, Maggie realized. The man had just lost a son. Of course he would look depleted and overwhelmed.

As Philip Lassiter ambled past, she found her body growing tense, waiting for some explosion of temper when he noticed Lewis Atkins. The same sort of outburst he'd had at the wedding, sparked by Alec's unexpected appearance. But there was none. Lassiter either didn't notice his old friend, or chose to ignore him.

She carefully glanced at Atkins, who sat with his eyes straight ahead, his hands resting in his lap. He showed no interest at all in his former partner — and present rival, if Alec and Claudia could be believed. If Maggie didn't know better, she would have never suspected that the two men knew each other.

Perhaps their parting was not as bitter as Lassiter's children believed. Or maybe their hatred had gone completely cold by now.

Once Jeremy's father was seated, the memorial began. Speaker after speaker painted a picture of Jeremy as a dedicated scientist, a gifted teacher, a good friend, and an able coworker — a young man with every advantage who was not above sharing his time and talents with those less fortunate.

Stewart Campbell, the principal at Rebecca's school, spoke about Jeremy starting a science club for children in a low-income neighborhood. In fact, he told the audience, that was how Jeremy and Rebecca met, through their mutual commitment to help others.

"To think that a man of his stature and brilliance would come to our little elementary school every week to teach and inspire these forgotten children. To share his love

131

of the natural world and the method of scientific discovery. I am sure that he's inspired many youngsters to follow his path. To take his place someday in the halls of scientific study . . ."

Stewart Campbell was not a bad speaker. But he was a bit didactic, Maggie thought, and long-winded at the podium. He seemed quite moved by his own speech, she noticed, and kept pushing the frame of his wire-rimmed glasses as they slipped down his nose, his voice growing thick with emotion.

Finally, he was finished, and a representative of the university stepped up, also praising Jeremy's intellect and gift for sharing his knowledge in one of the most rigorous scientific areas. "The university and medical school will sorely miss this outstanding scholar and scientist."

Claudia Lassiter got up and spoke for the family. She told a few anecdotes from childhood that softened and humanized the austere image created by the previous speakers. Jeremy also had a sense of humor and had been quite a prankster, often switching identities with his brother, Alec, who would somehow always catch the blame, Claudia reported. Alec was the older brother, by two minutes, she explained.

This detail drew a soft laugh from the

crowd and even a small brief, smile from their mother, Patricia. She glanced at Rebecca and squeezed her hand.

This was a different side of the young man, one that had not come across at their first meeting, she had to admit. But that was why these gatherings were important. You learned a lot about the person who had passed on and could honor his memory more completely.

Claudia also praised her brother's commitment to the family enterprise, At-Las Technologies, and his great contributions.

"He felt a deep, personal connection to every one of our employees. He knew them all by name, the names of their spouses and children. He may have seemed the classic, absentminded professor, with his head off in the clouds. But Jeremy was very much of this world and cared about the well-being of everyone who works in this company."

Maggie noticed Rebecca nod in agreement. She was proud of her late husband's fine qualities. At least that was some comfort to her.

Finally, the minister led the group in a short prayer. Maggie bowed her head, though she didn't close her eyes completely. She noticed Lewis Atkins had not closed his eyes, either, and now glanced over one shoulder.

What — or whom — was he looking at? she wondered. She couldn't help herself and discreetly followed his gaze.

The beautiful Erica Ferris. Of course. Erica met his glance for a moment, then quickly shook her head. She closed her large brown eyes and continued — or pretended? — to pray.

When the service was over, Maggie rose and looked around for her friends. But before she could make her way out of the row, Lewis Atkins drew her attention.

"It was nice meeting you, Ms. Messina . . . even under such sad circumstances. May I stop by your shop sometime, to say hello?"

Maggie was suddenly flustered. She still didn't know what to make of Lewis Atkins. Was he the villain of this drama . . . or just much maligned by the Lassiters? The family was no prize package, either. That was for sure.

"Please do. Anytime. Here's my card." She pulled one from her knitting bag and handed it to him.

He looked at the card a moment, then slipped it into his wallet. He then offered his card to her.

"Here's one for you. In case you'd like to Google me," he joked.

"I didn't think of it," she admitted. "But I guess I probably should."

Her frank reply made him smile. He seemed to like her all the more for it.

"Just remember, you can't believe everything you read on the Internet," Atkins reminded her.

"Yes, I know. Remember that if you Google me," she added as they parted.

As Maggie had expected, the line leading to Rebecca, Jeremy's mother, and the rest of the family could have circled a city block. Maggie had to get back to her shop and she doubted Dana or Lucy wanted to wait, either.

She found her friends and they made their way to the foyer, retrieved their coats, and gave the valet their car ticket.

"I'm sorry I didn't get to speak to Rebecca. But I'm glad I came," Lucy said.

"I'm glad we came, too. It was very interesting to hear everyone speak about Jeremy. That's a great benefit of these gatherings," Maggie noted. "Especially for people like us, who hardly knew him."

"Who was that sitting next to you, Maggie? You seemed to be getting along very well," Dana asked as Maggie's car pulled up.

"You'll never believe it." Maggie slipped

135

into the driver's seat. "It was Lewis Atkins, Philip Lassiter's former partner. We had an interesting conversation. He said he wants to stop by the shop."

She didn't relate that he suggested she Google him. She knew they would tease her mercilessly.

"That is interesting," Dana murmured in the backseat as they headed to town.

"I also got an earful, sitting behind Jeremy's brother and sister," Maggie added. "I didn't mean to listen in. But they weren't even trying to be discreet.

"It's funny how well we can hear when we really want to, isn't it?" Dana asked. "It's some amazing connection between our mind and body going on, I think."

"What did they talk about? Now you've made me curious," Lucy admitted.

Maggie smiled at her. "It was all very . . . juicy stuff. But I think I'm going to save it for our meeting tonight. I'll feel bad enough repeating it once. I don't want to be a complete gossip."

Dana laughed. "Very noble of you. If you only disclose it once, that doesn't count?"

"I suppose it does," Maggie said, caught in an ethical quandary. "Okay, my lips are sealed. I won't tell you what I overheard. That's the high road, right, Dana?"

"The high and boring road," Lucy said.

"Oh, you've tantalized us now. Just make sure we all promise not to repeat anything. I think I can live with that." Dana sighed and sat back in her seat.

"I can, too," Maggie decided. "People are fascinating. The things they say, their grievances and passions. What makes them tick. I'm sorry, I just can't help listening in at times."

"Don't apologize to me." Dana patted Maggie's shoulder. "I make a living at it."

Maggie laughed. Perhaps she should have gone back to school after her career as an art teacher and become a therapist. But she was better off running her shop and teaching knitting, she decided. More of a fiber therapist. She was helping people, too, she thought. A different path, to the same end.

That night, Maggie was the last one to arrive at Dana's house for their meeting. Dana greeted her at the door with a hug and hung her coat in the hall closet — tidy as a pin, Maggie noticed, with plastic boxes on a shelf above the rack, bearing labels such as "Baseball Caps," "Umbrellas," and "Waterproof Gloves."

"Where's Phoebe? Does she have a class tonight?" Dana asked.

"She has a paper due tomorrow and put it off until the last minute, as usual. She has to hunker down and pull an all-nighter," Maggie explained. "She did ask me to bring her some dessert."

"No problem. Lucy made a flourless chocolate cake. It looks like a killer."

"A slice of that should cheer her," Maggie agreed.

Lucy and Suzanne looked up from the knitting to greet her as she entered the great room adjoining the kitchen, at the back of Dana's house. They were seated on the cushy leather sectional that circled a large slate table. A fire flickered in the sleek, black marble hearth.

Lucy had started a new project, Maggie noticed, but she couldn't quite tell what it was. She'd put aside the shrug she'd begun for herself, right after the wedding. Understandably. It was an unhappy reminder of the newlyweds' tragedy and was a bit unnerving for everyone to look at it.

Maggie sat next to Lucy and took out her own knitting, and wondered how long it would take for anyone to ask her about it.

Lucy peered over at her project. "What are you working on now? I can't figure it out."

"An amigurumi," Maggie replied, knowing that was no explanation and no one in the room probably had the vaguest idea of what she meant.

"An ama — what?" Suzanne looked at her across the table. "Sounds like an appetizer at a Japanese restaurant."

Dana laughed. "I know what it is. A little stuffed toy, right?"

Maggie nodded. "Exactly. There are loads of different patterns. But I'm focusing on a spring theme. I'm going to knit up a bunch of birds and such and put them in the window for a display . . ." She dug around in her knitting tote. "Here's a picture."

She put a photo of the cute, colorful amigurumi birds and beasts on the table. Everyone immediately oohed and aahed.

"Oh, these are adorable. You'll have people asking right away how to make them." Suzanne picked up the picture to take a closer look.

"That's my hope. Business has been a bit slow lately. I was thinking of running a special: Birds of a Feather Knit Together. A two-for-one class." Maggie looked around, trying to gauge their reaction. "And maybe a contest of some kind? Win a free basket of yarns and needles and such. And a lesson or two?"

"That all sounds good to me," Lucy said.

"Maybe everyone is just making that transition from winter knitting to spring and summer?"

"Could be," Maggie mused. "The birds were a fallback plan. I had really wanted to do a spring wedding theme for the window using Rebecca's gown and the bridesmaids' shrugs that you all made. Maybe use some photos of the wedding. Nora even dropped off the gown after the wedding. Before . . ." She paused. Everyone knew what she was about to say. "Well, I certainly can't do that now."

"It would be hard to look at her gown or any of that right now," Suzanne agreed. "But I still want to hear about the memorial. I'm so sorry I couldn't make it." Suzanne stared straight at Maggie. "I hear you sat up close and personal to the Lassiters. And chatted up Philip Lassiter's old business partner. Who asked you on a date or something?"

"Oh, dear . . . I wouldn't go that far. He just gave me his card. Who told you that wild story?"

"He was definitely interested, Maggie. I'd be surprised if he didn't stop by the shop very soon." Dana set down a plate of freshly made hummus circled by little triangles of pita bread and alongside that, a bowl of cucumber yogurt dip and one of black olives.

"He was just being friendly. I gather he had ventured into enemy territory and was happy to talk to anybody. He did express great fondness and respect for Jeremy," she recalled. "Alec and Claudia seem to have mixed feelings about him. They call him Uncle Louie and it seems he was a member of the family while they were growing up. But the breakup with Philip Lassiter was definitely bitter. Claudia takes her father's side. But it sounded like Jeremy sided with Atkins in the feud. Strange, right? But he does have issues with his father."

Dana theatrically cleared her throat. "To put it mildly."

"And what about the sibs? You haven't filled us in yet on that conversation. You said it was very juicy," Lucy reminded her.

"I did say that, didn't I?" Maggie regretted that now, though it was true. "Well . . . if you all promise not to repeat anything, I'll try to recall. It was enlightening, I must say. Let's see . . . they noticed a lovely, dark-haired woman first, Erica Ferris. Seems she was Jeremy's former flame and worked with him at the lab. I thought she was a real knockout. But they both seemed to think Jeremy was very smart to break off the

141

relationship."

"I know who you mean." Lucy had noticed her, too. "She sat a row or two ahead of me and Dana and had on a black sweater set?"

"Yes, that was her. Claudia and Alec tore her apart mercilessly." She shrugged, working the small stitches on the mother bird pattern.

"Interesting. What else did they talk about?" Suzanne asked eagerly.

"Mainly about At-Las Technologies and the formula Jeremy had been working on. It seems there's a race with Atkins's company to perfect it and get it to the marketplace. I had no idea that was going on. Rebecca and Nora never mentioned it. But it makes sense if you think about it. The project has been a long time in the making and Atkins must have been at the company for the original idea and early research."

"And they may not have filed a patent yet when he left, so it wasn't protected," Dana added.

"It sounded to me like Jeremy still hadn't perfected it," Maggie told the others. "Alec talked about some missing pieces to the puzzle. But Claudia claimed Jeremy had it all in his notes and all they have to do is put it together."

"I guess the explosion and fire set them back," Lucy said. "He must have had a lot of notes in his lab."

"Maybe . . . maybe not. Claudia said he had saved notes off-site."

"That's what I should do," Lucy said. "I'm terrible about backing up my files. If my hard drive ever crashes, I'm in serious trouble."

"Lucy, I can't believe you're bad about backing up. That's your business," Dana reminded her. "I have the same issue with my office records. There are services you can use. Cheap, too. But a big company like At-Las must have had all kinds of built-in backup systems. And loads of security for their trade secrets."

"Yes, they must," Maggie agreed. "Who knows what's really going on? But it did give me a glimpse into the rivalries between scientists, how competitive they are, racing toward some big discovery. Sounds worse than professional sports," she said with a small laugh. "Especially since this one is potentially so valuable. From what Claudia said, it sounds like the fate of At-Las Technologies — and the family fortune — is hanging in the balance. Another reason Jeremy's death was such a blow."

"Oh, yes, they talked about that, too. Alec

made some sardonic remark about how their father would have kicked Jeremy out of the family, too, but he needed his brains too much."

Dana looked up from her knitting and blinked. "Wow, that sounds positively toxic."

"Oh, it was," Maggie said quietly.

They all sat knitting for a few minutes without talking.

"You know, if this was a movie or book, that explosion and fire that killed Jeremy wouldn't have been an accident," Suzanne surmised. "It would have been corporate sabotage or something like that."

"Sabotage . . . by whom? Lewis Atkins, you mean?" Maggie heard a certain defensive note in her tone that was surprising. Even to herself.

Lucy glanced at her. "I know you enjoyed his conversation. But he wouldn't be the first charming scoundrel."

"Of course not. But . . . well, I don't think so. He just didn't seem the type. The things he said about Jeremy . . . It sounded like he genuinely loved him and felt real grief."

Maggie knew she was defending him. But she felt she had an objective perspective on Atkins. She just didn't think he had any part in Jeremy's death.

"Maybe he didn't think Jeremy was there.

He probably knew about the wedding and thought the couple had left on their honeymoon and the lab was empty. Especially at that time of night."

"Well, possibly. He did know about the wedding," Maggie recalled. "But a lot of people knew about it and could have thought the same. It didn't have to be Atkins," Maggie pointed out. "Once you take a close look at this mix of personalities and past history . . . well, there are a few people who may have wanted to throw a wrench into At-Las Technologies' big project."

"That is true," Lucy agreed. "And I'm not at all sure this notion of corporate sabotage even makes sense. The notes for this super-secret formula had to have been backed up in a few different places. If anything, the fire and explosion would have made a mess and diverted the company's energy for a little while. But it wouldn't have destroyed the formula altogether."

"Not unless Jeremy didn't have it figured out yet. Maybe that's why he was working up to the last minute before his honeymoon trip." Suzanne took a slice of pita bread from the platter and chewed it thoughtfully.

"I'm sorry, ladies," Dana said. "As interesting as this corporate sabotage theory sounds, I have it on good authority that both the fire department arson experts and the insurance investigators haven't found anything to suggest the explosion and fire were intentionally set."

"On good authority . . . meaning Jack has talked to people about it?" Maggie asked.

Dana's husband, Jack, was a former police detective turned attorney and had a lot of law enforcement connections in town. If there was a hot case going on, Jack usually had the inside story, and Dana usually passed on what she could to her friends.

Maggie was glad to hear that, for some odd reason.

The notion of anyone — not just Lewis Atkins — killing poor Jeremy, just for the sake of some glue formula, was too heinous and cold-blooded to even consider.

"Let's talk about something a little more upbeat for a while," Maggie suggested. "Doesn't anyone have something positive to report?"

Nobody answered. Maggie looked around the room. Her gaze gravitated to Lucy. She knew that little smile by now, though her friend did her best to hide it behind a thick veil of wavy blond hair.

"Lucy? Do you have something to tell us?"

Lucy looked up from her knitting, staring around as if she'd just woken up from a nap.

146

"Well . . . actually, I do," she said slowly. "Matt and I were talking the other night and he's going to move in with me."

CHAPTER SIX

Lucy didn't expect the news to surprise anyone. Not after all their well-intentioned but needling remarks on this topic.

But her friends stared at her wide-eyed. All except Dana, who stitched away steadily with a small knowing smile.

"You've been sitting here the entire time and didn't say a word?" Suzanne's voice rose on a note of miffed surprise.

"I'm telling you right now, aren't I?" Lucy replied calmly. "We only decided last night."

"I think it's great." Dana's smile was warm and encouraging. "You two are definitely ready. When does he move in?"

"He needs to leave his apartment by April 15."

"That's not very long. What is it . . . two weeks?" Maggie said.

"Did our conversation last week inspire any of this?" Suzanne shot Lucy a look.

"More like an interrogation," Lucy reminded her. "But no . . . it didn't figure into things at all."

But, since Suzanne brought it up, Lucy wondered now if their prodding had, in a very tangential way, played some part. Did the mere fact that she'd started thinking about it somehow send a silent vibe to Matt? They were uncannily in sync at times. He said so himself.

"I never mentioned it," Lucy said. "Matt's landlord needs the house for his mother. She can't live alone anymore and is moving down from Vermont. Matt has to find a new place so he brought it up. I guess he'd been thinking about it, too."

"Of course he was. He's crazy about you," Suzanne insisted. "It won't be that different. I bet you guys barely notice."

Lucy was crazy about Matt, too . . . but she knew she would notice.

The rest of the evening went by quickly. When Dana brought out coffee and tea, Lucy served the cake she'd made. It was so rich, the first bite gave her a chocolate headache, but it was well worth it.

Maggie remembered to wrap up an extra-large slice for Phoebe. "Chocolate is one of her three food groups, you know that, right? Along with Greek yogurt and black coffee."

Lucy also took a slice for Matt. It was his favorite.

"So that's how you hooked him," Suzanne said between bites.

"Not quite. But it didn't hurt," Lucy admitted. "I hope he doesn't expect one of these every week now. I'll gain a hundred pounds in no time."

"But he'll love you anyway," Dana reminded her.

"Watch out, Lucy. You'll be comfortable old married people before you know it," Suzanne predicted.

Lucy just smiled. She didn't even want to think about that yet.

Lucy dealt with her anxiety about Matt's imminent change of address in her usual way. By making a list. On Monday morning she found a yellow legal pad and made a list of chores she needed to do before he arrived. "Clean closets" and "paint bedroom" were close to the top. Luckily, a break in deadlines gave her some time to prepare for this milestone.

Matt was busy packing most of the weekend, but they managed to fit in a stop at the hardware store to look at paint chips.

"I was thinking a soft, buttery yellow color. Something very Provence . . ." Lucy mused, twirling the rack.

"Hey, this one is nice." Matt pulled out a card. "I like that," he said flatly.

Lucy glanced at it. It was blue. Not even robin's egg, but a dreary gray blue. Vulture's egg blue, if she had to name it.

She took a breath. "Not so bad . . . but the curtains and bedspread and all that go better with yellow."

"I have a nice quilt we could use. It's gray and black with tan triangles and sort of stripes on the sides. That would go pretty well, don't you think?"

Lucy despised that quilt. She had to grit her teeth every time she looked at it. Luckily, whenever she stayed over, it was pretty dark in the room and she was too distracted to pay it much notice.

She was really hoping that particular household item would not make its way over her threshold . . . *their* threshold, she reminded herself.

The problem was that practically everything Matt owned was black, brown, gray, or tan. The "real man" color spectrum. Fitting his belongings in with hers was a decorating challenge. Or nightmare, depending on how you looked at it.

"You know," she said finally, "I'm not even sure we really need to paint that room right now. Why don't we just move your things and see how it looks?"

Matt agreed, since he didn't have time to help her, anyway. Lucy was fine with that. She liked to paint and figured if she did the work, she got to pick the color. Right?

When the week started, Lucy was so busy getting the cottage in shape, she totally neglected her knitting . . . and keeping up with her friends. She only left the house to go to the grocery store, and didn't walk to town once. It was too rainy to walk much anyway.

The sun finally appeared again on Wednesday. Lucy pulled back the drapes and squinted at her backyard. Everything looked so green, with spurts of grass pushing up from the dark earth and tiny buds on the trees and bushes. Birds hopped from branch to branch, driving Tink wild with their chirping.

She opened the window a crack and the dog pressed her nose against the screen, eager to do more than bird-watch. Lucy wanted to get outside, too. She leashed up Tink and headed for Maggie's shop.

When she tied Tink to her usual spot on the porch, she noticed Maggie had changed the window display. The clever kites were gone. A flock of colorful knitted birds had taken their place, hopping around a tree Maggie had fashioned out of cardboard, complete with paper leaves.

A few of the birds perched on branches, some in a nest of cottony white and tan roving. Maggie always had little chunks left on the spinning wheel and Lucy imagined she gathered them, much like a nesting bird herself.

A sign on the tree read LEARN HOW TO MAKE THESE ADORABLE FEATHERED FRIENDS . . . AND MORE. IT'S EASY AND FUN. TRY OUR NEW CLASS: "BIRDS OF A FEATHER." SIGN UP WITH A FRIEND AND GET A 50% DISCOUNT!

A large knitting tote filled to the brim with needles, yarn, and pattern books was settled next to the tree trunk. Another sign read ENTER TO WIN THIS FABULOUS START-TO-KNIT KIT. NO PURCHASE NECESSARY. ENTRY SLIPS INSIDE.

That was Maggie. She faced a problem squarely and took action. Not enough sales and traffic in her shop? Figure out a way to bring in more customers.

Lucy entered the shop. There weren't any customers around. But Maggie and Phoebe were busy rearranging the cubbies that held skeins of yarn built into one long wall on the right side of the shop.

"Hello, stranger." Maggie turned, her arms full of navy blue skeins. "Have you been on another deadline?"

"Sort of." Lucy sat down at the table and flipped open a new knitting magazine. "The Matt-moving-in deadline."

"Right, I almost forgot." Maggie put the navy yarn into a basket, then started to fill the empty space with some bright aqua angora.

"I've been cleaning like a madwoman. You'd think royalty was coming. Or maybe my mother," Lucy added, only half joking. "It's not like he's never seen the dust bunnies and dog toys under the couch."

"Yes, but you want to start off on the right foot. It's sort of a nesting instinct, if you don't mind me saying so."

"I think you have nests on the brain," Lucy tartly replied. "But I love the new window. I want to make some of those birds for Regina and Sophie," she said, referring to her nieces. "Even though they're probably getting old for that sort of thing."

"I love those little creatures. And I'm way older than your nieces." Phoebe came out of the storeroom, carrying a pile of boxes. More spring yarn, Lucy assumed.

"I'm going to make a few for my apartment. Maybe I'll make a mobile for the living room." Phoebe seemed so excited by the notion, Lucy didn't have the heart to comment. "You know, you could put sachet inside of them, too," Phoebe added.

"I never thought of that," Lucy said honestly.

She suddenly felt better about Matt's taste in home furnishings. Things could definitely be worse.

The shop door opened and Dana walked in. Lucy was surprised to see her. It was a little late for Dana's lunch break but too early for the end of her day.

She wasn't carrying her knitting tote, either, Lucy noticed. Surprising. In fact, she looked sort of disheveled. For Dana.

"What's up? Do you have a break this afternoon?"

"Yes, luckily. I'm supposed to be at a meeting . . . but I decided to come here instead." Dana waved her hands. "Gather round, I only want to say this once."

Maggie and Phoebe left the cubby and the cartons of yarn and came to the table. They all stared at Dana curiously. She seemed distressed. As if she didn't know where to start.

"Jack just called. He was at the police station, talking to a detective about some lawsuit he's working on. He overheard some big news. A man's body was found this morning in a motel room just outside of town. The police say it's Jeremy Lassiter."

Maggie gasped and put her hand over mouth. "Jeremy? How can that be? We just went to his memorial service. There must be some mistake."

"No mistake. The body was positively identified. His driver's license and passport . . . it was all in the room."

Lucy felt her mouth drop open. She couldn't speak.

"Wow . . . that is unreal." Phoebe pressed her hand to her head and dropped into a chair, like a marionette. She turned and looked back at Dana. "Maybe it was like, his twin brother?"

"They checked that possibility. Alec is alive and well, still visiting at his mother's estate. No, it's definitely Jeremy."

"How can that be? How did he die?" Maggie asked quietly.

"Strangled . . . with a woolen scarf," Dana added.

Lucy immediately recalled the scarf he'd worn the night he came to the shop. How he and Rebecca had joked about it. She guessed her friends were remembering that, too.

"That is so . . . unbelievable." Lucy was

stunned, and her thoughts whirled with possibilities. "So all this time, the explosion and the fire, his funeral . . . everything. He's been alive, hiding out?"

"Looks like it." Dana let out a breath and sat at the table, with her friends.

"I don't know what to say." Maggie was definitely flustered. "You'd better call Suzanne. She'll burst her buttons when she hears she's missed out on this news flash."

"You're right." Dana slipped her phone out of her jacket pocket. "I'll text her right now. But I'll just say we're all here and I have something important to tell her."

"Important . . . and unbelievable." Maggie sighed. Then she turned and started toward the storeroom. "I really can't get my head around this. I need a cup of tea. Anyone interested?"

They all were interested and Phoebe followed Maggie to the storeroom to help her.

"So Jeremy is dead . . . again." Lucy looked over at Dana. "It's so weird. I feel really bad. But I was already used to the idea that he was, you know, gone. So it's hard to feel anything. Except confused."

"I know what you mean. I feel confused, too. And curious. And maybe a little foolish? He did trick everyone."

Lucy was quiet for a moment. "Do you

157

think Rebecca knew? Could he have really done that to her, too? It looked to me like he really loved her."

"I had the same question. He did act as if he really loved her. But who can say what he was capable of now." Dana sounded upset. Maybe, Dana thought, as a psychologist she should have picked up some sign that Jeremy was not as guileless as he seemed.

"Oh, he had me fooled." Maggie bustled back into the room, carrying a tray with a teapot, mugs, and all the necessary ingredients. Her expression suddenly dropped. "Wait a minute . . . If Jeremy's ashes aren't in that urn, who do you think is in there?"

"Good point, Mag." The question gave her a little chill. Lucy hadn't thought that far yet. "I bet the police are wondering the same thing."

"Along with trying to figure out why Jeremy staged his own death. The body the police recovered at the lab . . . the body parts, rather," Dana quietly clarified, "were wearing Jeremy's clothes, his watch, his wedding ring. The victim's body was beyond recognition. But Jeremy was the only one seen going into the lab that night on the security cameras. And only one body was found after the fire. That's why they just as-

158

sumed it was him, without a DNA test."

"I guess they'll do that now. Better late than never." Maggie shrugged as she peeked into the teapot. Lucy was ready for some tea, but knew Maggie wouldn't pour it until the leaves had steeped long enough.

"Maybe if they're able to identify the John Doe in Jeremy's urn, they'll have some idea of why Jeremy ran and hid out," Dana offered.

"That's the real question. Why did he stage his own death?" Lucy asked the others. "Was he trying to avoid marrying Rebecca? If that was the reason, why not do the disappearing act before the ceremony?"

"That would make the most sense. But guys are totally illogical sometimes," Phoebe said.

"It would be the most elaborate and diabolical case of cold feet I've ever heard of," Maggie said as she poured the tea and passed it around. "Jeremy was nothing if not logical."

"He was obviously trying to escape something," Dana mused. "Which brings us back to wondering if Rebecca knew he was alive. Jack said the police want to question her. They went to the school where she teaches to give her the news. I guess she went back to work right away."

159

"Do you think that means she knew?" Lucy asked. "I mean, she wasn't so broken-hearted that she had to take a lot of time from work."

Maggie shrugged. "Some people return to their routines right away after a loss so they won't be alone with their sad thoughts. I don't think that means anything. I'd bet the police are talking to the Lassiter family, too."

"Oh, no doubt," Dana quickly answered. "The police have already interviewed everybody at At-Las Technologies about the explosion and fire. Now they have a whole new set of questions to ask them."

Maggie stirred some honey into her tea. It was suddenly so quiet, they could hear the spoon clinking against the inside of the mug.

"Jack thinks Jeremy staged his death because he knew someone was after him. But his murderer must have figured out the ruse, and gotten to him anyway." Dana reached across the table and took one of the oatmeal cookies Maggie had brought in on a plate.

"How awful to think Jeremy might have been hunted down that way. But the theory makes sense," Maggie conceded.

"I bet it has something to do with that glue formula," Lucy said. "It sounds like the Lassiters are obsessed with it . . . and

160

other people are, too."

"Lewis Atkins, you mean." Maggie glanced at her.

"His name came to mind. You're the one who overheard that he's their main competition." Lucy knew Maggie had gotten a favorable impression of Atkins and was usually a good judge of character. But look how Jeremy had tricked them.

"His name would be at the top of any list," Dana added. "But there could be others in this race. Players we don't even know of. It might not be about the glue at all. I don't think the police can narrow it down to just that one issue so quickly."

"Of course not . . . but . . ." Maggie sighed and didn't bother to finish her sentence. "I guess we'll find out soon enough."

Dana's phone buzzed and she checked the screen. "A text from Suzanne. She's with a client and can't get away right now. Guess I'll have to fill her in later."

"You'd better. Or we'll all regret it," Phoebe warned her.

"I hear you," Dana agreed.

"I should call Nora," Maggie said quietly. "The poor woman. She's been through so much the last few months. What could possibly be next?"

Maggie found the shop phone and dialed

Nora's number. Lucy could tell the message machine had answered. "Hello, Nora. It's Maggie. We just heard about . . . Jeremy. Give me a call if you like, anytime."

Maggie ended the call and looked back at her friends.

"She's probably with Rebecca . . . somewhere." Maggie's voice trailed off.

At the police station? With the Lassiters, planning another funeral? Lucy's head spun with possibilities.

The shop door opened and they all turned to see who was coming in. Lucy expected their missing buddy, Suzanne. But it was no one she recognized.

Maggie did, though, and waved to the two women. "Be right with you. We'll sit up front today," she added. "I'll bring some tea."

"Time for a class. I almost forgot." She glanced at her watch. "They're a little early but I'd better hop to it."

Dana and Lucy also decided to go and walked out together.

They stopped for a moment on the sidewalk in front of Maggie's shop before parting.

"I still can't believe it," Lucy said, holding on to Tink's collar. "It's so amazing. And confusing. I guess when Maggie talks to

162

Nora, she'll find out more."

"I'm sure she will." Dana tied the belt on her coat and flipped up the collar. Lucy felt chilled, too. The sinking sun had brought colder weather. Or maybe it was just the strange news. "I just hope Rebecca isn't pulled into this investigation. I'm not sure, but helping someone pretend that they're dead is probably against the law."

"I never thought of that. I guess she could get in trouble if she knew he was alive."

"It could be even worse than that. The spouse is the first person the police look at as a suspect," Dana reminded her.

"Rebecca is such a sweet person. How could anyone ever suspect her?"

Dana didn't answer. She did have a point. Lucy knew that much about murder investigations. Detectives look at the spouse first and, more often than not, are looking in the right direction.

"I'm glad Maggie called Nora," Dana said finally. "I have a feeling the Baileys need our friendship even more."

Lucy had to agree. Nora and Rebecca needed all the friends they had right now.

CHAPTER SEVEN

The explosion and fire at At-Las Technologies three weeks ago had been big news around town. A terrible tragedy for the family and the young bride was the common consensus.

But now that Jeremy Lassiter had been found dead again, people could talk of little else. Everywhere Lucy went — the dry cleaner, the Schooner, even at the library — she overheard speculation about the young scientist's motives for such a desperate act and gossip about the Lassiter family.

Which is all it really was, she kept reminding herself — speculation and gossip. The local newspaper hadn't reported any hard evidence or explanation for the bizarre events, though there were three articles and a sidebar about the story in Thursday's edition.

Lucy hoped that Dana, or even Maggie, would have more to report at their knitting meeting that night. It was Suzanne's turn to host, but the location was switched to the shop at the last minute. The ceiling in Suzanne's kitchen had fallen down and Kevin was already working on it.

"It didn't fall down completely," Suzanne explained when she called Lucy's cell phone to head her off. "I mean, not on my head or anything like that. Just a few chunks sort of plopped into the chili I was making for you guys. But Kevin pretty much has to pull the rest down." She explained how her teenage daughter Natalie had taken one of her three-hour showers and didn't turn off the shower faucet tightly, allowing gallons of water to leak.

When Lucy got to the shop she expected to find her friends waiting with take-out food — probably Chinese, their favorite default dinner.

Maggie, Dana, Suzanne, and Phoebe were all there, chopsticks poised over containers of steamed dumplings and cold sesame noodles. She had not expected to see Nora Bailey at the table as well.

"Lucy, come on back. We saved your seat," Maggie said.

Lucy greeted everyone and took her usual chair, between Dana and Phoebe. She met Nora's gaze, suddenly feeling awkward.

Should she offer condolences again about Jeremy?

Maggie quickly came to her rescue. "Nora needed a little company tonight so I asked her to join us. The past few days have been so difficult."

That was Maggie, the master of understatement, Lucy nearly said aloud.

"It's like a nightmare that just doesn't stop. I just had to get out of the house for a little while," Nora confessed. "Rebecca decided to stay with me again. She has some visitors tonight. A few teachers from school and her principal. They're actually sitting in the living room, watching TV. Rebecca will barely get out of bed to speak to anybody. But they didn't mind staying at the house with her. This second wave of news about Jeremy has just crushed her. And the police, with all their questions. They've barely left us alone since they found him. Again."

Lucy could not imagine it. What was it like to think someone you dearly loved was dead . . . then find out he'd been alive all that time? But now, learning he had actually died?

"Did Rebecca know he was alive?" Lucy felt rude asking the question so abruptly, but she couldn't help it. She knew everyone was wondering the same thing.

Nora looked down at her dish, fiddling with her chopsticks. "That's what everyone wants to know, isn't it? You'll probably read about it tomorrow in the newspaper, anyway. The police didn't tell Rebecca she couldn't talk about it. These things have a way of getting out." She took a breath and looked up at them. "Yes, she did know he was alive. That's why it's so much harder for her now."

Dana was the first to react. "When did she know? Right after the fire?"

"No, not immediately. Those days and nights of tears before the memorial service were quite authentic. She said he got in touch a few days after the service. He sent her a text while she was at work, during her lunch break. She didn't recognize the number and thought someone was playing a cruel joke. But he tried again and used a certain nickname that no one else in the world could possibly know, so she finally called back. Of course, she was so shocked. She couldn't believe it."

Nora's voice was low and faltering. Lucy and her friends sat perfectly still, hanging on every word. "He didn't get very far. He was just outside of town, in a motel on the highway. Imagine that. He could have slipped into his own funeral in a disguise and no one would have realized it," Nora said, and nearly laughed at the absurdity. Though her glee sounded on the edge of hysteria, Lucy noticed.

"He probably could have," Maggie agreed. "There were so many people there."

Lucy was suddenly wondering if he *was* there. How ironic that would have been.

"Why did he stay so close?" Lucy asked, thinking out loud. "He really took a risk being discovered."

"Rebecca asked him that, too. He said he was waiting to get in touch with her. He didn't want to make her go too far to meet him," Nora explained.

"Did he call anyone else?" Lucy asked quickly. She was already wondering who else knew Jeremy was alive.

"He might have. If the police know, they haven't told us," she replied.

"I don't know if they found a cell phone in his room," Dana said. "But now they have the number on Rebecca's phone and they'll track his calls. But when did he get in touch with Rebecca? You said a few day after the memorial and Rebecca was back at work. Was that Monday or Tuesday?" Dana asked, getting more specific.

"It was Tuesday. Of course he asked Rebecca to come see him. Right away. She told her principal she had a migraine headache and needed to leave for the day. Stewart said he thought she'd come back to school too soon and made her promise to take a few more days off. Little did he know. Lies on top of lies. I always liked Jeremy. It was his family that rubbed me the wrong way. Well, I guess the apple doesn't fall far from the tree. Rebecca was head over heels in love. Now look where it's gotten her."

Nora shook her head in dismay. It was clear that she deeply loved her only child and would do anything for her, suffer any pain or sacrifice, Lucy thought. But what could she do for Rebecca now? Except to help her navigate the aftermath of Jeremy's deception.

"So Rebecca went to see Jeremy at the motel that afternoon," Maggie said, getting her back on track.

"Yes, she went straight to the motel. Just out on the highway, not that far from town. She did call me," Nora added. "But only to say that she didn't feel well at school and needed to take a little ride somewhere, to be alone. And not to worry. But of course, I did," Nora stated flatly. "It wasn't like her to do something like that. But, with all she'd been through, I didn't argue. I just told her to call me that night and let me know if she was going home, or staying over somewhere. She stayed with me right after the fire. But after the memorial service, she went back to her own apartment. She insisted. I just wanted her to keep in touch."

Dana nodded sympathetically. "You had no idea where she was really going. How could you?"

"Exactly. I'm not even sure what I would have done," Nora said honestly. "Jeremy told her not to tell anyone he was alive. That his life depended on her keeping the secret."

Nora looked around the table, wide-eyed. For a moment, Lucy imagined the way Rebecca must have looked at the police station, with that same wide-eyed stare, telling this same story yesterday to a detective. Maybe more than one. Probably having to tell it more than once, too.

"Rebecca hoped that she could persuade him to come forward, and try to figure out his problem, without this elaborate pretense. But she loved him," Nora added. "So she did what he asked."

"But why did he stage his own death? Can you tell us that?" Dana asked.

"He never told her why. That's what she told me and what she's told the police. She says that he never got to explain. He promised he'd tell her everything after they got

170

away. But said it wasn't safe now for her to know."

"Wasn't safe . . . because someone was after him?" Maggie asked.

"I'd assume that's what he meant. I think the police assume that, too. He told her that they needed money, just enough to get away. But he had a way to get more and not to worry."

"Where was Rebecca supposed to get the money? From bank accounts?" Lucy asked.

"Yes, he'd put her name on all his accounts and investments before they were married. She already has access to those funds. His will has to go through probate. I don't think he wanted her to wait that long," Nora said.

"But if he knew he was going to run away, why didn't he take money with him?" Dana asked.

Lucy hadn't thought of that, but it was a good question. Jeremy had plenty of money. Dana was always so logical.

"She did ask him that," Nora replied quickly. "He said he didn't want a large withdrawal to look suspicious after his fake death. He was worried that it would raise a red flag to anyone investigating the fire at the lab and he knew that his bank records would be reviewed after he died, when his estate was in probate."

"That make sense. Jeremy was thinking ahead. He obviously knew how the arson and insurance investigators worked," Dana said, seeming satisfied with the answer.

"So what was his plan? Were they going to leave the country together?" Suzanne asked.

"He told Rebecca that they would," Nora answered, though she didn't sound convinced, Lucy noticed. "Jeremy was going to leave first and wanted Rebecca to meet him somewhere . . . Thailand . . . Switzerland . . . Dubai . . . he wasn't sure where it would be. Or so he said. He must have had a fake passport or knew where to get one. The police haven't told us if they found anything like that or any airline tickets in his room."

Nora's eyes filled with tears and she couldn't speak.

Lucy could see that it was hard for her to consider Rebecca's part in this bizarre, possibly criminal escapade. She was worried about the consequences for Rebecca, now that it was all coming to light.

Or maybe the tears had come just thinking about her daughter, living on the run, hiding in some distant land, possibly never to be seen again.

Lucy had no doubt that was the very opposite of the life Nora had envisioned for the newlyweds. Nora probably took it for granted that even after she married, Rebecca would stay close, living right in town where she would baby-sit her grandchildren and remain a big part of her daughter's life.

Jeremy had to seem a bit of a monster now, didn't he? He certainly seemed much more devious than anyone had suspected.

"Rebecca was supposed to gather up whatever money she could," Nora continued, "and transfer it all electronically into an account he'd opened somewhere . . . in Europe maybe. Or Asia. I'm not sure. He hadn't given her the account number yet. He was going to send it by text." She paused and took a deep shaky breath. "I wonder now if he was even planning on taking Rebecca with him. Or just using her. Now she's left to answer all these questions. Hounded by the police . . ."

Nora's voice trailed off. Her eyes filled with tears and she covered her face with her hands. Maggie patted her shoulder.

"I think he loved your daughter," Maggie insisted. "But that is a valid question. It seems to me, if the police find that Jeremy was going to desert Rebecca, too, that would help prove she wasn't involved in his scheme. Whatever it turns out to be."

Nora wiped her eyes and nodded. "Yes it

would. I agree. The problem is that somebody killed Jeremy before he told Rebecca what he was really up to."

"So she only saw him again that one time, before he was killed?" Dana asked.

Nora nodded and sniffed. "That's what she says. And I believe her. She told me that the police kept asking the same question. He must have had other visitors. Maybe even another woman. I won't assume anything about him now."

Neither would anyone in the room, Lucy thought.

"But the police think Rebecca was the last to see him alive and I'm afraid for her . . . I'm afraid she's in trouble . . . I'm afraid they're starting to think . . ."

Nora began crying in earnest now. Suzanne handed her a box of tissues.

"Who would want to kill Jeremy?" Phoebe asked bluntly. She had been quiet tonight, so far, Lucy realized. But now went straight for the bottom line.

"Did he have any enemies?" Dana asked, following up. "Anyone he was afraid of?"

"The police asked the same thing. Rebecca didn't know of any. There were always tensions at the lab. He was under a lot of pressure. Everyone was counting on his work to save the company."

"What about his work? Did he talk to Rebecca about it much?" Dana caught a bean pod with her chopsticks and took a bite. No one was very interested in dinner tonight, Lucy noticed. Especially now that it was getting cold. There were few things less appetizing than cold Chinese food, that was for sure.

"Oh, Rebecca didn't understand anything about chemistry. It all sailed right over her head. She did laugh about all the little notes and stickies he left around the house. He'd get ideas in the middle of the night. Or while taking a shower."

"I do the same thing. When I'm working on a new pattern," Maggie said. "Rebecca ought to save those notes if she finds any. They might come in handy."

"He did tell Rebecca about arguments at work," Nora added. "But it was a very stressful time for everyone there."

"Arguments with whom?" Maggie asked.

"With his father, mainly. But everyone argued with Philip Lassiter. The man has a very short fuse. Just like the way he acted at the wedding. Anyone can see how volatile he is." Nora's expression was tight and angry. Did she blame Philip Lassiter for all of this, Lucy wondered.

Philip Lassiter had a temper, no question.

But enough of a temper to have killed his own son? That seemed too extreme and awful to contemplate. But if he had discovered that Jeremy faked his death, and deserted the company at its darkest hour . . . well, he may not have been able to control himself.

"Jeremy's father is in the hospital," Nora added. "I guess you didn't hear that. The family kept it very quiet. He went in right after the memorial service. I heard he has some sort of chronic stomach problem and had an attack. He's in bad shape, they say. This news has caused a setback for him."

That seemed to answer Lucy's unspoken question. Philip Lassiter had a solid alibi, flat on his back in a hospital room.

"There are a lot of questions still to answer, Nora," Lucy offered. "Rebecca can't be the only person that the police are looking at. She was probably not the only one he called or the only one who visited him."

She couldn't be sure of that, of course. But she certainly hoped so.

"Don't worry, Nora. The police have to see that Rebecca is innocent. They'll find the person who did this." Suzanne's voice was full of sympathy.

"I would have said that myself at one time," Nora replied quickly. "But I'm not sure of that at all."

"It's very complicated. It's going to take time for an investigation to sort this all out." Dana's tone was calm and knowing. But she didn't make any bold predictions, Lucy noticed. "In the meanwhile, Rebecca ought to have some legal advice. Especially if she's asked to talk to the police again. Have you been in touch with an attorney?" Dana asked.

Nora shook her head. "It never occurred to us. She had nothing to do with his death. She was crushed by the news. She's just lost her husband . . . a second time."

"I understand. But it's the smart thing to do. Just to make sure her rights are protected." Dana took a card from her wallet and passed it across the table. "My husband would be happy to recommend someone. Give him a call."

"Thank you. We'll do that." Nora took the card and put it into her wallet, then sighed and sat with her hands clasped over her purse.

As if she were waiting for a bus, Lucy thought. A bus that was going to take her to a place she didn't want to visit.

"The police haven't released the body yet. When they do, there'll be another service," Nora added. "Just the immediate family,

Rebecca and the Lassiters. I'm not even sure if my brother will come back down from Vermont." She sighed and stood up, then put on her coat. "We'll get through it, I guess."

"Yes, you will." Maggie patted Nora's hand again and glanced around the silent table.

"Believe me, I know how it is to be unfairly accused of such an unthinkable act. You remember that nightmare I went through after Amanda Goran died," she reminded Nora. "I don't know how I survived it."

"I remember." Nora nodded. "Was that only a year ago? It seems like much longer."

It did seem as if much more time had passed, Lucy agreed. It had been an ordeal for them all. A local shopkeeper and rival knitting store owner, Amanda Goran, was found dead in her store and Maggie was the prime suspect. There were no eyewitnesses and very little evidence.

Maggie had nearly shut down her shop, overwhelmed by the gossip and false accusations. But she'd toughed it out, with a little help from her friends, until the real culprit was discovered.

The situation was not unlike Rebecca's, Lucy realized. Which made Maggie all the more sympathetic to Rebecca's cause.

"Is there anything we can do to help you?" Maggie asked.

Nora sighed and shrugged. "You've all been a great help, just hearing me out. I'm glad I came tonight. I needed to talk. My brother left right after the service and Rebecca is in such a state. She's so fragile right now. I can't talk to her frankly about all this anyway."

"We're here for you, Nora. Anytime," Maggie promised. "If only we could do more than just listen," she added, gazing around at her friends.

"Finding out who really killed Jeremy . . . that's the only thing that can really help us now. I'm afraid for my daughter, ladies," she said very quietly.

She stood up, ready to go. Maggie stood, too. "I'll walk you to the door," she offered.

Everyone around the table called out good night and good wishes. Nora's disclosures had left them all with an uneasy feeling.

It was an amazing reversal, Lucy thought. A few weeks ago, Nora and Rebecca had come here, bringing such high spirits and happiness with their wedding plans. Now it had come to this. An unthinkable deception and a murder investigation.

Once Nora left, they cleared away their dinner dishes and took extra care cleaning the table. "I hate it when my projects smell of Chinese food; you can never quite get it out," Dana noted.

"That's a bad thing?" Phoebe asked. "Josh likes me to do that on purpose."

Dana and Lucy just looked at each other.

Everyone took out her knitting. Maggie brought in a platter of sliced fruit. Phoebe stayed in the kitchen to fix a pot of tea.

"Poor Nora," Maggie said finally.

"Poor Rebecca," Suzanne added.

"Poor Jeremy," Lucy said. "He went through all that trouble to fake his death, but somebody wanted him dead for sure." Lucy turned to Dana. "It's just as you predicted. Sounds like the police consider Rebecca their prime suspect."

"Unfortunately. But when you look at the big picture, you can understand why. She stands to gain the most, as far as anyone knows right now. The first time he died, he left her with piles of money. Then he came back and told her to send it all to some mysterious bank account. And wouldn't say why he was running away, where he was going, or how they would be reunited. The police have to consider all that. She's the most obvious suspect, and, it seems, the only one who saw him alive."

"It sounds real bad for Rebecca when you

tell it that way, Dana." Suzanne seemed genuinely disturbed. "You sound as if you think the poor girl is guilty."

"I didn't say that. But let's try to be a tiny bit objective. Just look at the facts. Let's say, just for argument's sake, he did fake his death and she didn't know he was alive until he got in touch the other day. Now Rebecca is the only one who does know he's alive and knows where he is. And maybe she's gotten used to her new net worth of a few million dollars and doesn't like the idea of running off to Thailand or Dubai and living life on the lam."

"Dana, really. I've known Rebecca since she was a little girl. She's just not capable of such a thing," Maggie protested, sounding truly distressed.

Dana offered a small smile and shook her head. "We'd all like to think that we know what people are capable of. But the truth is, no matter how people act in public, we know so little about them. About what's going on under the surface. Case in point: Jeremy," she reminded them.

"I believe Rebecca," Lucy said, jumping in. "I really do. It's just unfortunate that Jeremy never told her what, or whom, he was running from."

"All we know for sure is that Jeremy set

fire to the lab to escape some threat by playing dead," Suzanne reminded them. "Maybe he had gambling debts or some horrendous secret he was running from."

"That might be true," Lucy agreed. "But I think it had to do with his work, his research. It keeps going back to that, don't you think?"

"I agree with Lucy," Maggie said firmly. "I think it's about this mysterious glue formula. Maybe he was trying to steal the invention and run away with it. It sounds like it was all his own work. Maybe he believed he had a right to keep it and didn't care about saving the family company."

"Employees doing creative work or research usually have to sign a disclaimer form, saying that everything they create or discover is the intellectual property of the company," Lucy pointed out. "Do you think his father made him sign something like that?"

"His father sounds pretty hard-nosed and there was a lot of tension between them. Maybe they argued about the formula, whether it belonged to Jeremy or the company?" Maggie suggested.

"His father might have argued about this with Lewis Atkins, too," Dana said.

"But from what you overheard at the

service, Maggie, his sister said Jeremy's research was on record. All they had to do was put the pieces together again," Lucy recalled.

"Unless Jeremy kept a lot in his head and never documented the complete formula," Maggie pointed out. "Remember those little scraps of paper Nora mentioned? It sounds like his formula was so sensitive and unique that one tiny missing ingredient would render it useless."

"No one's ever said if the formula was protected by a patent. But if it was so radical and valuable, it must be, right?" Lucy said. "I wonder if there's some way to look that up."

"There must be. Let me ask Jack about it," Dana said. "He's my go-to guy for legal research."

Phoebe had left the table to make more tea but now returned with both the teapot and a platter of fortune cookies that had come with the takeout. "Hey, we forgot the most important part of the meal. I'm going to spin it and everybody take one."

"Do you have to spin it?" Maggie watched the plate go round, bouncing on the table-top. "That's one of my favorite platters."

"That's part of the fun, Mag. It's like a wheel of fortune or something," Phoebe explained.

Finally the plate stopped. "Okay, everyone take a cookie," Phoebe instructed. "Let's open them at the same time."

Lucy felt a little silly, as did the rest of her friends, she noticed, but they all went along with Phoebe's instructions. The little exercise lightened the mood a bit.

They all tore open the cellophane wrappers at once, creating a small but irritating racket. Then they crunched open the cookies and read their fortunes.

" 'Your hard work will be recognized and suitably rewarded,' " Suzanne read. "Great. Maybe I'll sell a house this week. I'd settle for a rental," she added.

" 'The greatest wisdom is kindness,' " Maggie read. "That's not really a fortune. But it is true," she conceded.

" 'Beware of wolves in sheep's clothing,' " Dana read. She laughed out loud. "Well, one has just revealed himself. If you consider Jeremy in the wolf category."

Lucy's was short and to the point. " 'Trust your intuition.' Okay, I can go with that."

"Wait, mine's the best," Phoebe announced. She cleared her throat, then read it aloud. " 'If love is the glue that holds the world together, guilt must be the staples.' "

Dana laughed. "That is a good one. I

might use that in my practice sometime."

"It does ring true, doesn't it?" Lucy said.

"It's sort of uncanny if you ask me, with all this talk tonight about Jeremy's glue formula. A message from the fortune cookie gods that we're on the right track?" Maggie said playfully.

"So what are we saying here?" Phoebe asked. "Someone was after the glue formula and killed Jeremy in order to get it? Is that too obvious?"

"Not at all. I think that's a strong possibility. Even more likely than Rebecca wanting to hang on to the money she inherited," Dana conceded. "I'm sure the police must be following that line of reasoning, too."

"Too bad Rebecca can't tell us more about his work," Lucy mused. "That might help us figure out who was after him."

"There was one woman in his life who did understand," Maggie reminded them. "Who worked with him side by side in his lab. Until very recently."

"In his lab . . . and in his bed, if you believe what you hear at funerals," Dana quipped.

"I usually do," Maggie replied. "It would be fun to ask Erica Ferris a few questions. She could really shed some light."

Suzanne was paging through a knitting magazine and suddenly looked up at Maggie. "Why would she talk to us? She doesn't even know us."

"That's true, but . . . leave it to me. I'll figure something out," Maggie promised.

Lucy looked over at her, wondering what she had up her hand-knit sleeve. But she had long ago learned to never underestimate the owner of the Black Sheep Knitting Shop.

Dana gave Maggie a look, too. "Do you really want to get involved in this, Maggie? The police are on the job, in force. I don't think they really need our help."

"I'm not so sure about that. And I'm not doing it to help the police. I'm doing it to help Nora and Rebecca. You urged her to find a lawyer. So you obviously agree that they need some advocates?" Maggie asked.

Dana gave her a look. But didn't answer.

"I want to help them, too, if I can," Lucy said.

"Me, too," Suzanne agreed.

"Me, three," Phoebe echoed.

"I'm just concerned. Let's not get carried away and get ourselves in trouble again. Agreed?" Dana looked around at the circle of friends.

They all nodded solemnly. But Lucy thought she caught Maggie winking at her.

186

CHAPTER EIGHT

Maggie arrived at the shop the next morning and stood for a few moments on the front porch, thinking about cold-weather pansies. Shouldn't they be in the nursery soon? She was eager to brighten up the storefront with some flowers.

The new window display was attractive, she decided. The amigurumi birds were cute and the knitting tote looked bountiful. She wasn't sure if it had attracted any new customers, though.

But staring at it suddenly gave her an idea of how she might lure Jeremy's former flame and lab partner over for a chat. A long shot, but worth a try, she decided.

As usual, she'd arrived well before nine, and left the front door sign flipped to the closed position, SORRY WE MISSED YOU! WE'RE RESTING OUR NEEDLES RIGHT NOW.

She liked time alone in the morning to survey her cozy kingdom. She put on a pot of coffee and looked over the displays, making sure the stock was arranged to its best advantage. She turned to the counter next. A respectable pile of forms filled the basket by the register. Several people had thrown their names in to win the knitting tote in the window. She'd planned to keep it out there a while longer before announcing the winner.

But there would be two raffle baskets now. Fair or not, she already knew who the winner of the one in the window would be.

With the shop arranged to her standards, Maggie sat down with her coffee cup and the phone receiver, preparing for her performance.

She was glad Phoebe was not working this morning. It was best to do things like this alone, without answering a million questions. An audience would have made her too self-conscious.

She had already looked up At-Las Technologies online the night before and jotted down the phone number. She'd also Googled Erica Ferris, but didn't find out much more than she already knew. Erica did have a PhD after her name and had published many scientific articles. Most had to do with something called polymers. Maggie had Googled Jeremy, too, and found even more credits for articles on his pages.

Maggie dialed the number and was soon connected to Erica. "Dr. Ferris?" she asked boldly. "This is Maggie Messina. I'm calling from the Black Sheep Knitting Shop."

"Are you selling something? I'm not interested . . . How do you people get office phone numbers anyway? Isn't there some sort of law —"

"Please don't hang up. I'm not a salesperson. This is important." Maggie spoke quickly, hoping to catch her attention. "You've won a prize. A Black Sheep 'You Can Knit! Starter Kit' — a complete set of needles, a bag, how-to books, and enough high-quality yarn to complete two beginner patterns. And three free knitting lessons," she said quickly.

The scientist did not answer for a long moment. Now she really has hung up, Maggie thought.

"There must be some mistake. I never entered any contest at a knitting shop. You must have the wrong number."

"I don't. I'm sure of it," Maggie insisted. "Maybe someone entered your name without your knowing. Don't you know anyone who knits?"

She was going out on a limb here. But everyone knows someone who knits . . .

189

don't they?

"My sister-in-law, Janet. This must be her idea of a joke."

"Maybe Janet wants some company," Maggie suggested. "Or maybe she wants the set. I think we allowed only one entry per person."

There had not been any such rule. That last line had been truly inspired.

"But I'm not —"

"I can drop it off at your office, or your home," Maggie rolled on. "Or you could come to the shop and pick it up anytime. It's worth at least . . . two hundred dollars," Maggie added, exaggerating a bit. "If you don't want to give it to Janet, you could sell it on eBay, for goodness' sake."

Erica sighed. "All right . . . what time do you close tonight? I work pretty late."

"We're open tonight until . . . nine. At least. Don't worry. I'll wait for you," Maggie said.

Once she hung up, she wondered if it was wise to talk to Erica alone in the shop. Maggie somehow doubted Jeremy had been murdered by his old flame. But it wasn't completely out of the question. The woman could be dangerous.

Phoebe was working in the afternoon, but would not even be in her apartment upstairs in the evening. Her boyfriend Josh's band was performing at a bar in Rockport and Phoebe was needed to lead the cheering section, move equipment, and sell their self-published CDs. She would complain endlessly about her many duties as the unofficial manager of the Babies, but everyone knew she actually loved it.

Unless she called a friend to come over and act the part of a customer, Maggie would definitely be totally alone tonight for Erica's visit. If Erica Ferris had somehow found out Jeremy was still alive after the fire, she had good reason to confront him.

His siblings believed she still loved him and had never gotten over the breakup. What if she'd tried to convince him to take her with him, instead of Rebecca? When he'd refused — rejecting her for the second time — had she lost control?

Would a chemist be more likely to kill someone in a neater, more clinical fashion than strangulation with a knitted scarf? Or was that a cliché? Scientists were not immune to passionate, even dangerous liaisons. Even Albert Einstein had his torrid love affairs.

But Maggie eventually decided she would take her chances and deal with Erica on her own. If Lucy or Dana hung around in the knitting nook, pretending to be customers, Erica might feel self-conscious talking freely.

From their brief conversation, there was no doubt the young woman was very discerning. Not the type to let her guard down easily. But somehow, Maggie thought she could get Erica talking about Jeremy. He was one of her favorite subjects, wasn't he? And from there, the work they did together and the formula she'd taken part in developing with him.

Those must have been special, meaningful days for her, working side by side on an exciting project with the man she loved. She was probably proud of that time in her life.

Maggie left the knitting tote, along with the sign about the raffle, sitting in the middle of the front window, so it would all look very legitimate and convincing.

Not that it was a subterfuge . . . entirely, she reminded herself. Though this was costing her a few dollars and she would have to replace the prize tomorrow and eventually give it away to one of her real customers.

She hoped the effort was worth it.

As Maggie expected, the shop was empty when Erica finally walked in. It was nearly eight o'clock. But the sign that read COME ON IN, WE'RE STILL HERE STITCHING hung from the door and all the lights were on.

Maggie sat behind the counter, working on her bookkeeping.

She recognized the stunning brunette the moment Erica stepped through the door. She wore a red flair coat, black leather boots, and smooth kid gloves.

Maggie had to remind herself that the young woman did not remember her from the funeral. Or know that she had any connection to Jeremy and his family.

"You must be Maggie?" Erica approached her. She looked tired and annoyed to have to stop on her way home from work.

"That's me. Can I help you?"

"I'm Dr. Ferris. We spoke this morning. About the mysterious raffle prize?" Erica spoke to her as if she were senile. For goodness' sake, she wasn't that old.

"Oh, yes . . . of course. I lost track. I was just doing some bookkeeping." Maggie slipped off her reading glasses but didn't hurry to come out from behind the counter. "So, you've come for your prize. I'm glad. You might like it more than you think. Have you ever tried any knitting?"

Erica gave her another look. "It's one of those pastimes I'm saving for my golden years. Like bridge or Sudoku."

Maggie knew plenty of young people who enjoyed bridge and Sudoku. But she under-

193

stood Erica's gibe.

"Well, maybe you'll consider it. You've won everything you need to get you started and three free lessons. You may not want to pass along this bounty after all."

"Can you get the prize? It's been a long day," Erica said and glanced at her watch.

Maggie ambled over to the window and moved the backdrop for her arrangement.

"By the way, can I see my entry form?"

Maggie turned. "Entry form? Oh, you mean the slip of paper I pulled. It's around somewhere," she lied. "Do you want it back for your taxes or something?"

She hadn't the slightest idea if Erica needed it for her tax records or not. But she didn't know what else to say.

"I just wanted to see the handwriting. I still don't know who entered my name," Erica replied in a flat, logical tone. She sighed and flipped her silky hair off her shoulder.

Maggie turned back to the window display. "This will take just a minute. I've clamped it down with some masking tape, so it wouldn't spill out . . ."

"Right. No rush. Anytime this week would be fine," Erica mumbled under her breath. Then there was another pained sigh.

While Maggie hated to make snap judgments about people, the young woman's breathtaking good looks were totally at odds with her social skills. In short, she seemed to have an awful personality and the derisive comments of Jeremy's siblings rang true. She suddenly recalled their nickname for her. Icky, wasn't it?

"Here we go. Sorry that took a while." Maggie finally produced the tote. "Just one more thing . . . the free patterns and certificate for the lessons. I have to fill in your name." Still carrying the tote, Maggie ran back to the counter. She pulled out her gift certificate book and flipped the pages.

"You know, you look awfully familiar. I've been trying to figure out where I've seen you. Do you attend the First Congregational?" Maggie named the church she'd attended for the past twenty or so years. She knew very well Erica wasn't a member. But I have to start somewhere, she thought.

Erica shook her head. "I don't belong to a church. Sorry."

"No apology necessary. To each his own. I'm just thinking, it was some sort of service, I'm almost sure . . ." She shook her head, writing out the certificates. She could have put all three lessons on one ticket, but decided to drag it out.

"I remember now. Weren't you at Jeremy

Lassiter's memorial service? Last Friday?"

Erica had been peering over the edge of the counter, obviously wondering why Maggie was taking so long. She lifted her pointy chin and stared at Maggie curiously.

"Yes, I was there."

Maggie sighed. "What a tragedy. Such a young man. So brilliant. Did you know him well?"

"Yes, I did. Did you?"

"Not very well, no . . . But I'm friends of the family," she fudged. His wife's family, she should have said. "How did you know him? Oh, right . . . you work for At-Las Technologies. Did you two work together?"

"Yes, we did. In the same lab. But I think you already know that Mrs. Messina."

Maggie felt her stomach clutch. "I do? How would I?"

"I noticed you there, too. Now that you mention it. You're friends with his wife, Rebecca, and her mother, right?" Erica asked bluntly.

Maggie had talked to Rebecca and Nora for a long time when she came in. Erica did not take her seat until much later. But maybe she was standing somewhere in the room, talking to coworkers, with her eyes on Rebecca, of course.

"I think you must be the one who helped

her knit her gown. I heard all about that. How creative and craftsy she is. A craftsy little cow."

"You did? Where did you hear all that?" Now it was Maggie's turn to be surprised.

"At work, in the employee lounge, of course. Jeremy's wedding was an endless topic of conversation for some people. You'd think he was part of the royal family."

Maggie didn't doubt it. Employees in a family-owned company loved to gossip about the company owners. How that wedding talk must have galled and humiliated Erica. Everyone must have known she'd been tossed aside for Rebecca.

Why did she ever stay at the company? To stay close to Jeremy? She must have loved him very much.

"You know, I had to talk to the police. But I really don't have to talk to you."

"No, you don't. That's true," Maggie admitted, feeling sheepish.

"Is that what this is all about? Some silly . . . trick to lure me here?" Erica looked genuinely angry now. Maggie wasn't frightened. Though she did slip a pair of sharp scissors off the counter and into her skirt pocket.

"You don't have to speak to me about Jeremy. About any of this," Maggie admitted without answering the question. "I'm just trying to help Rebecca. The police are hounding her. I'm afraid they suspect her. I'm just trying to help her out a bit. Whatever else you might say about her, she's not capable of murder. Especially murdering Jeremy."

Erica's eyes narrowed. "Then you don't really know her at all, Mrs. Messina. If you can stand here and say that. She's capable of a lot of things. She stole Jeremy from me. We'd been together for more than two years and talked about getting married, until she came along. Did you know that?"

Maggie did know that. But in the version Alec and Claudia had related — which she'd learned by eavesdropping — Erica had not been painted as the sympathetic party. More like a spider, wrapping up her prey and sucking it dry.

What had Alec said? The best thing Jeremy ever did for himself was to get out of Erica's clutches.

"I think I did hear that you and Jeremy had been in a relationship, before he met Rebecca," Maggie conceded.

"She acts all innocent and sweet. But she's a ruthless, coldhearted witch. A total phony. Those outfits she wears. She always looks like she's about to churn butter. What did

Jeremy ever see in her? I couldn't get it."

Erica still sounded angry and stung. Remarkable, Maggie thought, all things considered. Erica stared at Maggie, as if expecting some explanation. Maggie didn't say a word.

"Do you really want to know why I never want to learn how to knit?" Erica asked. "Why I can't even stand looking at this stuff? Because it reminds me of her. All those ugly sweaters and scarves she made for him. He used to wear them to work, a new one every day. It made me sick just to look at them." Erica visibly shuddered. Then pulled herself under control just as quickly.

Erica truly despised Rebecca. Maggie had rarely seen such pure hatred up close and personal. Who knew what she'd told the police in her interview, if this was a taste of it. No wonder they were looking so closely at Rebecca as a suspect.

"Do you really think she killed Jeremy, Erica? Or do you just wish she'd be punished for what she did to you?"

Erica sighed and shook her head, her glossy locks tumbling about like a shampoo commercial. "Yes, I do believe she could have done it," she said. "But probably on impulse. She's too dumb to plan anything more complicated than a bowl of hot cereal.

Sweet little do-gooder Rebecca. Running around, making the world a sunnier place with her scrapbooking and volunteer work. How long was it going to take for him to get bored with that? Maybe he was bored with it already and she realized he wasn't going to take her with him . . . wherever he planned on going."

While Maggie had pictured Erica in that scenario with Jeremy, reacting badly to that news, she had never pictured Rebecca in that role. Interesting, she thought.

It certainly was possible, Maggie had to concede. But she quickly brushed the image aside. Even if Jeremy was trying to jilt Rebecca, she would never have reacted by killing him.

She wasn't so sure now about Dr. Ferris.

"Is that what you think happened? You were the woman close to him, for a long time. A woman at his intellectual level," Maggie added, purposely pouring on the flattery. "Rebecca says she didn't understand his work at all. She doesn't have a clue. Burning his lab, faking his death, that was a pretty desperate act. What do you think he was trying to accomplish?"

Erica's full lips closed in a tight line. "I really don't know. I moved to a different department after he hooked up with Rebecca."

"But you were close to him before that. He trusted you. You were one of very few, I'd imagine," she added, playing to Erica's ego again. "You must have some special insight into him."

Erica didn't answer at first, but finally, the flattery seemed to move her. "I was close to him. He did confide in me. Mainly about his father. Jeremy was always very angry with Philip. Maybe he was just trying to get back at his father, burning the place down and disappearing at the eleventh hour. Maybe it was his way of getting revenge for being controlled by the old man for so long. The lab was in trouble. The investors were very restless. They wanted to see some results. And you know that Lewis Atkins was working on this same formula, right?"

"Yes, I'd heard that." Maggie nodded. She really wanted to bring Lewis Atkins here next. Though she doubted that raffle trick would work on him.

She looked back at Erica, who had buttoned her red coat and was tugging on her leather gloves. Very nice gloves, Maggie noticed. They wouldn't have left any trace in a motel room. Or on a woolen scarf.

Maggie could tell her time with Erica had

201

come to an end. She tried for one last question.

"So, how did you feel when you heard the news that Jeremy was found in the motel? It must have been a great shock."

Erica laughed. "You're not very subtle, Mrs. Messina. The police were far more direct. You really want to know where I was when he was killed, right? I worked late that night at the lab. The fire didn't only affect his project, it set everyone back. It's all on the security cameras, my coming and going. The time and date, the works."

Erica shrugged, holding her gloved hands out in the air for a moment. "Claudia Lassiter called me at home very early Wednesday morning. Right after the police told his family. She thought I should hear the news personally, before I came to work."

"That's was thoughtful of her." Maggie was surprised, considering the way Claudia had spoken about Erica.

"I think she just didn't want me to make a scene. The Lassiters hate emotional displays." She paused and tugged on her gloves again. "It wasn't fair the way Jeremy died. The way his father made him waste his life on glue. It makes me very angry."

"No, it wasn't fair at all. None of it," Maggie agreed.

It was clear that Erica loved him and truly grieved. No matter what else you wanted to say about her. Maggie could see that.

Erica picked up her purse and turned to leave the shop. "That's all I can tell you. I have to go."

"Wait . . . don't forgot this." Maggie ran out from behind the counter, carrying the knitting tote. She held it out. "I want you to have it. Honestly. Give it away to someone if you don't want to keep it."

Erica finally took her prize. "My sister-in-law's birthday is coming up. I guess it will come in handy."

"You were here all alone with that woman? You took a big chance, I'm very upset with you." Suzanne made her scolding-mom face.

Maggie tried to look contrite but was secretly laughing. It was Saturday, nearly noon, and she had just finished relating her conversation with Erica to her friends. She'd sent a quick, early-morning e-mail, reporting that she'd lured Erica to the shop. They all wrote back that they'd drop what they were doing to meet at the shop and hear more about it. Claiming they had planned to come by anyway, for one reason or another.

Maggie quickly related the conversation she'd had with Jeremy's old flame. But now she had to endure their rebukes. Which she hoped wouldn't go on too long. She was rolling balls of yarn off her knitting swift and paused to slip on another skein.

"It wasn't a huge chance. But still. She is an unknown quantity," Dana agreed.

Phoebe just gave her a look. "Dumb move," she mouthed silently.

"My money would be on Maggie in that matchup," Lucy finally said. "So, do you think she did it? Sounds like she has a good alibi, with her coming and going at the lab documented by the building's security system."

"It's almost too good. A clever mouse has many holes," Maggie said quietly.

"I think the exact quote is 'A mouse does not rely on just one hole,'" Dana corrected. "But the clever ones know how to use them to advantage. Security videotape and clocks can be tampered with and she's worked at the lab for years. There must be ways in and out of the building that bypass the cameras. Jack says the police have figured out that Jeremy must have known how to do it. That's how he snuck a cadaver in to fake his death."

Phoebe made a face. "Where does a nice

guy like Jeremy grab one of those anyway?"

"Simple. Jeremy swiped his from the medical school," Dana explained. "He taught a chem course there, so he was able to get in and out easily and knew his way around the building. It probably wasn't too difficult, once he had it planned."

"He was extremely intelligent. So is Erica. They were at the same intellectual level. She made sure to point that out to me. A few times," Maggie said.

"Did you ask if she visited him at the motel?" said Phoebe.

Before Maggie could answer, Dana jumped in. "Jack says the motel clerk told the police he saw a female visitor the night before Jeremy was found dead. But the clerk described someone who fits Rebecca's description, with long fair hair, a bit taller than average. So we were correct in guessing that the police think Rebecca returned and left Jeremy dead."

"Somebody did. But I know it wasn't Rebecca," Maggie loyally maintained. "But I didn't ask Erica if she went there. I didn't bother. She wouldn't have told me the truth."

"Do you really think Jeremy would have called both Erica and Rebecca?" Suzanne seemed shocked by the idea. "He struck me as the loyal type."

"I don't think we can assume any high moral standards from a man who faked his own death," Dana reminded them. "He may have needed some special favor from Erica before he left the country. Maybe he needed something from the lab and knew it would be hard for her to refuse helping him?"

"Yeah, come to think of it, you're probably right." Suzanne nodded her head. "He knew that Erica would have been thrilled to hear he was alive, and sounds like Erica would have definitely taken a bullet for him."

"Or put a bullet in him. Depending on her mood." Maggie gazed around at her friends.

"Or strangle him from behind with his own scarf," Phoebe said, feigning a horrified chill.

"A scarf Rebecca had made for him, don't forget. Erica was adamant about how much she despised seeing Jeremy wear Rebecca's hand-knit gifts," Maggie reminded the others.

"Knitting rubbed in her wound?" Suzanne asked.

"Exactly."

The skein of yarn Maggie had been rolling came to an end and the little machine, now empty, kept whirring.

The women were quiet for a moment. Maggie put another skein on the swift and started to roll again.

"Lovely Erica may well have her secrets," Dana said. "But let's say she didn't do it. Who could it be otherwise? Who's left?"

"A long list. Which is probably good for Rebecca," Maggie said on an upbeat note.

Dana turned her knitting over and stopped to contemplate the question. "As far as possible female visitors, there's his sister, Claudia, and his mother, Patricia. He might have called one or both of them to let them know he was alive. And there's his stepmother, Sonia. But she seems the most distant and least likely to be in his confidence. She's also an ally of his father, the very person he was trying to escape."

"I think we cross Philip Lassiter off the phone call list. I'm sure Jeremy didn't get in touch to tell his dad he was alive and kicking," Suzanne said.

"True . . . but he might have called his brother, Alec?" Lucy looked up from her work, the idea just coming to her. "Jeremy showed a lot of loyalty to his brother at the wedding. He even crossed their father in order to have Alec stand up for him as the best man. And Alec is an outsider to the family circle. Jeremy may have felt safe contacting him."

"Good point, Lucy." Dana nodded. "I've been thinking about the way Jeremy faked his death, from a psychological point of view. It is a common fantasy. People do wonder how their loved ones and other social connections would react once they're gone."

"I do all the time. Whenever I get really pissed about how Josh doesn't appreciate me. Or how hard I work for his band," Phoebe admitted. "In my fantasy, he's on stage in a solo spotlight, weeping a little, saying, 'This one is for Phoebe. The greatest girlfriend who ever lived . . .' Or he's dedicating an entire concert to me. Oh, and there's a really good photo of me up on big screens next to the stage. A real glam shot —"

"Thank you, dear. I think we get the idea," Maggie interrupted. "Although, lifting the veil on your secret life this way does make me a little concerned."

Dana laughed. "I think you might say the same if we all had a turn confessing our fantasies, Mag. But that's just what I mean. We know that all the pressure to produce and save the family was on Jeremy. He must have felt resentful and under-appreciated.

I'm starting to think that he enjoyed watching the way his family reacted to his fake death. And was tempted to reach out to a few people in his life and let them know he survived. Not just Rebecca. Maybe Alec, too."

"Well . . . do we think Alec is a good twin . . . or an evil twin?" Phoebe peered around the circle pushing back a lock of her long dark hair. Maggie still wasn't used to the yellow streak. Phoebe had recently changed it, from her usual magenta. Which Maggie thought was more becoming . . . in some odd away.

"Does he have to be one or the other?" Lucy asked with a laugh.

"Identical twins are always one or the other. In daytime dramas and the movies," Suzanne said quickly.

"It's a bit more complicated in real life," Dana said. "But I'd say the Lassiters have all the necessary dysfunction to produce that classic combination."

"What do the police say, Dana? Has Jack heard anything about more visitors or phone calls? Or visits to the motel by Alec?" Lucy asked.

"Nothing more so far. Except for Rebecca going there. Which she admits, too," Dana replied.

"And which has her in a lot of hot water if they can't find evidence of anyone else visiting him there," Maggie added in a rushed, worried tone.

"Jeremy was very smart. He knew how to cover his tracks," Dana continued. "He purposely left his iPhone in the fire, along with his wallet and wedding band and many personal belongings, in the pockets of the stolen cadaver, to prove his demise. Then he bought a prepaid phone to use at the motel. The police found only Rebecca's number on that. But it doesn't mean he didn't contact other people with other means that are harder to trace. The police are still checking all the pay phones in the area, library computers, and other venues."

"Wow, that could take months," Phoebe said.

"It could," Dana agreed. "Hopefully, they'll get lucky. Unfortunately, there were no security cameras at the motel. Did I already mention that? The police only have the accounts of three different desk clerks who had shifts while Jeremy stayed there. And of course, they weren't watching the parking lot every minute."

"More like watching a mini-TV tucked in their office space somewhere," Suzanne said. "Or napping."

"Exactly. There were some other guests and employees of the motel. But they didn't have much to say. It was definitely the type of place where people come and go anonymously. And that's pretty much all the desk clerks saw — Jeremy, coming and going. Carrying bags from the 7-Eleven next door. Wearing low caps and sunglasses."

"And, most likely, the scarf Rebecca had made for him," Lucy added. "Sounds like he rarely took it off."

"Sounds like he slept in it," Suzanne added.

"Sounds sort of kinky —" Phoebe said.

"Enough said," Maggie cut in, calling a halt to that line of speculation.

"Hey, this sounds really obvious, but don't the police realize that when these desk clerks saw Jeremy coming and going it could have been Alec?" Lucy pondered aloud. "Jeremy was so smart, he may have even told his brother to wear an identical getup, something simple like a baseball cap and a dark-colored jacket?"

"His sister, Claudia, said that they used to trick the family, trading identities. That was one of the stories she told at the memorial service," Suzanne recalled.

"A common prank for twins in childhood. Not so common for adults," Dana re-

211

marked. "But in this situation, it would have definitely come in handy."

"It would have," Maggie said thoughtfully. "Alec may have been there several times, flying under the radar. Are the police looking into that line of investigation at all?" she asked Dana.

"If they are, Jack hasn't heard about it." Dana glanced at her. "I will ask him. He doesn't hear every little nuance. Just the high points."

"Or the low points, as the case may be with this squad." Maggie did not hold out great hopes of the local investigators finding Jeremy's murderer. They'd failed to figure out the murder not only of Amanda Goran but also of a dear old friend who had mysteriously drowned last summer, Gloria Sterling.

Maggie and her knitting circle had gotten tangled in that investigation, too. Which was probably part of the reason Nora had appealed to her for help.

"Maybe we should assume Alec did visit Jeremy but nobody noticed because of the twin thing," Suzanne suggested. "What then?"

"Yes, what then? Good question." Maggie sat with her thoughts, the yarn swift working like a second brain.

The little alarm on her watch went off and she checked the time.

"Oh, dear. I have to get moving. Sorry." Maggie apologized and quickly gathered up the balls of yarn she'd been winding. Phoebe ran over and helped her.

"You're all welcome to hang out as long as you like, of course," she added. "I have a class coming in a few minutes. The first session of Birds of a Feather. Anyone want to try it?"

"No thanks, this bird has to go show a house." Suzanne stood up and stashed her knitting in one fell swoop.

"This one has a yoga class." Dana stood and stretched.

"This bird needs to keep cleaning out her nest," Lucy said with a grin. "To make room for another bird to share it. Along with his electric guitar collection and assorted amplifiers. He wants to hang the guitars on a wall in the living room. Or the bedroom."

"You're kidding, right?" Suzanne stared at her. "You poor thing."

Phoebe seemed genuinely puzzled. "What's the problem? If Josh ever moves in here, I'd have an entire apartment filled with his amps and instruments."

"Upstairs, she means." Maggie tipped her head to look up at the ceiling with a bleak expression. "Heaven preserve me," she mumbled just loud enough for all to hear.

"Enough said. Have a good class, Maggie. Catch up with you all later." Dana led the way and the others followed her out. Just as a few of the new student "birds" were coming in.

Maggie smiled and greeted the new faces. She was looking forward to teaching this class. She'd be learning how to make these cute little creatures along with her students, but that was all right. That's what creative effort was all about. Discovery. Surprise. Inspiration.

The new faces and cheerful project would offset some of this gloomy talk about Jeremy's demise. That was for sure.

It was time to put all the questions about Jeremy's murder aside for a while. That was the best thing to do.

Sometimes a real insight could come to you in a flash, when you weren't thinking about a problem at all. Maggie hoped that would happen to her. There were so many questions about Jeremy's murder and so far, not nearly enough answers.

Chapter Nine

"See . . . what did I tell you?" Edie Steiber slapped the newspaper down on the counter in front of Lucy, practically sticking Lucy's nose in it . . . in her usual, subtle manner.

Lucy had dropped in at the Schooner on her way home to the cottage for an extra dose of caffeine. She needed a boost to face the mountain of old clothes in the guest room waiting to be sorted out for charity and a mountain of work she had to finish over the weekend that waited in her office.

As she waited for the coffee, longer than she wanted to, she was not sure what Edie was ranting about. She looked down and gave the article a glance, knowing she wouldn't be served until she at least feigned some interest.

"I knew that At-Las investment offer was too good to be true. My big toe was tingling. I'm glad I followed my own good advice and didn't listen to that kid who handles my portfolio."

While Edie squawked about airhead financial advisers and greedy, shameless hucksters robbing the life savings from vulnerable old people like herself, Lucy tried to translate the business jargon of the news article.

It was a short but chilling report, on page three, about an investigation by state and federal authorities into the business practices of At-Las Technologies. Particularly the investments recently solicited for research and development of a new adhesive formula, which the company contends will be a groundbreaking technology.

Investigators question whether the funds, earmarked for R&D, were used improperly by the firm and question the substantial returns some investors have already received, though no product has been formally announced or so far produced for the marketplace . . .

The news story continued. But Lucy paused and looked up at Edie.

Before she could even formulate her question, the older woman said, "In other words, Philip Lassiter was running a shell game. Using the money he collected from one guy to give a profit to the other. So he kept attracting more investors, see?

"Meanwhile, hard to say if any of that dough was used to make the doughnuts. More like he needed some quick cash to prop the place up until his golden boy, Jeremy, could figure out that blasted glue formula. And we all know the sad ending to that story . . ."

"Yes, we do, unfortunately." Lucy sighed. "Mind if I keep this copy? I don't have time to read the whole thing now."

"Sure, go ahead. I have a stack of 'em." Edie shrugged and rang up Lucy's coffee, which she'd finally poured out, smacking on a plastic lid. "I'm going to throw in the newspaper for free, hon. As long as you look me in the eye and say, 'Edie, you told us so. You were the first one that smelled something fishy in that deal.' "

Lucy was happy to comply. "You were the first one to sniff out that rat, Edie. No question."

Edie seemed satisfied and handed over the coffee cup. She pulled down her handmade powder blue sweater vest over her large stomach. The garment had a spring theme, Lucy noticed, with a bright yellow sun embroidered over Edie's right breast, a red bird in flight just below her left breast, and a row of multicolored flowers sprouting up from the bottom hem, tugged across her hips. She was a walking, talking garden of delights today, Lucy thought. Though she didn't dare tell Edie that.

"You know what P. T. Barnum said," Edie added. "There's a sucker born every minute."

Lucy could not argue with that. And didn't have time to, either.

Maggie's Saturday at the shop had been busy and passed quickly. Which was just the way she liked it. She'd taught a class in the morning and one in the afternoon and the fair weather had brought out more shoppers to Main Street.

The shop had not been overrun, as it was sometimes in the fall or right before the holidays. But there had been a nice flow of customers coming and going most of the day. She'd made a few very nice sales, too, and felt very encouraged as she sorted a pile of button cards and returned them to their proper drawers.

Phoebe had left early to help Josh with a gig. But Maggie didn't mind lingering to clean up. She liked the shop to be neat on Monday morning when she opened the door again. It was a far less stressful way to start the week. She did the same thing at night, before she went to bed, picking up around her house and setting up the coffeepot.

Besides, she didn't have anywhere to go but home to eat her dinner and read a book, or maybe find a movie on TV worth watching. And work on her knitting, of course.

The sharp tap on a windowpane in the front door drew her attention. She had already flipped the sign to the CLOSED side but there was always some persistent customer who wouldn't accept that message as long as there was a light left on or she could be seen through the window.

Her day's totals hadn't been good enough to miss a possible sale, so she wearily walked to the front and pulled open the door.

She was surprised to see Lewis Atkins standing there.

He looked very smart in a camel hair overcoat and dark brown muffler. The brim of a brown fedora was pulled low over his eyes. He wore his trademark bow tie and a look of satisfaction, she noticed. He was pleased to be surprising her.

"Mrs. Messina . . . hope you don't mind me dropping by to say hello. I was just in the neighborhood."

"No, not at all. Come right in." Maggie

quickly retrieved her usual poise and manners, stepping aside so her visitor could enter.

"My, what a lovely shop you have here." He politely removed his hat and walked in, gazing around at the interesting space she'd found for her store. He took in the groupings of antique furniture, couches and chairs, the armoire filled with yarn, and long worktable in back.

"What beautiful molding . . . and a bay window with a real window seat. This must have been some house in its day."

"It must have been," she agreed. "Fortunately, it was well preserved. The separate rooms suit my needs very well."

"I can see that. It all looks very cozy. And functional," he added. He appreciated the practical, logical side of things, she remembered.

He strolled over to the spinning wheel in the front room and gave the wheel a turn.

" 'Round and 'round she goes. Where she stops, nobody knows," he called out. Then he looked up at her and smiled.

Maggie smiled back, just to be polite. Even though he had told her he would stop by sometime to see the shop and say hello, she found his appearance at this hour somewhat . . . odd. Even unsettling.

She watched him, her arms crossed over her chest.

"How's business? I see you're running a contest," he tilted his head toward the window again. "Good idea. People always like something for nothing."

His observation was true. Though Maggie wouldn't have said it so plainly. "People like contests. At least I hope they do. I'm not sure if it's bringing in more traffic."

"Oh, I think it's bringing in traffic. You've got me in here, right?"

He caught her eye and smiled again. She felt a chill. She suddenly wondered if he and Erica were connected in some way and Erica had sent him.

She didn't feel comfortable asking him why he'd come. But a few other questions came to mind now that he was here.

"Terrible news about Jeremy. What a shock," she began. "You knew him well. Did you ever imagine he could plan such an elaborate ruse?"

Atkins narrowed his eyes, his gaze shifting to the side. "Oh, he seemed sunny and bright. And for the most part, he was. But desperate times inspire desperate acts. Jeremy disappearing down that rabbit hole was an act of self-defense. Self-preservation. It was a prison break gone wrong. The boy was driven to it. By his father," he said bluntly. "Philip Lassiter is the one to blame. No question in my book."

Of course Philip Lassiter would be the villain in any of Lewis Atkins's scenarios. But in this case, it was probably true.

"I never looked at it that way. Maybe you're right."

"No maybes about it," he replied. "Any other questions?"

In for a penny, in for a pound, Maggie thought, grasping her courage. "Did Jeremy get in touch with you, from the motel? I'm just curious," she added. "It seems like you two had a good relationship, in spite of everything that had gone on at his father's company."

"We did. I think so anyway . . . But curiosity was bad for the cat, Maggie. Remember? It was fatal."

His reply was alarming. But Maggie hid her reaction well.

"So, you're not going to answer me?" She shrugged. "That's all right. I understand."

He shook his head. "What's the difference? Sure, I'll tell you. You'll probably hear everything around town anyway. Jeremy did call me. He wanted to meet, to talk about the formula."

"To sell it to you, you mean?" she asked

quickly. She remembered how Rebecca had told them Jeremy said he could get a lot of money in a little while. But he didn't say how.

"That's right. He knew I was still trying to work it out. He told me he'd cracked it and he wanted to make a deal." Lewis paused, making her wait for the punch line. "I didn't go to meet him. I didn't believe him."

"You didn't?" Maggie was surprised.

He shook his head. "I knew he wanted to get back at his father, and giving me the formula was the best way to do that. But I still didn't trust him. I mean, it's hard to trust a man who faked his own death. Don't you think? No matter how nice a boy he'd always seemed."

Maggie considered Lewis's line of reasoning, and thought he was a wise person. Dispassionate, but wise.

"That does make sense." Dana had said almost the same thing, when they had been talking about Jeremy's possible disloyalty to Rebecca — we can't assume anything about the moral code of a man who would fake his own death.

"I also make it a rule not to do business with people who are desperate. And Jeremy definitely fell into that category."

Maggie nodded. "Yes, I suppose he did. I guess he was counting on the fact that the offer would be so tempting you'd lose all perspective."

Lewis laughed. "Mrs. Messina, you say that as if you don't think I'm smart enough to figure out the formula for myself."

Had she really sounded like that? She felt embarrassed. Well, maybe she was thinking that, a little.

"So, have you cracked it?"

He shook his head. "Not yet. But I'm getting there. Since we're on the subject, I'll tell you something else I told the police. I didn't want it so badly I'd kill him for it. It's just . . . glue. What would be the point of that anyway? Killing him after he gave it to me, or because he didn't give it to me? No . . . I'm not their man. I have a rock-solid alibi, by the way. I was at an opera in Boston, sitting there the entire night. *Carmen.* All four acts and a very late dinner afterward. Were you curious about that, too?"

Maggie feigned an innocent stare. "Of course not. It's just too tempting to talk about all this. With someone who knew him well."

"Yes, it is. People are fascinating. And you're also a very poor liar, Mrs. Messina."

"Well, thanks. I'll take that as a compliment, all things considered. And you can call me Maggie, if you like."

"Thanks. Call me Lewis." He smiled, looked around again, then put on his hat and adjusted the brim. "Nice talking to you, Maggie. I love the store. I'd imagined it a lot like this. Good luck with your business."

"Thanks for stopping by," she replied. And thanks for an enlightening conversation, she thought.

"No problem. I'll be by again sometime. In the meantime, you really ought to curb that curious streak. There are still a lot of unstable chemicals in this mix. And unstable personalities. You don't want it to blow up in your face, Maggie."

"No, I don't," she agreed. A few moments later, he said good night and walked out.

Maggie felt admonished by his words. But still curious. He seemed to have spoken freely with her. But she felt sure there was still a lot Lewis Atkins knew but had not disclosed.

On Sunday morning, Lucy found a long but interesting e-mail from Maggie, addressed to all her friends:

The bunch of you are always telling me I

225

need to socialize more. Just want to report that on Saturday night, I actually spent some quality time with an attractive, intelligent man. Who even likes opera. How rare is that?

Too bad he's on our short list of suspects. It was Lewis Atkins. He stopped by the shop. I'm not exactly sure why now. We had a long conversation. He's quite intelligent and interesting to talk to. I've decided that I don't think he killed Jeremy. And not because I'd like to go see him again. (Outside of a prison visit, I mean.) So don't you all start getting ideas. I'll explain next time you're in the shop.

Till then — I think we can cross Atkins off the list.

I remain alone but not lonely. (Except once in a while, on the weekend.) Honestly.

XO, Maggie

Lucy only had time to write back a short note.

Interesting! I may call you later tonight or just drop by tomorrow. Am busy with moving Matt's stuff today. Including the guitar collection. :(

Lucy and Matt had decided he didn't have

enough belongings to make it worth hiring a mover. He drove a small pickup truck and she drove a Jeep, so they figured it wouldn't take more than two loads to bring all his belongings to the cottage.

Yet once they started packing up the vehicles, the boxes and odd pieces of furniture seemed to triple. Matt was not the best packer, either, and items like lamps and even dishes seemed to be flying out of haphazard containers.

Most of the boxes held his books, and while Lucy had always appreciated Matt's literary interests, moving his library was definitely the downside.

"Remind me not to get involved with any brainy guys in the future." Lucy grunted as she hefted another box up to the truck bed. "I'm getting you an e-reader for your birthday. No question."

"You can leave those for me, Lucy," Matt said gallantly.

"No, I can't. I don't want you to exhaust yourself and hurt your back."

"That's my secret plan. Then you'll feel so sorry for me and give me a back rub."

She glanced at him, lifting another box. "You know you'll get one anyway, and a nice dinner, too. Hate to say it, but you're spoiled worse than the dogs now, honey."

Matt made a hurt face, then had to laugh with her.

"Yeah, you're right. And who's fault is that?"

Lucy smiled back but didn't answer. He had a point.

The last of the boxes was loaded in the pickup and Lucy brushed her hands off on her jeans.

"Okay, pal. Once you move it, it's a whole new ball game. Since you brought it up, I think it would be wise to set some ground rules. Cooking, cleaning, laundry. Division of labor? That sort of thing?"

"Division of back rubs?

"Yup, that's on the list, too. Maybe we should get one of those chore charts and hang it on the fridge. Like my sister has for her girls?"

"I'm good with that."

He nodded again. Then put his hands on her shoulders and looked into her eyes. He was smiling but still looked very serious.

"Was this a good idea? Tell me honestly."

She nodded and smiled. She felt nervous, too. But underneath that, happy. Incredibly happy, she realized.

"Absolutely. It's the best idea we've had in a long time. Honest," she said. She hugged him and he hugged her back even tighter.

"Glad you said that. I think so, too."

It did feel a little different Monday morning, waking up with Matt in the house, Lucy noticed. Not that he wasn't often there in the morning. But with all of his belongings around, most of it still in boxes, it just felt more . . . permanent.

Lucy knew this living together situation was going to take a little getting used to. It was nice to kiss him good-bye and know for sure that he'd be coming back at the end of the day to be with her. But she did feel secretly relieved when he left, so she could ease into her usual morning routine.

After a quick shower, she made her way down to the village with Tink. Her friends had agreed to meet for coffee and get the full report on Lewis Atkins.

Maggie was waiting for them, coffeepot in hand as Lucy walked through the door. "Come on back. Suzanne brought some horribly fattening crumb cake from the bakery. She just wants to torture us."

"And I brought some fruit and yogurt smoothies," Dana said, walking in right behind Lucy.

"If I drink one of those, will it cancel out the cake?" Maggie asked.

Dana shrugged. "I'm not sure. It couldn't hurt."

Phoebe wasn't up yet, Maggie reported. The rest of the group filled their mugs and gathered around the table. "So, tell us what happened, Maggie. You were very circumspect in your e-mail," Dana noted. "What convinced you that Atkins wasn't involved?"

"He has a strong alibi for the night Jeremy was killed, for one thing," she began. "He was in Boston at the opera."

"Right. Opera lovers can't be murderers. Everyone knows that," Suzanne teased. Lucy watched as she helped herself to a small piece of crumb cake, then sliced off the cake and ate just the crumbs.

"That's not why. But opera lovers probably comprise a very low percentage of violent criminals compared to other groups. To hockey fans, for instance," Maggie quickly added. "And he didn't deny that he's still trying to figure out the formula. But he believed Jeremy may have been, too. He didn't trust Jeremy to sell him the real thing."

"That's a good point," Lucy agreed.

"Even if he somehow got the information from Jeremy by force," Maggie continued, "or knew where it was stashed in the motel room and stole it, I still don't feel he has it in him to have ended Jeremy's life. I think Atkins felt too attached to him."

They all listened quietly, eating their unbalanced, balanced breakfast.

"You might be right, Maggie," Dana said finally. "Jeremy was killed in a very close, personal way. Strangled with a scarf around his neck. Not everyone would be cable of that act, especially with someone they knew so well. And had parental feelings for, which I think Atkins has expressed from time to time."

"Exactly my take," Maggie answered. "He did say something more before he left. He warned me to stay out of it. To stop snooping around. How did he say it again? Oh, right . . . he said there were some unstable chemicals and unstable personalities mixed up in the situation and it might all blow up in my face."

"Interesting." Dana sipped her smoothie. "Sounds like he's on some inside track, while still denying he had anything to do with the murder."

"It does, doesn't it?" Maggie paused for a moment. "I also had to wonder later how he even knew I was snooping . . . and why he really came here. We did exchange business cards at the memorial service. But his visit seemed prompted by something else. I think he has some connection with Erica Ferris and she told him about my raffle prize trick. Which I'm a little embarrassed about now." She laughed and took another sip of coffee.

"Hey, it worked, right?" Suzanne reminded her. "Don't argue with success. But you've got a point. Those two have a lot in common. She's still on the inside of At-Las and even worked with Jeremy. Maybe Atkins persuaded her to come over to his side of the glue wars and help him figure out the formula."

Lucy suddenly sat up in her seat, feeling the coffee kick in and her achy spots fade a bit. "I think you're on to something, Suzanne. They do make a good glue duo now. Maybe Atkins has been trying to win her over for a while. Ever since Jeremy dumped her, thinking she'd want to get back at him."

"But she turned out to be the loyal type, if nothing else," Maggie agreed knowingly. "But Jeremy's gone now. No reason to be loyal to At-Las or the Lassiters. Nobody there seems to like her. Claudia would have fired her given half a chance. Erica probably knows that."

"So . . . let's sketch this out. I'm getting a little confused," Lucy admitted. "We have Atkins and Ferris teaming up to figure out the formula. At-Las may have the complete formula, but they can't find it. They need to put it together from Jeremy's records, which are scattered."

"That's what they claim," Maggie added. "I'm just thinking back to the conversation I overheard at the memorial service. Claudia sounded very sure they could find Jeremy's lab notes and records and put it all together. Alec however wasn't nearly as sure," she added.

"I wonder where they're at with it now. It's been exactly two weeks since the fire," Suzanne pointed out.

"Wait . . . did any of you see that article in the newspaper about At-Las Technologies? Edie showed it to me Saturday morning. I have a copy somewhere in here. . . ." Lucy quickly dug through her knitting bag, a large, disorganized tote. As most of her purses and totes tended to be.

"I was so busy over the weekend, I forgot to tell you guys about it." She finally found it and pulled it out. Then passed it around and they all quickly read it.

"So Philip Lassiter is in big trouble. A Ponzi scheme with investors? That's heavy-duty." Suzanne nodded, licking cake crumb off her fingertip.

"Yes, looks like he's a regular mini-

Madoff," Maggie suggested.

"I'm sure his attorneys are telling him it would help his case if he could produce the finished product," Dana said.

"That's just what I was thinking," Suzanne agreed. "I mean, 'Got glue?,' Philip."

"Good question, Suzanne. I'm sure all the Lassiters are wondering the same thing. If only we could talk to Claudia and Alec," Maggie mused.

"Or sit behind them again at some event and eavesdrop," Lucy reminded her with her grin.

"Oh, that would be even better, wouldn't it?" Maggie agreed.

Her phone rang and she rose to answer it. "Phoebe probably," Maggie said in a softer voice. "Calling from upstairs to say she's still sleeping and we're making too much noise," she joked.

They all laughed. Though Phoebe had actually done that once or twice, when she'd been up way too late and wasn't due in to the store or at school until the afternoon. No wonder their punky little mascot was so thin and pale. She didn't get enough sleep, Lucy thought.

"Good morning. Black Sheep Knitting Shop. Can I help you?" Maggie answered sounding like a parody of a shopkeeper.

"Oh . . . hello, Nora. I thought you were someone else." She laughed, returning to her normal tone. "How are you? How's Rebecca? Oh . . . really? That's awful . . ."

The sudden note of alarm in Maggie's voice alerted Lucy and her friends to turn to her.

"What's going on? What happened?" Suzanne called out. "Is Rebecca okay?"

Maggie glanced at them, holding up her hand like a crossing guard, still listening to Nora's conversation on the phone. She looked very distressed, her eyes wide with concern.

". . . yes, I understand. I'll let you go. I'll try to stop by later. This afternoon or tonight." Maggie said good-bye to Nora and ended the call.

She stood by the counter, facing them, still holding the phone. "Rebecca's apartment, the one she and Jeremy lived in, was broken into last night. Just about everything was stolen. Or torn apart."

"Oh, my . . . that's awful. That poor kid. What's going to happen next?" Suzanne pressed her hand to her face.

"I assume she wasn't home at the time?" Dana asked. Lucy and her friends had already started clearing away the coffee and breakfast dishes, so they could all get to

235

work. Maggie walked over and joined in.

"No, she wasn't there. Thank goodness. She'd been staying a lot at Nora's off and on. But went back to her own house after the second funeral, the private one. Last night she just happened to be out with a girlfriend and found the place wrecked when she got home."

"It's awful to have someone break into your house. Some creepy stranger, touching all your stuff." Suzanne shivered, transporting the creamer and sugar bowl to the storeroom. "It happened to me once in college. I'll never forget it."

"Sounds like the creepy stranger did more than touch stuff. Nora said they hauled away a lot of her belongings. Books and CDs. Even Rebecca's knitting supplies, some bags of yarn and needles."

"How odd. You can't do much with someone's old books and CDs," Suzanne said. "Is there a big call for stolen yarn on the street these days?"

"That's what she said." Maggie shrugged. The table was cleared and cleaned. Suzanne slipped on her jacket and grabbed her briefcase and knitting bag.

"Luckily, her wedding gown wasn't there. Nora said she wouldn't have been able to stand it if the gown was taken, too."

"That was lucky. Where is it?" Lucy asked.

"It's here, in the storeroom. Nora gave it to me the day after the wedding so I could put it up in the front window. I told Nora I'd bring it over tonight. I'll take some knitting supplies, too. The poor thing. The thief took her bag, all the needles and paraphernalia. I don't think anyone could have hauled away her entire stash. He would have needed a moving van. Rebecca has the Mother of All Stashes, believe me. It was epic."

Maggie knew of epic stashes. Her own personal stock of yarn at home took up most of the second floor. Lucy could only imagine Rebecca's.

"Maybe this despicable person plans on opening a knitting shop. Sounds like you might have some competition, Mag." Suzanne checked her phone, tapping back an answer to a text while she continued to talk to her friends.

"It does sound like that," Maggie agreed. "I wonder what the police think of all this. I guess I'll hear more about that from Nora tonight."

The others were ready to go, too, and Maggie walked them to the front of the shop.

"I might be able to come if you'd like

237

company," Dana offered.

"I would like some company. Thanks for the offer," Maggie replied.

"I'd like to see Rebecca and Nora, too . . . but it's Matt's first real night in my house . . . our house, I mean," Lucy said, quickly correcting herself.

And nothing short of a house fire was going to keep her from welcoming him home and spending the evening with him.

"He finally moved in? I totally forgot this was the big weekend," Suzanne confessed.

"That's all right. I was being low-key about it." Just in case one of us got cold feet at the last minute, she added silently.

"For goodness' sake . . . you could have mentioned something. How was the move? Is it going all right?" Maggie touched Lucy's shoulder, genuinely sorry to have missed the milestone.

"The move went fine. I'm just a little sore in places. As for the rest, so far, so good." Lucy shrugged and glanced at her watch. "And it's been a whole . . . eighteen hours?"

"I'm sure it will be great," Dana said sincerely. "A little tip — after the first twenty-four, best to put the watch away." She smiled and winked.

Maggie and Dana decided to get in touch later in the day, to figure out a time for the trip to Nora's, and the friends parted on the sidewalk in front of Maggie's shop.

News of the break-in at Rebecca's gave Lucy plenty to think about on the long walk home — aside from what she should make for dinner.

The robbery must have something to do with Jeremy's murder. The thief must have been looking for something that had to do with the glue formula. Some scribbled notation, or hidden, computerized record. He — or she — didn't have time for a close search, so they grabbed whatever they suspected might hold the buried treasure.

Including the knitting paraphernalia, as odd as that seemed. She also wanted to know what connections the police were making between this event and Jeremy's murder.

Though she wondered if they had any more insight into this sticky mess than she and her friends did.

CHAPTER TEN

"Here we are. It's that dark blue house on the right." Maggie pointed to Nora's house and Dana pulled up to the curb right in front.

"Thanks for coming, Dana. I always seem to be visiting here under such difficult circumstances." Maggie sighed and opened the back door of the car to retrieve the garment bag that held the wedding gown and two shopping bags full of yarn she wanted to give Rebecca.

Dana came around and grabbed the other bag, which was filled with needles, a tape measure, rubber needle tips, and assorted necessary items. She shut the car and locked it.

"You're a good friend, Maggie, and very generous. But everyone knows that."

Dana's compliment was a comfort. But Maggie still felt she wasn't bringing Rebecca nearly enough yarn, or doing enough for the girl. And Nora. Their trials and tribulations were reaching biblical proportions. What would be next?

Nora greeted them at the door before they even had a chance to ring the bell. She must have been watching out the window.

"Here's the gown. Safe and sound." Maggie handed over the garment bag first.

"Rebecca will be happy to see this." As Nora hung the bag on a coat tree in the foyer, Rebecca came down the stairway to greet them.

"Maggie brought your gown back. It's a good thing she had it in her shop."

"Thank you, Maggie. I would have come by and picked it up."

"No problem. I wanted to stop in and say hello anyway. And bring this other stuff over," she added. "It's just some extra yarn and things I thought you could use. I felt so bad when I heard that your equipment and your yarn were stolen."

"Oh, wow . . . look at all this." Rebecca crouched down to examine the gift closer. "Maggie . . . you didn't have to do that. There's a ton of yarn here. Let me pay you something. Please?"

Rebecca was a rich woman now. Maggie had forgotten. "Oh, don't be silly. It's a gift. I have so much stock sitting around the storeroom. I'll never miss it. I'm happy to see it go to someone who will really use it."

Nora had led them into the living room, where Dana and Maggie took seats side by side on the couch. Rebecca sat in an armchair nearby. Nora remained standing. Hovering a bit, in her usual way, Maggie noticed.

"Have the police told you anything more about the break-in?" Dana asked. "Anything they found when they searched afterward?"

Rebecca shook her head. "No, nothing so far. The same detective working on Jeremy's case was called in. Detective Marisol Reyes. She seems very competent. Very intelligent, too," Rebecca added.

Dana and Maggie exchanged looks. Detective Reyes had been one of the officers who had investigated the death of her old rival Amanda Goran, and also took part in the case when Gloria Sterling died.

"We've met Detective Reyes. She is very competent. Sounds like she's been promoted, too," Maggie said.

"They sealed the apartment and Rebecca wasn't allowed back in. She's staying with me a few days," Nora added. "I didn't want her to stay there alone right now anyway. Who knows? It could be dangerous. That awful person could come back."

Maggie heard a lot of fear in Nora's voice. Anyone would feel the same, she thought.

"It was really . . . creepy," Rebecca admitted. "The place was totally trashed. I don't know how I'm going to clean it up."

"We'll get it back together, sweetheart. Don't even worry about that now. One thing at a time." Nora patted her daughter's shoulder. "I don't think the police have even finished sifting through, looking for clues about who did it, or why."

"But they're pretty sure it wasn't a random break-in," Rebecca added. "They said it could have to do with Jeremy's work. His research on the formula. I guess the person who broke in didn't know Jeremy very well. He didn't even have a home office. He kept everything on his laptop, and they found that in the fire . . . Unless he hid something from me. Which is definitely possible," she admitted sadly.

"That's what we were thinking, too," Maggie said.

"I suppose this helps take pressure off of you, as a suspect in the case," Dana added.

"I hope so," Rebecca agreed. "But my lawyer said we still need to be concerned. The police could see these situations separately — the search for Jeremy's notes and his murder might not be connected at all."

"Yes, that's true," Dana agreed quietly.

"It is odd that they took yarn and the knitting tools," Maggie said after a moment. "Do the police have any theories about that?"

"They asked me a lot of questions about that. If Jeremy had access to my knitting supplies. Did I ever notice him going through it. They seem to think he may have hidden something there." Rebecca appeared amused by that idea.

"You don't think that's possible?" Dana asked.

Rebecca shook her head. "I had just bought most of that yarn for the after-school program. I didn't open the boxes until after the fire at the lab. Until Jeremy was . . . was gone." She faltered over the last few words but seemed to calm herself quickly. "The big plastic tote with my knitting tools had been over at school until a few days ago. I was using all those things for the program there, too."

"Which means that Jeremy didn't have a chance to hide anything in the yarn or in those plastic storage totes," Dana reasoned out loud. "But the intruder who ransacked your apartment probably didn't know that."

"I guess not. They were just casting a wide net, it seems to me. They took almost everything that wasn't nailed down, or they ripped it to shreds." She paused and sighed. "Losing all that yarn does annoy me. I've been teaching the kids how to knit and we were going to start a new project. Which reminds me, Maggie. I wanted to ask you about those little birds and animals you have in the shop window. Are they hard to make?"

Maggie found the sudden change in subject abrupt. But Rebecca was probably worn out from talking about all her other troubles. Talking about knitting was almost as good a distraction from worries as actually knitting, she knew.

"Oh . . . the little amigurumi. No, they aren't difficult at all and perfect for children. They don't take long to make, so there's fast gratification. And lots of motivation when you show them the samples," she added. "You need round needles to make the body and a little polyester fluff to fill them. The wings or tails, or whatever, are knit separately and sewed on. The children will need some help with that step, but it's a good little lesson in using a tapestry needle."

"That sounds pretty simple." Maggie could see Rebecca considering the instructions the way a teacher does. Wondering if she could lead her young knitters through this uncharted territory without too much chaos and confusion. In addition to everything else she had to worry about right now, Maggie thought sympathetically.

"Oh, I can come by and teach the lesson for you some afternoon. I want to donate all the materials anyway," she added.

"Maggie, please. You have a store to run. You don't have any time for that," Rebecca argued.

"Of course I do. I have a very able assistant to mind the store. And I've been wanting to help you in some way, Rebecca. Ever since all this . . . all these traumatic events began. Please let me do it. I love working with kids and I'm not too bad at it," she added. Everyone knew Maggie had been an art teacher for more than twenty years before she opened her shop. One of the most favorite and well remembered, too.

"Oh, I know you'll charm them," Rebecca said with a smile. "They may decide they like you better than me."

"I doubt it," Maggie argued with a laugh. "But I have thought of doing some volunteer work somewhere in town. It was my New Year's resolution . . . again. What is it now, April? This gives me a chance to check that one off."

An inspiration to volunteer often struck Maggie. Usually, late at night, when she was sitting at home with nothing very pressing to take care of. In the bright light of day, when all the demands of her business and routine crowded in, the idealistic notion would melt away. But here was the perfect opportunity to follow through on her good intentions.

"Let me come and show the kids how to make the animals. What day should I come?"

"We usually meet on Wednesday and Friday afternoons. But you could come any day that's convenient."

"Let me check my calendar at the shop and I'll call you. It's no big deal," she added, sensing Rebecca might try to put her off again. "I'm sure you could use a little relief right now from all your responsibilities at school. I know how tiring classroom teaching can be."

"She could definitely off-load some of the extras. No question." Nora had come back into the room with a tray that held a teapot, cups, and a plate of cookies that looked homemade. "But she's very stubborn. Never likes to ask for help. She's always been that way —" Nora set the tray on the table and began to serve them. "— and there's that school play that she's working on." Nora gave her daughter a look. "Extra time at school rehearsing that, too."

Rebecca rolled her eyes. "The kids are such hams, it isn't very hard to rehearse them."

"They are at that age. Or painfully shy," Dana offered. "What play are you working on?" she asked curiously.

"Nothing too ambitious. Just a comic version of *Little Red Riding Hood*."

"Oh, that must be very sweet," Maggie said.

"It has been fun. They've been working on it for weeks. I didn't want to disappoint them. They're almost ready for prime time," Rebecca quipped, taking a sip of tea.

"She really didn't have to go back to work so quickly. Her principal was happy to let her take a leave of absence. Even to the end of the school year," Nora told them.

"Oh, I could never stay home that long. I would go crazy. At least I feel a little better working. It keeps my mind off of . . . of things I don't want to think about."

"I understand." Dana took the teacup Nora had poured for her. "It's good to get back to a normal routine after a loss. I'm sure it was hard, though. You're a very strong person, Rebecca."

Rebecca sighed. "I'm just doing what I have to do. For myself. And for the kids. I know they would feel abandoned. They're very young. They wouldn't get it."

Maggie understood, too, but also felt Rebecca had shown great resilience and maturity by returning to work so soon. She wondered if Rebecca was talking about her own feelings, too. She must feel abandoned by Jeremy. After all the plans they'd made for their future. The circumstances of his death had to feel like a great betrayal in some way, no matter how much she loved him. Maggie glanced at the bookcase and saw a framed photo of Rebecca and Jeremy, the one taken outdoors, the brilliant snowy background in stark contrast to their red cheeks and Jeremy's colorful, uniquely designed scarf.

Was that the same one he was wearing on his fateful night? Maggie shuddered and put the thought out of her mind. She preferred to focus on how they looked at that very moment, captured for all time. Content in each other's arms, without a care in the world, their future looking as cloudless as the backdrop of clear blue sky.

It was a lucky thing that we couldn't see into our own futures. How could we enjoy the simple but satisfying pleasures life offered from day to day? Hour to hour? Maybe the trick was to be mindful of each moment and find joy where we could.

She was not surprised that Rebecca did not pull out any wedding photos to show them, as most newlywed brides would have. Considering all she'd been through, those photos would be very painful to view for a long time to come, Maggie imagined. She and her friends still hadn't looked at the pictures Suzanne had taken that day. Maggie wasn't sure when she'd be ready for that.

A short time later, Dana and Maggie said their good-byes and were back in Dana's car, heading toward Maggie's house.

Dana turned to Maggie, taking her eyes off the road for a moment. "I'm glad I came tonight. I didn't get a chance to speak to Rebecca at Jeremy's service. She was still in shock. She seems to be doing much better. Considering all she's been through."

"Yes, she does. She's a strong girl. But I hope the police leave her alone and get on the right trail. There's only so much pressure anyone can stand."

"That's very true. Maybe the break-in at her apartment will convince them that she wasn't involved."

"I hope so," Maggie said quietly. "With so many people interested and involved in that glue formula, you would think the police could come up with at least one other likely suspect, besides Rebecca."

"And where is the formula? Even At-Las Technologies doesn't seem to know," Dana pointed out.

While Maggie could not figure out the answer to either of those pressing questions, she did not forget her promise to visit Rebecca's after-school program. She arranged to start the amigurumi lesson on Wednesday afternoon and left Phoebe in charge of the shop.

"I have my cell phone. Make sure you call if anything comes up," she instructed her assistant.

"Don't worry, I've got this covered." Phoebe had slipped Maggie's red tape measure around her neck and also Maggie's extra pair of reading glasses, on their sparkling, beaded cord. "How do I look? Official, right?"

"Officially . . . very silly. Are you supposed to be me or something?"

"Power corrupts. Absolute power corrupts absolutely." Phoebe recited a tidbit of wisdom from a poli-sci class.

Maggie shook her head. "If you get too bored being corrupted, you can unpack the

251

stock that came in yesterday. Instead of texting your friends all afternoon, I mean."

"I'm sure I can manage both." Phoebe smiled and gave her a little wave. "Have fun. Play nice."

Maggie waved and headed out.

It had been a while since she'd worked with children this young, third through fifth grade. But that was an easy age to deal with. Most of them still minded teachers. She was sure she wouldn't have a problem.

As she drove to the school, she wondered why she'd never offered a children's knitting class at the shop. Now that would be a great market hook — Mommy and Me Stitchery, she might call it. Or maybe just Kids Knit?

I should leave the fussy helicopter mommies out of it, she decided. The kids are easier and more fun without the parents.

Maggie arrived at the elementary school just as the children were being released for the day. There was a lot of noise and energy, a touch of spring fever in the mix, as well.

The parking lot was hectic and the hallway even worse. But she followed Rebecca's instructions and after signing in at the main office, soon found the school's large multipurpose room, which had a curtained stage on one end, but smelled distinctly like a cafeteria.

The room was nearly empty, but she saw two long tables set up with folding chairs near the double doors she had entered. Maggie had brought all the project supplies in her shopping bags. She put the bags down and was just taking off her coat when Rebecca appeared. A few children tagged after her, like pilot fish.

"Maggie, thanks for coming." Rebecca hugged her a moment. "I'm so glad you're here. I have to rehearse the play after school today, too. I'm so relieved I have someone covering the club. It's a little tricky being in charge of two groups of kids at once."

"Not just tricky. Sort of impossible," Maggie agreed.

"The rehearsal is in this room, too. Down at the other end. I could have managed, but it's just a whole lot easier having you here."

"Don't worry. I have it under control." As soon as Maggie said the words, she realized she was echoing Phoebe's tongue-in-cheek farewell. "Why don't you introduce me and then sort of slip away?"

"Great plan. I think that will work out fine."

The children had already begun to arrive and Maggie helped Rebecca get them settled in their seats, then gave out a snack.

While they ate, she took out the samples of amigurumi animals, which she knew would capture their attention. They didn't even notice when Rebecca left to join the children who had gathered near the stage and were putting on costumes on the other side of the room.

The after-school club had a basic knowledge of knitting so she wasn't starting from scratch. She gave out the patterns and supplies, and walked around the tables, helping them get started. Some children were more proficient than others, of course. But all were capable of casting on and reading the pattern. She was impressed.

By the end of the meeting, a little over an hour, a few of the kids had made a good start on the bird's body. Most were knitting slower than that and one or two had jumped ship and were fooling around, chasing each other around the big room.

As the children gathered their knapsacks and jackets, Maggie cleaned up, collecting the extra yarn and needles and her sample animals.

She strolled down to the other side of the room, where the play practice was still going on. Rebecca was not only the director but dressed as the big, bad wolf, wearing a rubber wolf Halloween mask, a furry vest, and rubber claws.

When she saw Maggie, she pulled off her mask and gave the young actors a break.

"How did it go? I'm so sorry, I didn't get a chance to come back."

"That's all right. The kids were great. Very well behaved. Most took their projects home and said they would try to finish on their own. I think they'll all end up with some sort of cute creature. Although the finished products might not look exactly like the samples."

"That's even better," Rebecca replied with a smile. She was a good teacher, Maggie thought, valuing originality most of all.

Maggie noticed the school principal, Stewart Campbell, enter from a door on the far side of the room. The kids called out to him in a friendly, relaxed way. Then he sat on the edge of a table, chatting and joking with them, sharing a bag of corn chips.

When Rebecca looked over, he waved at her and began to walk toward them.

"Stewart's here. I can go in a minute. I just have to talk to him a sec. Want to walk out together?"

"Sure. I'll wait for you."

"Hello, Maggie," Stewart greeted her. "Nice to see you again. Rebecca told me that you were going to visit and give the

255

kids a special lesson."

"I just wanted to help Rebecca a bit. I showed the children how to make amigurumi animals." Maggie pulled one from her knitting bag and showed him.

"Cute. I bet those were a big hit. And Rebecca sure needed the break." He turned to Rebecca. "I've told Rebecca we should find some other teachers to take over these after-school projects. I think she's doing too much right now."

He was genuinely concerned, Maggie noticed, echoing Nora's sentiments exactly. A good principal appreciates his teachers, and Rebecca had to be one of the best in the school. He was also a personal friend, Maggie recalled. A longtime colleague, which must have made it easier in some ways for Rebecca right now.

"I'm all right, Stewart. Honestly." Rebecca glanced at him, then pulled off her rubber claws. "If you can finish the rehearsal today, I'll get going."

"Of course I can. I told you I would and here I am." He took the mask and claws, and then the furry vest Rebecca wore over a dark blue dress. "Actually, I've been looking forward to this all day," he added, glancing at Maggie. "It's more fun than sitting in an office."

Maggie knew teaching could be fun if you didn't have to do it every day. But he was a good sport to help Rebecca. Not every school principal would have stepped in this way.

Maggie waited at the tables while Rebecca walked back to the stage with Stewart. She chatted with the principal a few more minutes, then returned with her coat and book bag.

"I think I have everything. I hope so," she said breathlessly. "Wait a sec . . . let me check. Sorry." Rebecca set her book bag on the table and leafed through a stack of folders. It looked like papers she needed to grade.

Maggie watched Stewart organizing the children to run through the last scene or two. He was also dressed up as a character now. Wearing a long funny overcoat, wire-rimmed glasses, and a strange hat. The kids were laughing hysterically and he hammed it up for them. He must have been a good classroom teacher. Which is why he appreciated a teacher like Rebecca, she realized.

"Okay, I'm good. Sorry about that." Rebecca hoisted up her bag and they started off again.

"I hate to give unwanted advice," Maggie said as they walked along, "but I'm starting

257

to think your mother is right. And so is your principal. You're doing an awful lot around here. You're stretching yourself very thin."

"I know, but it helps me to keep from thinking about Jeremy. About what happened . . ." Her voice trailed off on a sad note as she pushed through the double doors.

Rebecca wore her long pale hair in a knot at the back of her head today. It had mostly come undone, Maggie noticed, framing her pretty face with soft curls. She suddenly looked very young and vulnerable.

They walked down a long school corridor, one that had been filled with jostling kids and high-pitched squeals a short time ago, but was now empty and silent. So quiet Maggie could hear the echo of their steps on the linoleum floor. The typical pale green color, she noticed.

"We're just concerned about you, Rebecca. That's all."

"The kids will perform the play for their parents next week. Then I'll only have the one club and my regular class. That's not much," Rebecca said.

"If you say so," although Maggie wasn't completely convinced.

They came to a heavy metal door that led to the parking lot. Maggie pushed this one open and they walked out into the brisk air and late afternoon sunshine.

Maggie's green Subaru was parked nearby. She took out her keys and unlocked the hatch, then stored her bags of supplies.

"I'm coming back on Friday to help the children finish the animals. Please don't argue with me," she said.

"All right. Thank you. But I owe you one."

Maggie turned back to Rebecca, but before she could answer, she heard the doors of a sedan parked nearby open and slam.

A man got out from behind the wheel, and a woman exited from the passenger's side. Their gaze was fixed on Rebecca and they walked straight toward her. Very quickly, Maggie noticed. Their body language alarmed her, and she suddenly felt alert and wary.

Maggie quickly recognized Detective Marisol Reyes, though the other face was unfamiliar.

"Detective Reyes, can I help you?" Rebecca sounded scared.

These were the detectives investigating Jeremy's murder and they looked as if they were on official business. Very official. Maggie took a step closer to Rebecca so they faced the two police officers shoulder to shoulder.

"We have new information in the investigation, Rebecca. We need to ask you some more questions." Detective Reyes spoke in an even, serious tone.

"About what? What's come up exactly?" Maggie knew she had no right to interfere, but couldn't help herself.

"Hello, Mrs. Messina." Detective Reyes turned to Maggie. "I had a feeling we'd run into each other before this case was over. Rebecca told us how you helped with her wedding gown."

Maggie wasn't sure where that detail had fit into the long story. But the police had questioned Rebecca several times now. They must have retrieved plenty of irrelevant information. You never know what will be important, a police detective had once told her. Maggie could see that was true.

"Well, here I am, Detective." Maggie shrugged. "Doesn't the girl have a right to call her attorney? What is this about anyway?"

"It's about the night Jeremy Lassiter was murdered. Mrs. Lassiter has told us several times that she visited her husband at his motel room once, in the late afternoon. Almost twelve hours before the crime was committed. We've just found some video from a security camera at the convenience store next to the motel that shows Mrs. Lassiter in her car much later that night."

Maggie felt as if she'd had the wind knocked out of her. "Are you sure it was her car? Are you positive?"

"The model and plates are a match. Mrs. Lassiter can be seen pretty clearly through the windshield, too."

Rebecca's eyes had filled with tears and she covered her face with her hands. Her book bag fell to the ground, the stack of papers covered with large, childish handwriting spilled out, the sheets flying off across the parking lot.

Rebecca quietly sobbed and Maggie put her arm around the young woman's shoulder.

"Detective . . . please. There must be some mistake. Some explanation . . ." She saw a flicker of sympathy in Detective Reyes's dark eyes, but Maggie could see she had come to do her job and was not going to be swayed. "Well, what if she was sitting there? It doesn't mean anything," Maggie insisted.

The officer with Detective Reyes moved forward a step, preparing to take Rebecca's arm and lead her away, Maggie thought. Detective Reyes froze him with a look.

"Rebecca, you really need to come with

us now. It will be much easier if you co-operate," Detective Reyes said quietly.

Rebecca calmed herself and nodded.

"All right. I guess I have no choice."

She slipped from Maggie's hold and walk toward Detective Reyes and her partner. Then turned and looked over her shoulder. "Please call my mom. She'll know what to do."

Maggie nodded and bit her lower lip. She dreaded calling Nora with this news.

Poor Nora. Poor Rebecca.

It was going to be a long night for all of them.

CHAPTER ELEVEN

By the time she closed the shop on Thursday, Maggie was exhausted. She'd stayed close to Nora the night before, well past midnight, while Rebecca was held for several hours and then questioned for several more.

Finally, Rebecca's attorney reported that the police had decided not to charge her. A monumental relief. But Rebecca was still a "person of interest" in the case, Detective Reyes reminded her. Perhaps even more so now.

After working all day on little sleep, Maggie just felt like going home, grabbing a quick bite, and falling into bed. Maybe dozing off while watching the news first. She didn't even factor in knitting, which was rare.

But it was Thursday and her friends were gathering at Suzanne's house for their weekly meeting. Beyond sending a short e-mail, Maggie hadn't found a spare minute all day to update anyone on Rebecca's night in custody. So she felt obliged to join them, even if just for a little while.

Maggie loved the Cavanaughs' big, old rambling colonial. Suzanne had found it and convinced her husband to buy the place before it had even hit the market. It had plenty of space for their big family and "great potential," a classic promise of real estate blurbs.

Suzanne and her husband, Kevin — who had made some money years ago fixing and flipping houses — had not been daunted at all by the state of disrepair. Kevin owned and ran a construction company and renovated houses for a living.

Now, years later, they were almost ready to admit that the house might be finished in time for their retirement years. The classic story of the shoemaker's children going barefoot, Suzanne liked to say. Kevin never had time to work on their own house and never wanted to hire anybody to do the work he could do for free.

But ongoing construction did not hamper Suzanne's hostessing style in the least. She still managed to cook and entertain with great flair and creativity, even if she had to don a hard hat along with her apron.

Tonight there were no acute emergencies.

Just the usual ladders and paint cans in a hallway, and a wall ripped open, Maggie noticed as she walked in.

"Hi, Mag . . . we're back here!" Suzanne called out. She soon appeared in the wide entrance to the great room at the back of the house, the first and most complete addition.

"Wow, you look beat. Late night with Rebecca and Nora, huh?"

"It was long and difficult," Maggie said honestly. "But Phoebe had a big exam today so I had to stay in the store."

"Come sit down." Dana patted a couch cushion. "We'll take care of you. Suzanne, get her a glass of wine."

"Just some tea, please," Maggie said. "Wine might make me nod off right here."

"Not before you tell us what happened with Rebecca. I've been dying to hear about it all day." Suzanne walked into the kitchen, which was separated from the family room area by a big island. Maggie watched her put a kettle on. "Before we get into Rebecca, I wanted you all to know I didn't make a huge dinner. Just a lot of small plates. We're doing tapas night, okay?"

"Sounds perfect to me." Maggie was so tired, she really wasn't in the mood for a heavy meal.

"Your small plates are always better than everyone else's big plates anyway," Lucy said.

That was certainly true. Suzanne could whip up an impressive meal, from pesto to paella, with ease. Including a table setting and cocktails to match.

"Well, we'll see. There are a few surprises . . . You go ahead, Maggie. I'm listening," Suzanne said, bending low to grab some dishes out of the refrigerator. "Did Rebecca really go back to the motel that night? I didn't understand from your e-mail."

Maggie had already told her friends how she'd been standing in the school parking lot when the detectives approached and asked Rebecca to go to the station with them. And why they'd taken her.

"Rebecca did drive back to that area. There's no question about that. But she says she never went to the motel. She says she sat in the car in the convenience store parking lot for a while. Maybe half an hour? Then drove away."

"Is that what the video shows?" Dana asked.

"It shows the car driving off. The problem is that there are no cameras in the motel lot," Maggie reminded her friends. "So the

266

police only have the eyewitness accounts of the night clerk. And the lot isn't very well lit, either. He says that an hour or so after Rebecca was in the convenience store lot, he saw a woman fitting Rebecca's description leaving Jeremy's room."

"Did he see what kind of car the woman got into?" Dana asked.

Maggie shook her head. "He didn't notice. Unfortunately for Rebecca. For all we know, he could be entirely mistaken and this mystery woman was coming out of another room."

"But I'm sure the other guests, in the rooms near Jeremy, were contacted and interviewed by now," Dana said astutely.

"Yes . . . they were. They all deny they had any visitors in the middle of the night. But people will lie about things like that. For all kinds of reasons. They don't understand a young woman's life is at stake. Or really care."

Maggie knew she sounded upset. But she was. She couldn't help it. She was convinced that Rebecca was innocent and could have never harmed a hair on Jeremy's brainy little head.

"That does sound bad," Lucy agreed. "I guess the police can make a case that Rebecca parked somewhere nearby and walked to the motel?"

"Something like that," Maggie agreed.

"But why did she go all the way back, in the middle of the night, and not go over to the motel?"

Suzanne had returned and began to deliver her platters of tapas, which all looked delicious and smelled divine. Maybe I'm hungrier than I realized, Maggie thought, eyeing the ramekin of plump shrimp covered with green sauce, another filled with grilled chorizo, and one with slices of vegetable frittata.

"She wanted to talk Jeremy out of the idea of running away. She had some time to think after the initial shock of finding out he was alive," Maggie said. "At first, she'd agreed to all his instructions, caught up in the moment and happy to do anything for him. But once she really thought about it, she wondered if there was some other way."

She speared a shrimp with her fork and swirled it in the green sauce. The subtle scent of garlic was totally tantalizing as she lifted it to her lips. She paused in her conversation to savor it, then continued.

"I think once Rebecca thought about it, she didn't want to take part in Jeremy's escape plan. Why did they have to lie to everyone? Hurt so many people they loved by running off to some foreign country, living in hiding, with little or no chance of ever returning here? Leaving all her friends and family and the work she loved? Rebecca was just not that type of person. It didn't sit well with her. She didn't even want to get married by a justice of the peace, remember? It was so radically different from everything she'd imagined her life with him would be."

"I can see that," Dana nodded. She was a vegetarian and went straight for the marinated artichoke hearts and the vegetable frittata. "Jeremy's plans were all very much against the grain of Rebecca's character."

Maggie decided to try the chorizo next, though she rarely ate cured meats. It looked too good to pass up and she was too tired to deny herself. She slipped a few bites on her dish and added a slice of crusty French bread on the side.

"Yes, they did go against the grain of her character," she replied to Dana. "Defrauding the insurance company felt very wrong to her, too. No less keeping the secret that he'd survived the lab fire. Dana was right. Faking your own death is a crime, as well," Maggie added.

"Do you think she went over to the motel and had that conversation with him, and left him totally alive," Lucy said, "then someone else came by soon after and killed him?"

"That would explain the desk clerk seeing her there — I mean, seeing some woman leave his room," Suzanne said, quickly correcting herself.

Suzanne set down a few more dishes. The ingredients were getting more exotic, Maggie noticed. A bowl of mussels in what appeared to be a zesty vinaigrette and a platter of puffy, toasty-looking croquettes. She wasn't sure what they were made of, but at this point, it hardly mattered. Everything was so delicious.

"The police asked her that. About a thousand times, I'll bet." Maggie knew how it was to be interrogated. She hated to remember. She took a sip of tea as if to wash away the memory. "They were trying to make her admit she was in his room during the time frame of his death, I'm sure. But she stuck to her story and insisted that she never went back to the motel. She says that at the last minute, she chickened out. Jeremy had made her swear she wouldn't come back. He said it was too dangerous. He didn't want to risk being found, that his life depended on it. Rebecca says that she didn't want to put him in any danger. Or even upset him. She decided she'd call him from school the next day. But of course, by then, he was dead."

"Wait . . . are there any security cameras at her apartment complex? Maybe there's some video of her car coming back, before the time frame of the murder . . . or so close it would have to shed reasonable doubt," Dana added.

Maggie knew Dana was trying to be helpful. And it was a very good point. But she shuddered at the reference to a jury and the terminology. Was Rebecca that close to being arrested?

"Yes, well . . . the problem is that Rebecca didn't go straight back to her apartment. She says she drove around for a while, thinking. Feeling very upset and confused. She wanted to wake Nora up and tell her everything. But she finally decided not to do that, either. It seemed too disloyal to Jeremy. There are security cameras at her apartment complex," Maggie added, finally answering Dana's question. "But by the time Rebecca got back, the police say she could have . . . Well, let's just say the timing doesn't give her an alibi."

"Oh, dear. That makes it even worse, doesn't it?" Suzanne shook her head and forked up a bite of artichoke. "Sounds like she's lucky the police let her go."

"Her attorney convinced them that sitting in a car in a 7-Eleven parking lot is not a crime. Even though there's a sign that says no loitering." Maggie sighed, and helped herself to more of the tasty offerings. She hadn't tried the grilled asparagus spears yet, she realize, nor the sautéed circles of squid. Or was it octopus?

"Suzanne, you've really outdone yourself. This is delicious," Maggie said sincerely.

"It is indeed. A real feast," Dana agreed between bites of asparagus. "A big part of the problem is that Rebecca lied in her interviews," she said. "The police were already looking at her and this may have convinced them she's the one. It's certainly strengthened their case."

"Why did she lie about it? Did she ever say?" Lucy leaned over to help herself to another bite of the chicken-potato croquette.

"Rebecca said she was afraid to tell them. She knew Jeremy had been killed around the same time and didn't want them to suspect her. She didn't get out of the car and didn't think anyone saw her there. So she didn't think anyone would ever find out she'd gone back."

"The real problem is that now the police may stop looking into any other leads and just hone in on her, trying to get more evidence to make a case." Dana knew how these investigations went. But this time, Maggie wished Dana didn't sound half so sure and knowledgeable.

"And make charges stick in court, you mean?" Suzanne said.

"Yes, I guess that's what they're working toward. And the only reason why they let her go," Dana added. "The police need to make a strong case that will hold up in court. So they'll focus on her until they get one. Right now, it's all circumstantial and there's only one questionable eyewitness, the night clerk who saw a woman from a considerable distance, in very poor lighting. A good attorney could very easily make hash out of that in a courtroom."

Maggie realized that, too. "Yes, but if they keep digging and digging . . . Oh, I know she's innocent. I'm sure of it. But I'm worried now. I really am," she admitted.

Dana reached out and put her hand on Maggie's shoulder, but didn't say anything more. Maggie noticed her other friends exchanging concerned glances.

"I'm sorry. I didn't mean to get so emotional. I am very tired." She suddenly felt as if she might cry and knew that wouldn't help anything. "I'm just afraid that Dana is right. If the detectives close in on Rebecca, they may never find the real person who did this."

They were all quiet for a moment and Maggie was afraid that they agreed with her. And felt equally as exhausted . . . and hopeless.

"I think Rebecca is innocent. If the police have stopped looking, we have to keep at it and figure out who really did it. Or at least figure out some angle that gets Rebecca off the hook," Lucy said quietly.

"Lucy's right. There are a lot of loose ends here. What about the break-in at Rebecca's apartment? Do the police think she did that, too? It's just ridiculous." Suzanne shook her head in frustration and finally pulled out her knitting.

The tapas dishes had been so interesting and delicious, and the conversation so intense, no one had made much progress with her knitting tonight, Maggie noticed. But they were all slowly getting to it.

"I know I keep saying this. But all roads lead back to that glue formula." Lucy picked up her knitting, too. She'd gone back to the shrug she was knitting for herself in a pale shade of turquoise.

"I agree. The secret formula is the glue that holds these folks together," Suzanne laughed, paraphrasing the fortune cookie motto.

"That reminds me, I think we should consider Jeremy's family again," Lucy suggested. "I'm not saying any of them killed him. But I think they could shed some light."

"Funny you should say that, Lucy." Dana sat up and started searching her knitting tote. "I was looking through some old e-mails this afternoon and came across this invitation . . ." She pulled out a sheet of paper. "It's a hospital event. I get invited to a lot of them. I hardly ever go."

In addition to her private practice, Dana worked a few hours a week at the local hospital, Harbor General, and had patient privileges there.

"This one did catch my eye," she continued. "The board is honoring a favorite donor. Look who it is . . ."

The sheet came to Maggie first. She peered down at it through her reading glasses. "Patricia Moore. Jeremy's mother. She's being honored for her leadership in helping to bring quality health care to the area and her charitable contributions?"

"That's right. When I called up about it, the woman in the fund-raising office said that Ms. Moore had canceled the appearance due to the family tragedy. Then recently reconsidered, so it's back on. She wants to dedicate a large gift in honor of Jeremy, to build a center for treating pediatric cancer. She's going to announce it at the event."

"That means the rest of the family should be there. Claudia and Alec," Lucy said. "We haven't spoken to either of them yet."

"Don't you think Rebecca is invited?" Lucy asked. "I mean, she is Jeremy's widow."

"Nora said Patricia always liked Rebecca and was happy when they got engaged," Maggie reported. "And Patricia and her children have stuck by Rebecca so far in all this. But maybe this last incident has given them doubts."

"That would be . . . unfortunate," Dana said. She didn't elaborate.

"You mean, if it ever goes to court, it would be to Rebecca's advantage if Jeremy's family was on her side," Maggie filled in for her.

"Well . . . yes. That is true," Dana admitted. "I'm not sure if attending this event will really help us. But why not?" She shrugged. "We might learn something. If only what Patricia and Jeremy's siblings think about Rebecca right now."

"I'd like to go. I think it could be fun. All those rich people, giving away money," Suzanne laughed. "It is amazingly generous. I wish I could do that," she added on a more serious note. "That's where Jeremy must have learned to give back to the community."

"It wasn't from his father. I think we can be pretty certain about that," Maggie said drily.

"What's going on with the investigation into At-Las Technologies?" Lucy looked up from knitting. "Has anyone seen more in the paper?"

"Not a word," Dana said. "But that could mean anything. The other shoe hasn't dropped yet in that situation, either."

"We might hear more about that at the hospital event, too," Maggie suggested. "When is it, Dana? I didn't notice."

"Sunday afternoon, three to five," Dana read off the sheet. She looked up at her friends. "I'm clear. Jack will be out playing golf all weekend. He's ecstatic about the spring weather."

"I have two open houses. But I can sneak over for a little while," Suzanne said.

"Phoebe will be away this weekend," Maggie told the others. "But I can go. How about you, Lucy?"

"Oh, Sunday should be fine . . . I just have to check with Matt."

She'd practically mumbled that last part. But they'd all noticed.

Suzanne actually laughed. "She has to check with Matt. Isn't that cute? I don't think I ever heard her say that before."

"Suzanne . . . stop," Dana warned her. But she was smiling, too, Maggie noticed. "Just ignore her, Lucy."

"I usually do." Lucy sounded a little miffed and made a silly face at Suzanne.

"Oh, my. Look at her." Suzanne laughed. "Hey, just for that . . . no flan for you."

"Wait . . . I was just kidding. You know that. What are you, the Flan Nazi, now?" Lucy sounded genuinely upset and suitably contrite. But Suzanne's flan was worth groveling for. Maggie would have done the same.

"I know . . . I just wanted to rattle your cage," Suzanne confessed. "I'll give you a piece of flan to take home for Matt. I'm sure he's home missing you right now. Does that make up for teasing too much?"

Lucy seemed pleased with the peace offering. Maggie was relieved. This was not a time for her good friends to rub one another the wrong way. They had to stick together, suit up in their finery and high heels, and

278

get out there to help Rebecca.

"Mrs. Messina . . . how nice to see you again." Maggie had been lingering on the edges of the cocktail party, scanning the crowd for her friends, when a familiar voice made her turn.

Lewis Atkins. Looking his usual dapper self, in a navy blue pinstriped suit with a pale yellow vest and red bow tie. She was surprised to see him there. Then realized that any foe of Philip Lassiter's would be an ally of his ex-wife Patricia's.

Their divorce had been especially acrimonious, Maggie had heard from Nora. And so had Lewis's parting from Philip. Nothing like a common enemy to draw people together.

Lewis had always maintained a good relationship with Jeremy and was wealthy enough to support the cause, so his inclusion on the guest list did make sense from that angle, as well.

"Hello, Lewis. You were going to call me Maggie, remember?"

He smiled and nodded. He enjoyed their verbal sparring, no question. "I do remember, now that you mention it."

He took in her appearance and she felt he approved. Instead of the predictable black dress and pearls again, Maggie had opted for a slim-fitting navy blue dress with a V-neck, and her real gold earrings and a bangle to match. The only problem had been, when she pulled on the dress at the last minute, the neckline was a bit lower than she recalled. Or had it somehow stretched out at the dry cleaner? But it had been too late to do anything about it.

For damage control, she'd grabbed a charcoal gray wrap with a touch of angora she'd knitted for herself. It was a perfect décolletage camouflage and a tasteful look for a fundraiser, she thought.

"May I get you a drink?" he said politely.

"I'm fine for now. Thank you. Just waiting for my friends."

"Nora and Rebecca Bailey, you mean?" he asked in that same polite tone.

"Uh . . . no. Some other friends." She left it at that, feeling she didn't have to explain herself to him.

She happened to know that Rebecca and Nora had been invited, but were not coming.

Rebecca felt too self-conscious about all the gossip swirling around her now. She'd told Maggie the attention from the police investigation was making her life very difficult. Miserable, actually. Parents were calling the school, demanding that she be fired. Or, at least, sent on a leave of absence until the situation was resolved. But the school administrators were sticking by her — especially the principal — and she had the teacher's union on her side, too. Maggie was glad she did not cave in to the pressure.

But it was so cruel, Maggie thought. Rebecca was such a wonderful teacher and really loved her work and the children. All she had left now was her job. Would that be taken from her, too?

Maggie did not disclose any of this information to Lewis Atkins. She didn't even consider it.

"How are you doing, Lewis? Any progress in the lab?"

"Progress?" He looked confused for a moment. Then narrowed his eyes and smiled. "On the formula, you mean?"

"You told me you were smart enough to figure it out. I'm just taking you at your word," she said, challenging him.

"Good tactic, Maggie. We men always like to prove ourselves don't we? And brag about it. Maybe I have figured it out. Maybe not," he toyed with her. "This is a time to honor Patricia and Jeremy. Not boast about my accomplishments."

"Very true," she said smoothly.

Was he trying to play the modest type? He was definitely the double-talking type. He had artfully sidestepped a frank answer to her question. Though she hadn't really expected one.

Score one for his side. She'd call it all even.

She noticed Dana enter and waved to her. "Excuse me. There's one of my friends. I'd better catch up with her."

"Sure thing. See you later." He smiled and raised his glass to her for a moment. Two green olives floated in his martini glass. They suddenly looked like two eyeballs watching as she walked away.

As Maggie strolled through the crowd to meet Dana, she took in the large, open atrium where the reception was held, part of a new wing that Patricia Moore had also helped to build.

Maggie had noticed from a sign that the space was normally used as a special lounge for the families of surgical patients. But it had obviously been closed for a few hours for this party.

The glass walls, constructed with abstract-shaped pieces of glass in different shades of blue, were at least two stories high. Tall potted palms and arrangements of exotic flowers made her feel as if she were walking through a greenhouse. One filled with tables of fancy hors d'oeuvres and waiters passing trays of sparkling champagne in fluted glasses.

By the time she and Dana met, they were both holding champagne cocktails and delicately toasted hello.

"Here's to Rebecca. Let's hope this evening helps," Maggie murmured.

"I'll drink to that. Looks like you've already started. Lewis Atkins found you quickly, didn't he?" Dana noticed. "You two seem to have plenty to talk about."

Maggie pulled her stole a little closer. "We were just chatting. Nothing important to report. He's too smart to disclose anything truly helpful. I did ask if he figured out the formula yet."

"My, you're a bold one." Dana smiled at her admiringly.

"Never underestimate the element of surprise," Maggie reminded her.

"Or cleavage," Dana added, her gaze slipping to Maggie's low neckline.

Maggie tugged at her dress, then just closed the stole over her chest again. "It's not that low. Just a bit much for me."

Dana laughed. "What did he say? Did he beat out his rivals yet in the glue race?"

"He gave me some double-talk. I have no

idea. I guess he's not totally dazzled by my charms. Have I lost my touch?"

"You're just getting started, if you ask me," Dana assured her.

Lucy and Suzanne came in together and spotted them quickly. By the time they reached Maggie and Dana, and admired one anothers' outfits, the speeches were starting. They faced forward to watch Patricia Moore receive her award.

She was introduced by the hospital's head of fund-raising and development, who left no accolade unturned.

Jeremy's mother walked onto the stage to a loud round of applause. She shook hands with the woman who had introduced her and stood behind the podium with a modest smile. Maggie thought she was the very picture of quiet confidence, equanimity, and grace.

Patricia looked out calmly at the audience, though a certain shadow of sadness lingered in her features.

"Wow, what a class act. She could play herself in the made-for-TV movie," Suzanne whispered.

Maggie nearly laughed out loud, but restrained herself. As did the rest of her friends, thankfully.

Patricia first recognized and thanked

everyone involved in giving her the award, noting that so many others among the audience would be as worthy, or even more, of the honor. She felt fortunate to be able to play a small part in bringing quality health care to the community, and vowed continued commitment to that cause.

She soon went on to talk about Jeremy, and the generous endowment that would bear his name, earmarked for a new treatment center for pediatric cancer.

"My son Jeremy was a brilliant scientist, who would have been a brilliant physician or perhaps dedicated his career to medical research. That was a dream of his. He even began medical school. But instead of following that path, he eventually chose to enter the family business and serve the community in a different way. By discovering new technologies to improve our quality of living . . ."

"Translation," Lucy whispered, "his father forced him to go into the family business and invent new ways for the Lassiters to make money."

Maggie nodded in agreement, but shushed her all the same.

Lucy's joke was an exaggeration, of course. But not a very large one. Here was another, even more toxic reason why Jeremy wanted to get back at his father. He'd been robbed of his dream, to study medicine. No wonder he prized his part-time teaching post at the medical school. He must have relished being part of that atmosphere. Maybe he even hoped to resume his medical studies someday in some far-off land?

Patricia soon concluded her speech, rallying the audience to join in this worthy cause and become part of the solution. Or some such call to arms with her closing words.

Maggie was a bit distracted by the sight of Claudia and Alec, hovering near their mother. Of course they would be here, too. Maggie doubted she'd be lucky enough to overhear an extended conversation between the two again, but decided to cruise up in their direction anyway, as soon as the speech ended.

Of the three people she guessed Jeremy had been in contact with during his motel hideout — Rebecca, Atkins, and Alec — his twin brother was the only one they had not spoken to yet.

Maggie doubted she'd get much out of him, especially in this sedate setting. But it was worth a try, she thought.

Alec stood a short distance from his mother, shaking hands as people approached, accepting congratulations. Once again his resemblance to Jeremy was stunning. How painful that must be to their mother, Maggie realized. Though in some odd way, maybe a comfort, too?

"Mr. Lassiter, I just wanted to offer my congratulations . . . and my condolences on the loss of your brother."

"Thank you very much . . . I'm sorry, have we met? You look very familiar."

"I was at Jeremy's wedding . . . and the memorial service. I'm a friend of Rebecca and Nora Bailey. My name is Maggie," she added.

"Nice to meet you, Maggie. I knew I'd seen you somewhere. How is Rebecca? I thought I might see her tonight. I'm afraid I haven't been a very good brother-in-law. I should call or visit her," he acknowledged.

"Yes, you should," Maggie agreed bluntly. "She'd appreciate that. And it might help dispel some of the rumors that are flying around town right now." Maggie watched his expression, wondering where he fell on the question of Rebecca's guilt or innocence. "The police seem to think she's responsible for your brother's death. Did you know that?"

"I've heard something along those lines. I don't really believe that, though," he added quickly.

"Neither do I. There's no solid evidence for it. Not a shred."

"I can't see how Rebecca could have done such a thing. What possible reason could there be?" Alec's expression was somber.

"Detectives can always seem to find a reason, however flimsy, when they want to make the pieces fit. Did your brother have any enemies, Alec? Anyone who wanted to do him harm? Who was he hiding from exactly?" She took a step even closer. She couldn't help herself. "I'm only asking this because Rebecca is under such great pressure now from the police. There might be something you know that can help her."

Alec considered her questions. Then slowly shook his head. "I loved Jeremy, but we really weren't that close anymore. I've been out in Santa Fe for years now and I rarely come east. I have zero interest in the family business. Literally . . . and figuratively."

His father had made sure of that. Maggie wondered why Alec had been exiled from Philip's royal court. But that story would have to wait for another day. She would have to ask Nora sometime. She probably knew.

"That happens. Even very close siblings grow apart." Maggie's voice was laced with understanding. "But he did call you from the motel, to tell you that he was still alive. So you two must have had some relationship left."

Alec, who had just sipped from his flute of sparkling wine, stopped midswallow. He coughed and covered his mouth with his hand a moment.

"How do you know that?" he asked in a low tone.

"Oh . . . I just know. That's not the point. I think you may have even visited him there, too. No one would have recognized you. They would have mistaken you for Jeremy."

Alec stared down at her, starting to look annoyed, she thought. Had she gone too far?

"I can only tell you what I told the police. I never went there. I never saw him alive after the lab fire."

"All right . . . but why did he call? Did he just want to talk to you? Did he ask you for help? Was someone pursuing him?"

"I wish he had asked for help. He might still be alive," Alec said sadly.

"I'm sorry to press you like this," Maggie said honestly. "But I feel Rebecca's fate is fragile right now."

He nodded and sighed. "Yes, I understand. But I can't think of anyone who could have found him there and harmed him." Maggie saw his glance dart away for a moment, back to his mother. Patricia was talking with Lewis — a relaxed, friendly conversation.

"Not even because of the formula he'd been working on?" Maggie pressed again.

Alec's glance snapped back to meet hers. She sensed he could tell what she was thinking — Lewis Atkins had a strong motive to harm Jeremy. Even if he had a good alibi for the night of the murder. Lewis might have hired someone to pressure Jeremy to give up the information but the coercion got out of control.

Alec shook his head. "If you mean Uncle Louie, you're totally mistaken. Uncle Louie loved us. Especially Jeremy. He doted on him. He could have never harmed him."

Maggie had gotten that same impression. But now she wasn't so sure. The equation seemed to boil down to Lewis Atkins. No matter how many ways she tried to add it up.

"The only person Jeremy was trying to escape was my father. And probably the federal investigators who are swarming all over At-Las Technologies right now. I think Jeremy was trying to duck out the back door before the ax fell." He sighed and glanced over at his sister. "Now Claudia is left holding the bag. Which would be laughingly ironic if it wasn't so unfair. She's the only one of us who truly loves the business. But Philip never gave her any respect or credit. No Y chromosome. Too bad for her."

Maggie could easily see that. She and her friends had speculated about most of Alec's disclosures. But it was different hearing it from him. It confirmed their hunches, which was important.

"Now, if you'll excuse me, please, I have to join my mother and sister for some photographs. It's been interesting talking to you, Maggie. Good luck," he added.

Maggie quietly thanked him. As she watched him walk away, she wondered if he would ever make good on his promise to visit Rebecca. Or if that was just fine talk, what he knew she wanted to hear. She wondered how deep Alec Lassiter's sincerity reached, once you scratched the surface of his smooth manner.

Turning away from Alec, Maggie noticed that Dana was talking to Patricia Moore, and Suzanne and Lucy were in a group, chatting up Claudia.

Her friends knew how to work a room, didn't they? Maggie was pleased. There would be a lot to discuss on the ride home, and with any luck, a few more insights and clues to help Rebecca.

CHAPTER TWELVE

Maggie heard sirens. Sirens and alarms. Everything was going off at once and she jumped out bed, fumbling for the lamp on the bedside table but only succeeding in knocking it over.

She ran out of her bedroom with her feet bare and downstairs, sniffing the air for smoke. The siren was even louder in her house, but now she could tell it was the burglar alarm. A small light was on in the kitchen, over the stove top. She quickly looked around the living room. Everything looked normal. Had someone broken in? Was someone in the house right now?

And what was that other noise, outside? It sounded like a car alarm . . . her car.

But before she could check the driveway, she heard the phone ring and ran to the kitchen to answer it. It was the alarm company. Maggie quickly gave them her password. Her heart was beating so fast in her chest, she could hardly speak.

"Yes, the alarm went off . . . but I don't see anything strange . . ."

"We have a report from sensor number fifteen. That's a window in the back of the house on the ground floor," the operator told her. "Do you want to check? I can hold on."

"All right, I'll take a look," Maggie said reluctantly, walking to the family room at the back of the house. "Are the police coming? I hope you've called them . . ."

"The police are on their way, ma'am."

"Well, that's some reassurance if there's a burglar in here," she mumbled. She quickly peeked into the room, flashing on the overhead light with one hand without actually stepping through the doorway. The windowpane was broken, she noticed, but the window was not raised. As if someone had started to break in, but changed his mind.

She explained this to the operator. "Okay, ma'am. I've made a note. You can shut the alarm if you like. I'll hold on."

The operator spoke in a patient tone. It calmed Maggie down a bit. She didn't think an intruder could get in a broken window. Could he?

She put on more lights and turned off the

alarm. Then she heard a knock on the front door and saw flashing lights through her living room window. It was a police cruiser.

"The police are here. Thank you for staying on the line with me," she told the operator.

She grabbed a rain jacket off the coat tree and pulled it on over her nightgown. She opened the door and faced two young male officers in uniform. One was tall with fair hair. He reminded her of the boys in high school who went out for basketball. The other was shorter and stockier, with a weight lifter's biceps and bulky neck to match.

They stared back at her, both holding big flashlights.

"Mrs. Messina?" the weight lifter said. "Your home alarm went off?"

"Someone tried to break in the back window. I'll show you," she offered, opening the door. "Maybe they tried to steal my car, too," she added, shouting over the alarm.

"I don't think that's a problem, ma'am," the stockier officer replied. "Did you see your car yet?"

Maggie shook her head. Something in the officer's expression told her she needed to take a look. She stepped out of the house and quickly looked in the driveway. The tall blond one helpfully slanted his flashlight at her car.

Someone had been working hard while she had been asleep, she realized. Her little green SUV was covered with shaving cream, broken eggs, and a massive tangle of yarn, stuck in handfuls all over the mess. As if that wasn't enough, a trash bag — or two — had been ripped open, the unsightly, rank contents poured all over the hood, windshield, and roof. All four tires had been deflated and a sheet of white paper, like a huge parking ticket, was stuck under a windshield wiper.

At first she stood stone still, taking it all in. The smell alone was totally nauseating. She didn't realize that she was barely breathing and shaking uncontrollably until she tried to take a step or two forward, to see what was on the note.

She was about to pull it out from under the wiper arm when the dark-haired officer stepped in her way.

"That's evidence, Mrs. Messina. We need to leave it there for now," he explained.

"Yes, I understand." Still, she couldn't help leaning over as far as she could without brushing her jacket on the mess. No small feat. But she could manage to read it. It had been written in large block letters with a black permanent marker, which compensated considerably for her lack of reading glasses.

time to clean up your own mess, maggie. stay out of everyone else's. or you'll be very sorry.

Even the note stunk. As if the vandal had purposely rubbed it in something particularly foul-smelling.

"Can you shut off your alarm with a remote?" the tall officer asked.

"Oh, yes . . . of course. Just a minute." The sound had been going on so long, she hardly noticed it. Odd how that happened. She was sure her neighbors did, though. She noticed more than a few lights on in the houses nearby, though it was somewhere around three in the morning.

She found her remote inside the house, then quickly shut off the car alarm from her front step. Then she walked down to talk to the weight lifter officer, who seemed to be in charge. He already had his pad out to take her report. She would ask him to call Detective Reyes, she decided. The sooner this incident was connected to Jeremy's murder investigation, the more it would help Rebecca.

Lucy had gotten up early and was just about to start painting the bedroom when Maggie called. She and Matt had moved all the furniture to the middle of the room before he left for work, but she still had a lot more prep to do.

Lucy nearly let the message machine take the call, but the distress in her friend's voice was alarming. She ran to the phone and Maggie quickly told her about the car being trashed and how the police had come at three in the morning.

"I went back to bed for an hour or two. But I couldn't sleep. Detective Reyes is on her way over. She should be here any minute," Maggie added.

"I'm on my way, too," Lucy said and hung up without waiting for Maggie to reply.

She was definitely dressed for dirty work, she realized as she grabbed her keys and ran out to the driveway. She drove to Maggie's house and parked on the opposite side of the street. Lucy saw a blue-and-white police car and a gray sedan parked right in front of the house. Two uniformed officers were in the driveway, circling Maggie's car, which looked like an unbelievable mess and smelled even worse than it looked. A Hal-

298

loween prank gone over the top, Lucy thought.

One of the officers took photographs and the other made notes.

Maggie stood in the driveway also, closer to the garage, talking to Detective Reyes. Lucy recognized her right away.

The detective looked the same, her long dark hair pulled back into a tight ponytail, wearing a conservatively cut navy blazer, gray slacks, and sensible heels. Medium height, slim and strong, she was Lucy's exact idea of a female detective, projecting an air of calm intelligence and professionalism.

Nothing like the women in law enforcement so often seen on TV — actresses who looked more like runway models, chasing the bad guys in five-inch heels, wads of glamorous hair swirling as they whipped out firearms and hit their target every time.

From what Lucy had seen, police investigation was slow, often frustrating work. Distinctly unglamorous and more intellectual than physical. With few car chases or shoot-outs involved, either. Though Detective Reyes, with her fit figure and perfect posture, looked prepared for any of those possibilities.

At least Maggie was able to deal with a

familiar face about all this. Though Lucy was sure the entire bizarre situation was very upsetting.

"I understand, Detective. I really do. But we're all so concerned about Rebecca Bailey," Lucy heard Maggie saying as she approached. "It seems to me your investigation is narrowing in on a totally innocent young woman and ignoring so many other possibilities."

Detective Reyes gave Maggie her full attention, her leather-bound notepad in one hand, a pair of used plastic gloves in the other.

"I know you're concerned, Maggie. But you must sit back now and let us do our job. That note is right. You're putting yourself, and your friends, in danger."

Maggie didn't answer. Lucy couldn't tell if she was taking the police officer's advice to heart. Or just waiting her out.

"We're going to give this incident a very thorough look and see how it might be connected. Consider yourself lucky. It could have been worse," Detective Reyes added in a serious tone. "I'm assigning a patrol car to watch your house for a while. Cruise by a few times during the night. Until the investigation is concluded."

"Oh . . . that's not necessary. Really,"

Maggie argued with her.

"I think it is. I'm sorry, you don't have too much say about it, Maggie. It's our job to protect you."

Detective Reyes gave Maggie her card. "Please call me for any reason at all. And just a tip, it's best to get that egg off the car ASAP."

The detective spoke to the uniformed officers for a moment, then they all got back into their cars and drove away. Lucy looked over at the Subaru again. She could not recall a more putrid-looking nor more foul-smelling mess.

Maggie joined her, covering her nose and mouth with her hand.

"Seen enough? Let's go inside. I can't stand looking at it, or smelling it anymore."

While Maggie made a pot of coffee, Lucy searched on the laptop in the kitchen, looking for the best way to remove egg from a car.

"I've heard it is bad for the paint," Maggie said, pouring them each a cup of coffee. "But I don't think I've ever had to deal with it. Maybe once, long ago, on Halloween."

Lucy found the answer and showed it to her. "Vinegar and water. We should have guessed. The universal cleaning solution."

Maggie peered down at the screen through

her reading glasses. "Detective Reyes was right. It says to clean it off right away or it will damage the paint. I have to get all that trash off first. It might be too late anyway," she murmured. "I really need to take some pictures for my insurance company. I hope I have some paint damage coverage."

A short time later, they were outside wearing plastic gloves and carrying trash bags. Maggie kept telling Lucy to go home and do her work. But Lucy couldn't leave her with the hideous mess.

"At least Phoebe is there to open the store," Maggie said as they started on the car. "Monday mornings are slow. I think she can handle it."

"I'm sure she can. She puts on a good space-cadet act. But she's pretty responsible." Lucy picked off bits of garbage and placed them in her bag. "Any ideas who did the job on your car?"

"Oh, I have a few," Maggie pulled off a chunk of egg-soaked yarn and dumped it. Lucy had a few theories, too, but wanted to hear Maggie's first.

"I'd have to put Lewis Atkins at the top of the list. Just because he's the only one who warned me, face-to-face, not to meddle. I had to tell Detective Reyes that, of course. Now she'll have to go talk to him."

Lucy could see Maggie felt embarrassed about that. But what could she do? Maggie hadn't gone running to the police right after their conversation. But this was different.

"I thought you were tending to believe what Alec Lassiter told you, that Lewis loved Jeremy and never could have harmed him."

Maggie worked quickly, picking off the garbage and spoiled yarn, Lucy noticed. But she paused and shook her head, her short brown curls bouncing around her face.

"See, that's the thing. It all gets muddled. I do believe Alec. I heard Lewis talk about Jeremy with my own ears, at the memorial service, in such a tender, loving way. It is hard, if not impossible, to believe Lewis would have tracked Jeremy down and harmed him. Or even hired someone to do it while he sat and enjoyed an opera." Maggie sighed, looking at a hunk of shaving-cream-soaked yarn. "I'm not even sure this trick-or-treat-type trashing is his style. He seems too neat and methodical a person. Though whoever did this car may have ransacked Rebecca's apartment. Even Detective Reyes had to admit the two incidents might be connected."

"We keep forgetting about Erica Ferris," Lucy reminded her.

"Yes, out of sight but not out of mind. She does hate knitting or anything even vaguely connected. Maybe this masterpiece is her artistic statement . . . yarn combined with garbage and rotten eggs?"

"I know what you mean. I was wondering the same thing."

Lucy heard a car approaching and turned to see Suzanne's huge SUV turning into the driveway. She parked behind Maggie's car and jumped out from behind the wheel. Dana hopped out the other side.

They were dressed in their oldest jeans and sweatshirts, Lucy noticed. Suzanne waved bottles of white vinegar in both hands, as if she were bringing vintage wines to a picnic in the country.

"We're here . . . with vinegar to spare. I bet you don't have nearly enough."

"We haven't even gotten to the vinegar yet." Lucy stood back from the side of the car she'd been working on. "We're still picking off the litter."

"Didn't the police take it away, as evidence?" Dana looked perfectly serious asking the question.

"They took a few samples. That's all they needed to track the forensics of this" — Lucy pulled up a bit of trash with her rubber-gloved hand — "old spaghetti?"

Suzanne drew closer and peered at the specimen. "Looks like linguine to me. Whole wheat, I'd say."

Maggie rolled her eyes. "Thank you, Watson. I'll have to call Detective Reyes later and tell her that. Maybe she can trace the garbage to an Italian health food restaurant. I don't even buy whole wheat linguine." She looked over at Suzanne and Dana again. "You guys didn't have to come over like this. I appreciate it, really. But shouldn't you both be at work now?"

"I don't have any appointments until the afternoon," Dana replied. "Besides, we couldn't leave you alone with this, once Phoebe told us what happened."

"I told her not to sound the alarm," Maggie said. "I didn't want to bother everyone."

"I have today off. Just some follow-up calls to make," Suzanne said. She looked over at Maggie's car. "What a mess. This is the handiwork of a truly sick puppy."

"Couldn't have said it better myself." Dana pulled some plastic gloves from the box sitting on the lawn and handed a pair to Suzanne. "Do the police have any idea who did it?"

"Not that they were willing to share with me," Maggie said. "But we have one or two," she glanced at Lucy.

"I had a feeling you would say that." Dana made a queasy face, wiping off a handful of gunk from the tailgate. "Let's spin some theories, ladies. It will distract us while we work."

With all four of her friends working, cleaning Maggie's car did not take nearly as long as Lucy expected. The scent of the white vinegar solution was almost as bad as the trash smell, but in a different way. Most of the egg came off, but the paint was damaged in spots. It made Maggie's car look like a camouflaged vehicle.

"You can go undercover much easier now, Mag," Lucy told her.

"There's always an upside, if you look long enough, right?" Maggie said drily. "But don't tell Detective Reyes," she added.

After the cleanup, Suzanne and Dana headed off to resume their postponed schedules. Lucy went home to shower and change, then returned to Maggie's house to drive her into the village. The car was cleaned off, but the tires were still flat. A roadside assistance service was coming and Maggie was pleased to hear they could make the repair without her being home. She decided to cover the back window with a wooden board and leave that repair for another day.

Maggie's house was a long walk into town and she was tired from the ordeal during the night and the cleanup. Lucy didn't mind the extra favor. She was too distracted to get any real work done in the afternoon anyway.

When they reached the shop, Nora Bailey was waiting.

"Maggie, I'm so sorry about your car. What an ordeal." Nora gave her a quick hug. "Rebecca and I feel responsible. It wouldn't have happened if you weren't trying to help her. Please let us pay for the repairs. We really want to do that," Nora insisted.

"Don't worry, Nora. My insurance might cover all of it. It's not your fault or Rebecca's. I think the blame falls squarely on the nut job who came over last night."

"Well . . . that's true. But you know what I mean," Nora sat on the love seat in the small side room, and took out her knitting.

Lucy sat in an armchair nearby and leafed through a new knitting magazine with spring patterns and projects. She was almost finished with the shrug and wanted to try something new.

"Alec Lassiter called last night. He and Rebecca talked for a while. He said he'd felt bad about not being in touch lately. Some-

307

thing about being a bad brother-in-law." Nora shook her head. "He said he met you at some fancy party and you made him feel guilty."

"Oh . . . I didn't mean to . . . Well, maybe I did a little," she admitted.

Maggie had slipped on her glasses and was going through the mail. Phoebe was in the back helping a customer choose yarn to fit a pattern she had out on the worktable.

"I only said it would help tamp down some of this nasty gossip if he and his family stood by Rebecca right now. And people could see Jeremy's own family believed she was innocent."

"It would help. But I think the Lassiters have their own worries. Alec's sister and father probably need his help right now even more than Rebecca does. Have you seen the newspaper this morning? Oh, you must have been too busy," Nora said.

Lucy put the magazine in her lap and looked over at Maggie. She had a copy of the newspaper in her hand, along with the rest of the mail. She put down the envelopes and unfolded the paper.

"It's on the second page, I think . . ." Nora put her knitting aside and walked over to Maggie, so they could read the article with her. Lucy did the same.

Maggie quickly opened the paper and found the news article. "Here it is . . . a big headline. 'Investment Scandal Rocks Mighty At-Las.' "

Maggie held out the paper so Lucy could read it, too. Nora had already seen the news and stood by waiting.

The article reported that an emergency board meeting was being held that morning. " 'It is expected that Philip Lassiter will be ousted as the chairman and CEO. The move comes in reaction to his alleged mishandling of investments earmarked for research and development of a new resin product, touted as a miracle adhesive,' " Maggie read aloud in a shocked tone.

" 'An investigation, mounted by federal authorities, is expected to be completed within hours. Sources close to the investigation predict Philip Lassiter will be charged with luring investors into a pyramid, or Ponzi-type scheme, over the past two years or more. The elaborate scheme included false financial statements and earnings reports on bogus advanced sales of an adhesive product that the company claimed was not perfected yet but already in demand.' "

Maggie looked up at them, sounding breathless. "I can't say that's a complete surprise. Jeremy's brother told me last night the ax was about to fall. Sounds like it's coming down right now."

"And heads are rolling," Lucy finished for her. "So Philip is a mini-Madoff, after all. Does it say anything more about the glue formula?"

"Let me see . . ." Maggie scanned the article again, which she hadn't completed. "Wait . . . here's something. 'Philip Lassiter's son Jeremy Lassiter invented the formula but had not finalized the product for production and marketing at the time of his death.' Not that anyone knows of," Maggie added. She took a breath and continued.

" 'Claudia Lassiter, vice president of operations and marketing, maintains that the company can produce the product, but the staff is still trying to reconstruct her brother's records and laboratory notes.' "

Maggie sighed and looked up at both of them. "Just like Alec predicted. His sister is left to shoulder all the responsibility. Look down here." She pointed to the bottom paragraph. "Philip Lassiter is in the hospital again. '— admitted late last night,' " she read aloud, " 'and according to the family, is being treated for a chronic stomach ailment.' "

"That's the second time in a month. He

310

went into the hospital right after Jeremy's memorial service," Lucy recalled.

"That's right. He was there when Jeremy was found in the motel," Nora added.

"Do you think the company can survive this?" Lucy looked at Maggie and then at Nora.

"It sounds like Jeremy's father will be arrested," Nora said. "There will be a trial. And the company will have to pay back all the people they've cheated."

"Which will probably push At-Las all the way under. The company must be leveraged and running at a loss already. Why else would Philip go to such lengths to bring in more cash?"

"He believed it was all going to be paid back, and more. When they started selling the new glue," Lucy reasoned. "If Claudia can finally figure out the formula, maybe she can salvage something."

"If she's not sent to jail first, you mean," Maggie said quietly. "She may be involved in this, too. We don't know. It's very complicated. But clearly another dark day for the Lassiters."

"I don't know much about either of them, Alec or Claudia," Nora said, returning to her knitting. "They both treated Rebecca well. I don't wish them any harm. As for

Philip Lassiter, I think he'll get what's coming to him. What he's dished out to everyone else his entire life — including his own children. And that is nothing good."

Nora was the first person Lucy heard voice that prediction. But hardly the last. The town was buzzing with the news of Philip Lassiter's downfall. There were few, if any, sympathizers.

"Schadenfreude," Matt observed one night during dinner. "Taking pleasure in someone else's pain. Especially your enemy's. People do like to see the high and mighty knocked down to size."

It was not pleasant to watch, but true, Lucy thought.

Of course Edie Steiber visited Maggie's shop to brag about how she was approached by the bogus investment offering, but between her tingling big toe and her big gut, she wisely turned down the opportunity to be robbed blind. "Like the rest of those poor suckers. Seniors like me, mostly."

The following days brought more news. Lucy read the articles each morning, before she spread the newspaper out on the floor for her painting project.

Claudia was arrested in her office and led from the building in handcuffs. There was even a photograph, though her head was ducked away from the camera. Philip was also arrested, right in his hospital bed. But his medical condition was far more serious than the family had revealed.

The truth was finally disclosed. He was suffering from stomach cancer, which had been kept hidden from the public for more than a year. He was in the last stages and there was nothing more to be done. He confessed that there was no glue formula. Jeremy had not completed it before he faked his own death. Philip was sure it could be perfected and had pressed his son to continue the research so he could satisfy his investors and save his company.

But Jeremy had given up and tried to escape the entire mess. And had nearly succeeded, Lucy thought, reading the latest report in the newspaper.

It was very doubtful Philip would live to stand trial. Police officers were posted outside his room. Not that he presented any great flight risk, Lucy realized. But there were so many enraged people in town who might do him harm. Investors who were cheated out of hundreds of thousands of dollars, a life savings for some of them.

All for the promise of cashing in big on the miracle glue.

But there was little mention of the missing formula in the latest news reports, Lucy noticed.

Lucy finally took a break from painting on Wednesday afternoon. All she had left was a second coat on the molding and doors and she was home free. She washed what she could from her hands and face, but didn't bother changing her splattered jeans and sweatshirt before heading out to Maggie's store.

It was a full-blown spring day, no doubt about it now. She'd been working with the windows open but feeling the warm sun on her face and breathing in the fresh air was a world of difference from the paint smell.

Even Tink and Walley had a bounce in their steps today. Though walking down to town went a bit slower with the two of them — two noses stopping to sniff at every opportunity.

She tied them on the porch of the shop, noticing a big splotch of paint on Tink's tail.

"Tink . . . what did you do? How am I supposed to get that out, cut your tail off?"

The dog stared up at her, already working on her chewy bone. All Lucy could think of was what she might have smeared in the house with her tail swinging around like a giant paintbrush.

She had wanted to check out yarns and patterns for a new project today anyway, an afghan that would match the new wall color in the bedroom. She had forgotten a paint chip, but at least she had Tink's tail.

"Welcome back, stranger," Maggie greeted her. "Are you still painting the bedroom?"

"It's almost done," Lucy reported. "I needed to use primer and two coats. We're covering a dark color with a light one."

"Sounds like a professional job. It's hard to find a woman who's handy around the house. I hope Matt appreciates that."

"Oh, he does." Lucy smiled and quickly changed the subject.

"Speaking of paint jobs, any word from the insurance company about your car?"

Maggie's Subaru looked like a large spotted reptile with wheels. She was mortified to drive it and had to get a new coat of paint or a new car, no question.

"I just called Detective Reyes and left a message. Seems the insurance company wants another case number or police report or some other official document for the claim. They never stop asking for more information. I think it's a ploy to tire you out and get you to give up on collecting

315

your money."

Lucy agreed. She'd jumped through those hoops herself.

The shop phone rang and Maggie checked the number. "Oh, this could be her right now." She picked up and greeted the detective. Then sat listening for a moment, her expression changing to surprise and concern.

"Really? I don't know what to say. I'm shocked. I spoke with him a few times and had some suspicions. But now that you say it, I can't believe he's the one . . ."

Maggie caught Lucy's gaze and held it, still listening to the detective. She covered the phone with her hand. "Lewis Atkins . . . the police went to his house on a tip . . ."

But suddenly she was drawn back to the conversation with Detective Reyes. "Yes, I will do that. I promise. Thank you for letting me know, Detective."

Maggie hung up the phone and shook her head in disbelief. "It's just so . . . surprising."

"What did she say? Did they arrest him for Jeremy's murder?" Lucy walked over to the counter where Maggie stood.

"Not exactly. Sounds as if they'd like to . . ." Maggie paused and took a breath. "They got a tip to look in a shed on his property and found Jeremy's iPad, the one Rebecca says he had with him in the motel room and was not found after the murder."

"Oh . . . that's pretty damning." Lucy was surprised to hear that about Lewis Atkins, too. There was something about him that she liked. Maybe it was the bow ties. He just didn't seem like he'd ever hurt anyone.

"But someone could have just planted the iPad in the shed. That wouldn't have been very difficult, right?" Lucy said.

"That's what Lewis claims happened. But the police got a warrant and searched his house, and found a lot of items from Rebecca's apartment. Apparently, he was the one who broke in."

"Wow . . . that sort of nails it, doesn't it?"

Maggie sighed. "It seems so."

"Has he said anything in his own defense, or tried to explain any of this?"

"I don't know. Detective Reyes didn't get that far and I didn't want to nudge her. I was surprised she told me anything about it. But she knew that I'd hear it from Rebecca and Nora. And she did say it practically tied in with my car vandalism, so she didn't feel it was inappropriate to include me in the news."

"Did Atkins admit to vandalizing your car, too?"

Maggie shook her head. "He completely denies it. He even laughed. He did say I was smart but nosy, and probably deserved it."

"Oh . . . really? That's a lot of nerve."

"It is, isn't it? He didn't mince words. That's probably why I liked him," Maggie admitted. "I guess we'll hear more from Dana. Let's fill her in right now. She'll tell Jack to check in with his precinct pals. With any luck, by tomorrow's meeting we should have the whole story."

Maggie was right. As usual. By Thursday night, Dana was ready to tell them the whole story about Lewis Atkins's apprehension and confession.

It was Lucy's turn to host the meeting, but with the boxes from Matt's move still cluttering up the cottage and the painting supplies filling up the rest, her friends gave her a pass.

They met at Maggie's shop instead, and Lucy brought along the dinner she'd planned for them — sautéed arugula, tomatoes, white beans, and grilled shrimp. Lucy thought it was a nice spring recipe and hoped her friends agreed.

Phoebe was at a class and was coming late. They were sorry she was missing the big story, but they couldn't wait to hear

Dana tell them what she'd heard about Atkins's arrest.

"All right, here's the scoop," Dana began soon after she'd sat down and pulled out her knitting. "You all know the police went to Atkins's house on an anonymous tip. They found the iPad in a shed, hidden in a bag of birdseed. Atkins denied he'd put it there. Or that he'd ever seen it. They had a warrant and searched his house, and found all the stolen belongings from Rebecca's apartment in his basement."

"What did he say about that? Did he deny ransacking Rebecca's house, too?" Suzanne sounded huffy, personally insulted, Lucy thought.

"He made a full confession. He admitted that he was looking for notes about the formula, of course. Some hidden note or secret message Jeremy had scribbled to himself. Or a memory card or flash drive stashed somewhere. He said he was really desperate to get his hands on anything and had given up on trying to figure out the combination of chemical chains himself."

"But Philip Lassiter just confessed that there is no formula and Jeremy never finalized it. That's why he was pressing him so hard," Lucy reminded the others. And why Jeremy's father may have pressured the young scientist into faking his own death, she thought.

Dana tilted her head to one side, neatly casting a series of stitches for a new project. "Atkins is convinced that Jeremy had lied to his father about that. Atkins believes Jeremy did complete it and had it with him when he died. Or had hid it somewhere. In fact, he's certain of it. He said it was just something in Jeremy's voice when he called him and tried to sell him the formula. A certain cocky tone he only used after a big scientific success. But, just as he told Maggie, he didn't trust Jeremy to sell him the real deal."

"Yes, that's what he told me. That's why he said he was trying to figure it out on his own," Maggie recalled.

"Atkins says that Jeremy didn't leave the real formula at At-Las, either," Dana added. "That's why Claudia and her staff were pulling their hair out, trying to put together his notes and backed-up files and replicate it."

"He might have even left a completely false set of lab notes there. Just to throw them off the track," Lucy said.

"That's right, Lucy. Like many people at that level of intelligence, he was capable of being very deceptive," Maggie observed.

"The police are still holding Atkins. But

he vehemently denies killing Jeremy. He claims he was only after the information but didn't find it in anything he took from the apartment. He also said he couldn't hurt Jeremy and claims that he loved him."

"Well . . . it wouldn't be the first time. 'You only hurt . . . the one you love . . .' " Suzanne sang a few phrases of the old standard, in her airy, off-key voice.

"Thank you, Tony Bennett," Maggie replied quietly. "Rebecca already told us Jeremy didn't have a chance to hide anything in the boxes of yarn or the container of knitting tools Atkins stole. She said all of that wasn't in her apartment until after the lab fire."

"True, but did Jeremy hide a memory card in something else? Something that wasn't in the apartment when Atkins broke in?" Lucy asked. "How about the wedding gown?" she said suddenly. "With all those folds of lace, Jeremy could have easily tucked something into a seam, or in the hem line?"

"That's brilliant, Lucy." Dana looked at her friend with awe.

"It is a clever insight," Maggie agreed. "I thought of that, too. Right after the break-in. I checked every stitch of the gown before I gave it back to Rebecca. I didn't find a thing . . . Go on, Dana. You were saying

321

something else about Atkins?"

"The iPad seems to be enough physical evidence to link him to the murder. And there is a record of at least two phone calls between the men while Jeremy was at the motel. But Atkins has been forthcoming about that. So far, that's all they have. No fingerprints in the room and he has a good alibi. They've only charged him with breaking into Rebecca's place."

"I guess if they keep digging, they'll find something," Lucy said. "Maybe someone at the motel will remember seeing him that night. Or seeing someone he hired to go after Jeremy?"

"Maybe not. I'm still not convinced he did it, or was behind it." Maggie's voice was quiet but firm.

"Really? I thought he was at the top of your list," Suzanne reminded her.

"Atkins has wandered around my list, from top to bottom and back again since I met him," she admitted. "I just feel there's some missing element we're not seeing. Something the police aren't seeing, either."

"Like the missing ingredient in Jeremy's formula?" Suzanne prodded her.

"Yes, just like that, now that you mention it. It doesn't mean that there isn't one. Just because nobody can figure it out."

Maggie had gone into her stubborn mode, Lucy noticed. It would be hard to convince her to change her position now, short of a signed confession from Lewis Atkins. And even then, she might say it was coerced by the police or the signature forged.

"Speaking of witnesses at the motel, what about the mysterious woman who was seen leaving Jeremy's room? The one the police were so sure had to be Rebecca." Maggie looked up from her knitting at Dana. "What do they say now about that bit of evidence? Where does that fit in with Atkins?"

"They are not saying much, Maggie," Dana replied. "I guess if Atkins is ever brought to trial his defense attorney could use that eyewitness to muddy the prosecution's case." Dana wore a small smile. "Is your big toe tingling, like Edie Steiber's?"

"It is," Maggie insisted. "Maybe the condition is contagious."

Lucy began to clear away the dinner plates and everyone else soon got up to help. The arugula and shrimp dish had been a hit. But Suzanne's dessert — a gorgeous tart — definitely stole the spotlight. Plump red raspberries in perfect rows sat on an airy pink filling. It looked like something out of a magazine, too pretty to eat. Though Lucy

323

knew they would force themselves to enjoy it.

"How do you whip this stuff up?" Lucy asked. "You could work in a fancy bakery."

"I could," Suzanne agreed. "But after a few weeks, I'd be trapped in there. I wouldn't be able to fit through the door. No, it's much better if I make this stuff and my friends eat it."

Suzanne was doing just that, serving the slices of tart to her friends when the shop door opened. They all turned, expecting to see Phoebe, coming in from her late class just in time for her favorite part of the meal.

But it was Nora Bailey. Maggie had mentioned earlier that she was coming by after dinner, to sit and knit a while. They all welcomed her as she took a seat near Maggie and took out her knitting.

"Nora, good to see you. You're just in time for dessert." Maggie pushed her things aside to make more room for Nora's yarn and pattern. "Suzanne made something with berries. It looks delicious."

"It's a tart with berry mousse. I can't believe I found raspberries at this time of year. But I had to buy a whole bunch. I couldn't resist them."

"It sounds wonderful. I'll just have a tiny taste, though," Nora said, accepting a sliver on her plate. "Rebecca cooked a big dinner for us tonight. Then she went out with a friend from work. She's feeling so relieved now that the police have arrested Lewis Atkins. She's moved back to her own apartment, too."

Atkins was arrested for the robbery, Lucy wanted to clarify. Not Jeremy's murder . . . yet. But she didn't want to seem so nitpicky. Nora was obviously so happy and relieved herself.

"I'm glad for that." Maggie's tone was sincere, Lucy thought. She was happy that Rebecca was off the hook. They all were.

"Everyone at school is singing a different song, too," Nora reported. "Her class finally put on their play and all the parents who came apologized to her. Well, not all, but a lot of them did," Nora reported with satisfaction. "It was really an adorable little show. I went over to help with the refreshments and take some photos."

She dug around in her knitting bag and removed an envelope, then took out some photos, which she showed to Maggie first.

"Rebecca was the wolf. The kids loved that . . . and here's her principal. He surprised the kids and dressed up as Little Red Riding Hood. He really brought the house down . . ."

Lucy watched Maggie nodding, stitching away, eyes glazed over as she looked at the photos, a sagging smile on her face. Maggie had seen her share of school plays, that was for sure. Another version of that classic tale, even with a surprise star turn by the school principal, could not impress her very much.

"Can I see?" Suzanne eagerly reached for the photos. "I loved it when the kids were in little plays at school. They're all getting so big now," she said. "Though Natalie says she might join the theater club next semester. She's a wonderful dancer, too. She's really got the Broadway bug."

There was no more conversation about Lewis Atkins, or speculation about his guilt or innocence. Perhaps they all felt self-conscious with Nora there, Lucy realized. She seemed so sure that Atkins was guilty and so happy her daughter was no longer a suspect, no one had the heart to consider other possibilities.

It was just as well, Lucy thought as she drove home that night. There was no final answer to this question. They would just have to wait and see if the police came up with more evidence that linked Atkins to the murder. Or, if he confessed. Which was also a possibility.

She knew where Maggie stood. But

thought her friend's usually clear judgment was clouded on this one. He was charming and smart and she was probably even a little attracted to him. Though she'd never admit that. Not even to her good friends.

CHAPTER THIRTEEN

Lucy didn't think she'd be returning to the knitting shop the next day, but she was out doing errands and needed to change the yarn she'd chosen for the new afghan. Tink's tail had not been the best way to match the paint color and the shade was a bit off.

When she went in, Maggie had just finished teaching a class, Birds of a Feather, again, which was turning out to be very popular. The student knitters strolled out together, chatting, some of them already admiring their newly knitted amigurumi birds.

Lucy walked to the back of the shop, where Maggie was clearing the table, putting away needles and bits of polyester filling.

"That class turned out to be a hit. The town is going to be filled with those little birds."

"It's going viral, as the kids say," Maggie agreed. "It would be great advertising for me. If only they were knitting little black sheep."

"I think that could catch on. You just have to figure out the pattern."

Maggie nodded. She seemed distracted. A bit edgy, too, Lucy noticed.

"Listen, I have to change that yarn I bought for the afghan. I need a different shade. It didn't match the new paint that well."

"No problem. You know where everything is." Maggie swept some tiny clippings of yarn off the table with her hand. "What color did you finally agree on? You never said."

"Sort of a wheaty, golden shade. I think the paint is called Amber Waves." Who names this stuff, Lucy always wondered. That was a job she'd like to have someday. "It's not as cheerful as the yellow I wanted. But it's not Matt's Vulture Egg blue, either."

Maggie finally smiled at her description of the compromise.

"Sounds very warm and cozy. Bedroom colors are important. Sets the tone for . . . a lot of things."

While Lucy sifted through the baskets of yarn, looking for her color, Maggie went over to the counter and pulled out a folder. "Come here a minute, I want you to look at something. Tell me what you think."

Lucy left the yarn and walked over. "Is something bothering you, Maggie? You don't seem yourself today."

"Something is bothering me. Look at these pictures a minute. Nora left them behind last night." She took out the photo that showed Rebecca's class play. Even the children on stage were doubled over with laughter at the sight of the school principal dressed as Riding Hood.

There were a few photos that included him, facing the audience and standing with his back turned. There was one where he raced across the stage and swatted at the big, bad wolf with an umbrella.

"I don't remember Riding Hood chasing the wolf away. But that's a very empowering ending for little girls," Lucy remarked with a smile. "He's quite a comedian, isn't he?"

"Yes, the classic type, going for the broad laugh one minute, crying the next. Take a look at this photo," she said, pulling out another.

Lucy recognized the scene, Rebecca and Jeremy's wedding. It was a picture Suzanne had taken of the flower girl. "Look in the background. Do you see him there, sitting on the aisle?"

Lucy realized she was supposed to be looking for the school principal again and found him easily. This time his face was covered with his hands, his head bowed as he sobbed. He looked bereft, as if he was sitting at a funeral.

"Wow, he looks so sad. He's not just, you know, moved by the wedding and all mushy the way Suzanne gets."

"No, he's crushed. His heart is broken, Lucy." Maggie picked up the other picture again, from the class play. "I bet he felt a lot better when he heard that Jeremy had died in the fire and Rebecca was a widow. But when Jeremy popped up, alive again, and he'd lost his second chance, Stewart Campbell had to do something about it," Maggie concluded. "I think that Stewart, dressed in his Little Red Riding Hood wig and an old coat and maybe one of Rebecca's knitted hats that she donated to the costume box, was the mysterious woman who visited Jeremy at the motel . . . and took his life."

Lucy stared at her, then looked back at the photographs. Could it really be? It seemed so . . . absurd. And yet, when she looked at the photos and considered everything they knew, it did seem plausible. The pieces fell into place.

Even more so than Lewis Atkins murdering Jeremy over the formula.

In fact, all that rivalry would have provided the perfect screen for the crime.

". . . and I'll tell you another thing I found out today," Maggie added, looking even more sure of her hunch. "I called the school district food service and asked if the cafeteria at Rebecca's school ever served whole wheat linguine." She smiled. "The lady on the phone said that they had it on the menu very recently. In fact, just in time for the leftovers, packed in the cafeteria trash, to end up on my car."

Lucy stared at Maggie and blinked. "How did you ever figure that out?"

Maggie shrugged. "I knew the car smelled like something so familiar to me — beyond the rotten eggs. And I looked at the photos of the play again this morning and thought about that multipurpose room at the school where the stage is. That room's also used as a cafeteria. It all came together for me then. Even trashing the car that way is a childish expression of anger, don't you think?"

"I think you're right. Have you told anybody about all this? Have you called Detective Reyes?" Lucy asked quickly.

"I called a little while ago, before the class. She heard me out. But didn't say much. She told me to scan the photos and e-mail them, and she'd look into it."

"Oh . . . that's sort of deflating. Here I am, thinking you just broke the case wide open and she'd rush over to the school and drag him out in handcuffs."

Maggie shrugged. "I think she will follow up. In her thorough, methodical way. It's just not like it is in the movies, Lucy."

But only a few hours later, Maggie found out that Detective Reyes had proved her wrong. The able detective's police work was very much like the movies.

Nora Bailey called Maggie that night, just a few minutes before eleven, and told her that Rebecca and a group of friends from her school had been out at a Mexican restaurant in town, helping Rebecca celebrate that the police had arrested Atkins. Nora named a hot spot where Maggie knew the margarita happy hour was a popular Friday-night draw. She could imagine the scene.

"They'd just sat down to dinner when two police officers came in and arrested Stewart Campbell. They took him out of the restaurant in handcuffs, saying he'd murdered Jeremy. Rebecca was so upset. No one can believe it. There must be some mistake,"

Nora insisted.

Maggie didn't know what to say at first. She wondered if she should tell Nora that she had instigated this shocking turn of events.

"I don't know what to say, either," she answered honestly. "What did the police say? Did Rebecca hear anything?"

"She went to the station and tried to help him. She called his wife, Pam. She was terribly angry at Rebecca, for some strange reason, and said some really hurtful things . . . Oh, I don't understand anything."

Maggie sighed. "Nora, I think Stewart had an intense attachment to Rebecca. It's not impossible to imagine that he resented Jeremy . . . and may have even been happy when it seemed Jeremy was killed in the fire and Rebecca was single again."

"No . . . do you really think that?"

"I do," Maggie said sadly.

But before Maggie could explain what she'd seen in the photos, Nora suddenly said, "I'm sorry. I have to go. That's Rebecca on call waiting. I need to talk to her."

"That's okay, Nora. I'll talk to you tomorrow."

Maggie hung up, greatly relieved. By the time she spoke to Nora tomorrow, perhaps Stewart will have made a full confession.

She wouldn't doubt it. He didn't look like the type who would stonewall. Just the opposite, in fact.

Maggie had just opened the shop on Saturday morning when Detective Reyes walked in. Wearing Saturday-looking clothes, Maggie noticed: a sweatshirt, jeans, and sneakers, in place of her usual tailored pants and blazer.

"I was on the way to my daughter's soccer practice and just wanted to stop by a minute," she explained.

Maggie had never pictured her taking time out from solving crimes to be a soccer mom. But today she certainly looked the part. "Are you the coach?"

"Just an assistant. That's enough work." She smiled, then looked serious again. "We took Stewart Campbell into custody last night. You'll read about it in the newspaper anyway, so I'll tell you now. He confessed to killing Jeremy and even vandalizing your car."

Maggie took a breath. She wasn't surprised, but after feeling puzzled by this for so long, it all seemed to fall together so fast.

"I did hear late last night that the police took him in for questioning. Nora Bailey called me. She was shocked, of course," she added.

"So was Rebecca. She never suspected a thing." The detective caught herself. She said a bit more than she'd intended, Maggie realized. She checked her watch and stuck her hands into her sweatshirt pockets. "Well, I have to run. I just wanted to tell you that and thank you for your input . . . though I'm not encouraging any more knitting club involvement in murder investigations. I hope you understand that."

Behind her stern tone, Maggie detected a note of good humor. Or she hoped she did.

"I understand, Detective." She nodded contritely, though she didn't promise it wouldn't happen again. Knitters had to do what knitters had to do.

Detective Reyes took a step toward the door and paused. "I'm still wondering . . . how did you put that all together? I have to be honest, it was staring me right in the face. And I didn't see it."

"Oh . . . I'm not sure. I didn't see it at first, either. But I did spend time at the school one afternoon and had seen Stewart in a costume. Maybe it just stuck in my subconscious or something. There was always something a little off about him. Something that made my big toe tingle," she added with a grin.

"Your big toe?" Detective Reyes asked in her serious way.

"That's just a joke around here. Never mind." Maggie shook her head. "Have a good game. I hope your girls win. If they want to knit any uniform accessories in team colors, let me know. I'll give you all a good discount."

"Thank you, Maggie. I'll keep that in mind."

A few minutes after Detective Reyes left the store, Phoebe walked in. She'd been at her boyfriend's house but was on time for work today . . . almost, Maggie thought.

"You just missed Detective Reyes," Maggie told her. "The police questioned Stewart Campbell last night and he confessed to Jeremy's murder."

"Wow . . ." Phoebe's sleepy, slacker expression was suddenly alert. "That is so totally weird. What did he say? Why did he do it? How did Stewart even find Jeremy?"

Maggie started setting up for a class and put out a basket of round needles. "Good questions. She didn't let me in on any of that. Maybe she's not allowed to go into the details."

"Right . . . but Dana always can. Is she

coming over this morning?" Phoebe asked eagerly.

"Not that I know of, but I can always call her." Maggie smiled and picked up the phone. "She has yoga this morning," she recalled, "but maybe she'll drop by right after."

Dana happily agreed to drop by and she did have the scoop about Stewart's confession. It was a big break for the county detectives and everyone in law enforcement in town was talking about it. Jack had already heard a lot of the details during an early-morning golf game.

By the time Dana arrived, Lucy and Suzanne were at the shop, too. They often stopped in on Saturday afternoon, just to hang out and knit a while, so Maggie alerted them to Dana's visit.

"We might as well get together all in one place, at one time and hear the last chapter of this saga. When I don't have anything going on here with real customers," Maggie said.

Dana strolled in, still in her yoga outfit, with a take-out bag from her favorite health food café.

"Well, here I am. I normally don't like to talk about negative things right after yoga. Definitely ruins the mood. But the class was even talking about Stewart Campbell. I guess this is big news," she said as she took a seat.

"I just had my hair done. The salon was buzzing," Suzanne reported. "Everybody's heard that he did it. But nobody knows how and why and all that. What's the story, Dana? Was he madly in love with Rebecca? That's what Maggie thinks."

"Something like that. I wouldn't call it love. More of an obsession. He and Rebecca were friends in college. They dated briefly. She decided it wasn't working for her, but they remained friendly."

"Bad idea, right there. That never works out." Suzanne shook her head.

"Suzanne, please, let her finish? And it can work out. Sometimes," Maggie added.

Dana glanced at both of them. "So time passes, they end up teaching in the same district and become friendly again. Or at least, cordial acquaintances. Eventually, he's promoted to principal and transferred to her school. Last year, I think that happened. By now he's married to Pam . . . and unhappy. Rebecca is single, and Stewart decides he's still in love with her. Maybe even more so. But Rebecca meets Jeremy, right under Stewart's nose. There's a whirl-wind courtship and before Stewart can get his act together to win her over again, she's engaged to be married —"

"— and Stewart has lost out again," Suzanne finished for her.

"Exactly. Which is why he looks so heartbroken in those wedding photos," Maggie reminded them.

"But when he heard Jeremy was killed in the fire, he believed he'd been given another chance. He would be there for Rebecca, show her how much she needed him, how she really belonged with him anyway. That was his plan," Dana told the others. "It was going along fine. Until Rebecca got the text from Jeremy and found out he was alive."

"How did Stewart find out about that text message? Did Rebecca tell him?" Lucy asked.

"No, she didn't tell anyone. But Stewart had been sitting next to her in the teacher's lounge. They were having lunch and he noticed her reading a message that disturbed her. A short time later, she came to his office and claimed to have a migraine, and said she needed to leave for the day. He was very solicitous, of course, but sensed that something was up. He followed her when she left the building. He told the police he just wanted to make sure she got home all right . . ."

"Yeah . . . right. Tell me another one." Phoebe rolled her eyes.

"Of course, he followed her to the motel and caught sight of Jeremy there," Dana continued. "He says he went back that night, intending to just talk to him. He claimed that he had no idea what Jeremy was up to. But it was already a crime to fake his death and he didn't want to see Rebecca dragged into something that would ruin her life, too." Dana paused. "He was angry about that. I guess in some way, he felt he wanted to protect her. Or defend her. He said Jeremy didn't deserve her or care about her. He was an egomaniac, and all he really cared about was his glue formula."

"Well . . . he had a point there. Jeremy was obsessed with the glue formula at the end. That much is true," Maggie agreed quietly.

"So? They fought over Rebecca and Stewart killed him?"

Dana squinted a bit. "He didn't explain it exactly that way. Jeremy told Stewart that Rebecca was going to leave the country with him and he had to stay out of it. He offered to pay him for his silence. Which really put Stewart over the edge. They fought and Stewart claims Jeremy was trying to kill him, so he wouldn't give him away. He

341

claims he strangled Jeremy as self-defense."

"He can say anything he likes now." Lucy shrugged. Her afghan was coming along nicely, Maggie noticed. She liked this second yarn color better than the first, too.

"Well, not exactly. There's forensic evidence that will support or refute certain aspects of Stewart's story. Just the marks the scarf left on Jeremy's neck for instance. They might show that Jeremy was strangled from behind. Which is rarely the case in a situation of self-defense."

"That's right, Dana. I never thought of that." Maggie was eating her lunch, too — some lentil soup she'd brought from home. "So he must have tried to make it look like a break-in, or a robbery? The police said initially Jeremy's cash and watch were missing and some other items. And the iPad, of course."

"Yes, that's what he did. When he realized Jeremy was dead, he panicked. He took whatever valuables he saw around the room and messed it up a bit. Then he dashed out. That's when the desk clerk saw him, mainly from behind."

"Still in the wig and long coat? Gee, what a nut job." Suzanne shook her head.

"Yes, I think he said the wig had fallen off, but he stuck it back on. Detective Reyes got a warrant last night and found the wig and coat at school. He returned them to the costume box. Stupidly," Dana added. "Fibers from Jeremy's scarf were found on the coat and Riding Hood's velvet gloves. No surprise there, of course."

"So this all would have worked out for him, actually, if he hadn't chosen to disguise himself as a woman. Who the police then suspected was Rebecca. She was the last person he wanted the police to go after," Maggie reasoned.

"Exactly. As the investigation began to focus on her, he got more and more rattled. Now he was going to lose her again and it would be his own fault. So he reasoned out the next best suspect in the situation and planted the iPad in Atkins's garden shed," Dana told them.

"Did he know Atkins had broken into Rebecca's house and had all her stuff in the basement?" Suzanne asked.

Dana shook her head. "That was just blind luck. But the police thought they'd finally nabbed the killer. Atkins had plenty of motive. He also knew Jeremy was alive after the lab fire and where he was hiding."

"No wonder Stewart was out celebrating in Margaritaville last night," Suzanne replied.

343

"Celebrating too soon," Lucy added.

"He should have played the wolf instead of Riding Hood," Phoebe observed.

"It's all . . . well, such a tragedy, really." Maggie shook her head. She kept thinking back to the night Rebecca had been in the shop, trying on her gown. How happy she and Jeremy had seemed together. Their whole lives ahead of them. It didn't seem possible that it had all gone so wildly off the rails. With so many lives broken in the aftermath.

"Not for Lewis Atkins. I bet he's a happy man today. I bet he's out celebrating tonight," Lucy predicted.

"He looks too classy to pick some blender drink joint with a DJ." Suzanne glanced at Maggie. "So you were right about him after all, Maggie. He didn't do it, just like you said."

Maggie shrugged. "I had a hunch, that's all." But she was secretly pleased that hunch had proven to be true.

"So Jeremy wasn't murdered over the glue formula," Lucy said. "That's what we all expected. That's what we were all looking for. That's why we didn't see what Maggie saw. It wasn't about the glue after all."

"In fact, it seems as if there is no formula. Despite what Atkins says. Nothing was found on the recovered iPad, or any of the belongings stolen from Rebecca and Jeremy's apartment. The Lassiters haven't been able to come up with it, either, and they have the most resources and information. You might say the quest for that formula ruined that entire company. Now that Claudia and her father are facing trial, the entire place has been shut down," Dana pointed out.

With all the focus on figuring out Jeremy's killer, Maggie had lost track of the scandal at At-Las. But it sounded as if it was proceeding just as she expected.

"If there ever was a formula, it looks like the secret was lost with Jeremy," Dana concluded.

Maggie nodded. "That might be true. Unless Lewis Atkins can figure it out someday. It seems to be his grand obsession."

"He's got the rest of his life to work on it," Lucy said. "Maybe we'll read in the newspaper one day that he finally solved the puzzle."

"Maybe we will. The newspaper prints good news, too, sometimes. Doesn't it?" Maggie asked her friends.

Of course, that question required no answer.

■ ■ ■ ■

Maggie heard from Lewis Atkins much sooner than she'd expected. He appeared in the doorway of the shop later that day. Once again, just before she was about to close up.

"Lewis . . . what are you doing here?" She stared at him, unable to hide her surprise.

"I came to thank you, of course. I heard how you helped the investigation and got me off the hook, Maggie. You should be very proud . . . and I am truly grateful."

"I'm just glad to see the right person arrested. But I am glad I helped you," she admitted.

"You did. In two ways, in fact. While I was stuck in jail, staring at the blank walls, having nothing to think about but how I might be stuck in there for the rest of my life, the police kept asking if I'd strangled Jeremy. They kept showing me the picture of him. With that . . . that scarf Rebecca made for him, all around his neck."

He gestured with hands around his own neck. She could tell it was very difficult for him to describe this. But he needed to, for some reason.

He took a breath. "Then they'd put me back in the cell, to think some more. You know, trying to force a confession out of me." He paused and looked at her. "And it came to me. Where Jeremy recorded the formula. It was just like . . . a bolt from the blue . . . from all the colors in the rainbow. That boy, he had some amazing mind."

Lewis looked down and shook his head. Maggie thought for a moment he might start crying. But finally he looked up at her and smiled again.

Then it hit her, too. "The formula was in the scarf Rebecca made him," she said quietly.

Lewis nodded, his head bouncing like a bobble-head doll.

"That's right. Every time he took a step forward in his research, he'd ask her to make a scarf. The colors were all coded, for different chemical chains . . . well, it's hard to explain if you don't know a lot about chemistry. But that last scarf he had on, the one he wore everywhere. It wasn't just because he loved Rebecca so much. That was the one that holds the complete, final formula. I got the police to show me the picture of it one more time, just to make sure. I memorized the color sequence and wrote it down. It wasn't too hard to crack Jeremy's code because I already know most of the formula. It all works out. Perfectly."

He blinked at her, his small brown eyes bright and sharp under his shaggy eyebrows.

"Lewis . . . I'm so happy for you." If anyone deserved the dubious honor of carrying on the glue legacy, it was Lewis Atkins. No question.

"What next? Will you apply for the patent now?"

"Well . . . I'm not sure. I have to think it over. The scarf actually belongs to Jeremy's widow, Rebecca. To me, that means she owns the formula. Technically. Though the police will hold the scarf as evidence," he added. "She still has the pattern Jeremy wrote down for her. But it's unlikely she would have ever understood its significance without me. I've already told her what I discovered. We'll work it out I suppose."

"I'm sure you will." Maggie was impressed. The race to figure out the formula seemed so intense, even cutthroat. But it wasn't really about the profits, was it? Not for Lewis. For him, it was mainly about the intellectual challenge.

"That sounds fair," she added.

"I try to be." He cleared his throat and adjusted his bow tie. "Solving the puzzle, that's the main thing for me. I don't know what I'll do with myself, now that I figured this one out."

"I have a feeling you'll think of something. Maybe you should take up knitting," she said jokingly.

He stared around at the array of yarns and supplies. "Maybe I should. Then I can disguise all my secret formulas," he quipped.

EPILOGUE

"I like the guitars, Lucy. Nice touch." Dana glanced around the living room, taking in the new decor. Lucy couldn't tell if she was teasing or not.

"It was either in here or the bedroom. But the guitars were a deal breaker." Lucy gazed up at the collection that hung over the fireplace, still wondering if they looked as bizarre as she'd first thought. "I'm actually used to them by now. Which really scares me."

"You have to compromise when you live with someone. No question," Dana reminded her.

"How true," Suzanne agreed. She was already sitting on the couch and took out her knitting. "And once things calm down a little, you can quietly move them into another room . . . and then out to a garage sale."

Dana gave Suzanne a look, but Lucy

laughed. She wasn't sure that would ever be true. But the advice gave her hope.

Phoebe was appalled. "A garage sale? Are you crazy? Those babies are classics. They're really worth something."

"Matt seems to think so," Lucy said.

"Yeah, I'm sure he does," Suzanne rolled her eyes. "Whoops — I hope he isn't hiding out in the next room or something. He's going to think we're terrible." Suzanne looked suddenly self-conscious. A rare state indeed, Lucy realized.

"All clear. He's meeting a friend for some racquetball and dinner," Lucy said.

It was Thursday night and Lucy's turn to host their weekly meeting. There were still piles of unpacked boxes around, but she didn't want to put her friends off forever. She'd never told Matt he had to vacate. It had been his idea entirely, but probably a good one — at least for this first time, when her friends were critiquing their combined decor with such enthusiasm . . . and volume.

There was a quick knock on the front door and Tink jumped up to investigate. She didn't bark at all when Maggie walked in. Just sniffed her leg, looking for a pat.

"Sorry I'm late, everyone. I got held up at the shop." Maggie brushed aside the dog with one hand and handed Lucy a foil-covered dish with the other.

"What this? You didn't have to make dessert. It's Phoebe's turn."

"They're oatmeal cookies. Rebecca just dropped them off at the shop." Maggie put her coat on the rack near the front door and joined the others, carrying her knitting tote.

"You just saw Rebecca? How is she?" Dana put her knitting aside and slipped off her glasses.

"She'd doing all right. All things considered. She's decided to take a few months off. She didn't want to go back to the same school where she'd worked with Stewart."

"Understandably. But didn't she have tenure there? That's hard to give up," Suzanne said.

"She's inherited so much money, her job security doesn't matter anymore. She's still committed to teaching and wants to continue in some shape or form. She might go out west to a reservation. Or to Central America and do service work someplace where teachers are really needed."

"Wow . . . now I know that girl is special. If I ever inherited a pile of loot, the last place you'd find me is in some muddy village in the middle of nowhere. I mean, that's what a checkbook is for. Sending donations."

Lucy had to laugh at Suzanne's honest, unedited reactions.

"Won't she be called to testify at Stewart's trial?" Dana asked.

"She told me she probably would be called, if there is a trial. Stewart can still decide to plead guilty and forgo a trial. His lawyer is working on a mental health angle," Maggie added.

"Oh, he like *totally* qualifies for that one." Phoebe gave a little fake shiver for effect. "Stalking Rebecca and dressing up in drag to kill her husband. How crazy can you get?"

"Actually, a lot crazier," Dana said knowingly. "If he has no other history of mental health issues, that evidence might not convince a jury. He might be smarter to work out a plea deal with the prosecutor. How would Rebecca feel about that, knowing he killed Jeremy and might get a reduced a sentence?"

Maggie took out her knitting. "She knows that could happen and doesn't want to see Stewart suffer. She says it won't bring Jeremy back and she's convinced Stewart is a sick man. She feels very sorry for him and blames herself in part for what happened. By being so friendly and never realizing he harbored deep feelings for her."

Dana seemed distressed to hear that.

"That's too bad. She can't hold herself responsible for Stewart's actions. Even if he'd been totally honest about his romantic hopes. Which he was not."

"I told her that," Maggie said. "She's been seeing a therapist to help her deal with all this, so I'm sure she's heard it already. It's going to take time for her to process things, and move on. She's decided to stay with Nora for now, until she feels better and knows what she wants to do. Nora has been through a lot, too," Maggie added, sympathizing with her friend. "But she feels so relieved that Rebecca has been exonerated and is happy to have her home again, at least for a little while."

Lucy was sure that Nora must be counting her blessings right now. She couldn't imagine what Nora would have done if the police had brought charges against Rebecca. Thankfully, it had never come to that.

"What about the formula? Did Rebecca mention Lewis Atkins?" Lucy asked.

"Yes, she did. She said they'd agreed that Lewis could bring the glue to the marketplace and they'll share the proceeds, fifty-fifty. Generous, I thought, considering that Rebecca owns the formula," Maggie added.

"I bet she's totally sick of glue by now," Phoebe piped up. "I bet she can't even stand hearing the G-word. No wonder she wants to run off to some distant place, where they probably don't even have glue."

"I think you're right, Phoebe. I'd feel the same by now, too," Lucy agreed. "What about her in-laws, the Lassiters? I saw on the news that Claudia and her father are out on bail right now, but will have to stand trial in a few months. If her father lives that long."

"Rebecca didn't have much to say about them. She still has a good relationship with Patricia, Jeremy's mother, and his brother, Alec. But she's had no contact at all with Claudia or Philip Lassiter in weeks, practically since Jeremy's funeral. His second funeral," Maggie clarified.

"Now that she's gone into business with Lewis Atkins, producing the prized miracle glue, I doubt they'll ever speak to her again," Lucy predicted.

"Unless it's through lawyers. I wouldn't put it past the Lassiters to go after Rebecca and Lewis Atkins, and accuse them of stealing the formula. Even if Claudia and Philip end up behind bars," Suzanne predicted.

"I hope Rebecca doesn't have to deal with that, too," Dana said. "But I guess stranger things have happened."

"Speaking of strange things, I have another

tidbit to share. This one is quite unexpected," Maggie warned them.

"Wait, let me guess. Lewis Atkins invited
you out on a date . . . to the opera in fact,"
Suzanne embellished. "And you couldn't
find it in your heart to refuse. Especially
since it turns out that he's not a murderer
after all, but in fact, a brilliant scientist and,
potentially, a millionaire."

Everyone turned to look in Suzanne's
direction. Lucy was the first to speak. "Wow,
what a scenario. That was positively . . .
inspired."

Lucy thought Maggie might be annoyed
by Suzanne's teasing, but she looked
amused.

"I'm sorry, Suzanne. That is not what I
was going to say. But if he did invite me to
the opera, I guess I would accept," Maggie
admitted. "As long as it wasn't Wagner.
Meanwhile, I was going to tell you that
Erica Ferris sent me an e-mail. It turns out
she's decided to take up knitting after all
and wants to sign up for her free classes."

"Oh, give me a break. I think she's just
too selfish to let go of that big knitting tote
she won," Suzanne said.

"Could be," Dana agreed. "Or maybe all
that gorgeous yarn and the shiny new
needles made her curious and she couldn't

resist at least trying it. Another victory for you, Maggie."

Maggie shrugged, but she did look pleased with herself, Lucy thought.

"You know me, ladies. Just trying to make the world a better place . . . one knitter at a time."

"And doing a pretty good job," Lucy said.

"And solving a crime, or two, on the way," Dana added.

"With a little help from your friends." Suzanne smiled and looked around at everyone.

"That about covers it," Phoebe concluded. "So, what's for dinner?"

NOTES FROM THE BLACK SHEEP KNITTING SHOP BULLETIN BOARD

To all my dear friends and fellow knitters —
The new Birds of a Feather Knit Together class had so much interest, we're full up for this month's sessions. Sorry if you wanted to try it. I'll be posting a schedule for more classes soon. Please put your name on the waiting list next to this note.

In the meantime, here's the link to the pattern for those adorable birds in the shop window. I made the Bluebird (though it doesn't need to be blue, of course) and the Chubby chirps. You'll also find instructions for a dog, dinosaur, monkey, frog, and turtle. These small, fun projects — called amigurumi — make a unique little gift. Or a nice way to amuse a child on a rainy day instead of turning on the TV or video games. Babysitters and grandmas, take note :) Here's the link: www.allfreeknitting.com/knitted-amigurumi.

I'm so glad to see the real birds have

returned and everything is starting to bloom again. But that's no reason to put aside your knitting. There are so many spring project ideas and bright new yarns on display at the shop.

Our knitting group had great success with an easy, wraparound shrug. A simple, flattering design, and the long, crisscross belt adds interest. Do you have a wedding or formal event coming up? This shrug is a great cover-up for an off-the-shoulder gown or dress. Or you can make a whole set for a bridal party, like we did. But that's another story entirely. . . . Here's the link: www.berroco.com/exclusives/embrace/embrace.html

Let me know how it turns out. Happy spring and happy knitting.

Maggie

NOTES FROM THE BLACK SHEEP KNITTING SHOP BULLETIN BOARD

Hey, Everyone —

Fast, easy, tasty dinners (and healthful wouldn't hurt, either). That's what I'm looking for now that I have to cook a real meal *almost every night!* (No more goofing off with scrambled eggs or cold cereal. Rats!) Matt cooks for us, too, on his assigned nights. And yes, everything is going along amazingly well. Why didn't we think of this sooner?

The knitting group loved this recipe and everyone wanted a copy, so I decided to post. If you don't want to use shrimp, you can use chicken or chicken sausage. Or just add some extra beans, which supply good protein all on their own. Some wholegrain pasta will make it a heartier dish, if anyone in your house is extra hungry.

Let me know how you like it.

Lucy

ARUGULA WITH TOMATOES, WHITE BEANS, AND SHRIMP

2–3 tablespoons olive oil

1 large or 2 medium-size yellow onions, enough to make 1 1/2 cups (or use a red onion, if you feel adventurous)

3–4 cloves garlic, peeled and chopped

1 pound shelled and deveined shrimp (pat dry with paper towel before cooking)

1–1 1/2 cups grape (or cherry) tomatoes, cut in half

1 large can (14–17 ounces) cannellini beans, drained (don't rinse)

6–8 cups arugula, washed (about 12–15 ounces, or two bags or boxes)

salt and ground black pepper

1/2 tablespoon thyme, oregano (to taste)

1/2–1 cup low-sodium chicken broth (optional)

1–2 wedges fresh lemon

1 cup cooked whole-grain pasta (optional)

Heat 2 tablespoons of oil in large flat skillet

or wok-style pan. Add onion and sauté a bit, then add garlic. Cook 1–2 more minutes until onion is soft and clear. If it's getting brown, turn down heat.

Add shrimp. Brown on both sides and sauté until shrimp is cooked through. Raise heat (add 1 tablespoon of oil, if necessary).

Add tomatoes and beans. Cook until tomato is warm and soft, another 2 minutes or so. Right before serving, add arugula in handfuls. The greens will wilt and cook down. (Beware: If the dish sits, they will virtually disappear.)

Season with salt, ground black pepper, thyme, and oregano. If the mixture seems dry, add a little broth. Squeeze in fresh lemon juice to taste. You can also serve with a cup of cooked whole-grain pasta.

Dear Fellow Chocolate Addicts —

Did you hear the news? Chocolate is now officially a health food. I'm not kidding.

I can't make this stuff up. I didn't need a scientist to tell me it's good for my mental health, that's for sure. If I don't meet my daily requirement . . . well, let's just say it's not pretty. But enough of my semisweet, or even dark, confessions.

If you're like me, and chocolate is one of your three basic food groups, this cake will deliver your daily dose, and then some. And it's also gluten-free. How healthy can you get?

Lucy is famous for this recipe. But I actually gave it to her a few months ago. Look what happened. She's practically engaged. Yes, I'm taking credit for the cake and that, too. Just wanted to share the magic . . .

Suzanne

FLOURLESS CHOCOLATE CAKE

6 tablespoons butter
5 ounces good-quality semisweet chocolate
4 eggs, separated
1/4 cup granulated white sugar
optional toppings: cocoa powder, confectioners' sugar, fudge sauce, raspberries

Preheat oven to 350 degrees. Prepare a 10-inch springform pan: grease inside surface and cover bottom with circle of parchment paper.

In a double boiler, melt butter and chocolate (see note below). Stir until smooth and blended. Pour into a large mixing bowl and set aside to cool.

Beat egg yolks with a whisk or fork. When chocolate mixture has cooled completely, beat egg yolks into chocolate mixture with a whisk or fork. (If chocolate is not completely cool you'll get lumps.)

Pour egg whites into a mixing bowl and

add 1 teaspoon of the granulated sugar. Beat with an electric mixer until foamy. Add the remaining sugar slowly and continue to beat until egg whites stiffen and form peaks, about 2 or 3 minutes. Carefully fold egg white mixture into chocolate–egg yolk mixture. Make sure white and chocolate are mixed but do not overblend, or egg whites will fall and cake will be too dense.

Pour into prepared pan and bake for 20 minutes. Check to see if cake needs more time. Sides should be cooked and pull away from pan, but a toothpick or sharp knife inserted in middle of the cake should be a little damp. Do not overcook.

When cake is done, cool for about 15 minutes on cake rack. Then slip a sharp knife around edge of pan to loosen and remove outer ring of pan. Invert cake on a dish and remove parchment paper. Cake can be dusted with cocoa powder or confectioners' sugar before serving. Or can be dressed with fudge sauce and a few raspberries tossed on top.

If you are serving this cake for a special occasion, you can decorate by wrapping a wide satin ribbon around the rim of the cake and placing small flowers on top or on the side of the platter.

Note about double boiler: If you don't

have a double boiler, make one with a small pot placed into a larger pot of boiling water. Or use a heatproof glass or metal bowl. Take care that none of the boiling water splashes into the chocolate mixture or it will seize.

ABOUT THE AUTHOR

Anne Canadeo is the bestselling author of more than thirty books, including the other novels in her popular Black Sheep Knitting Mystery series, *While My Pretty One Knits; Knit, Purl, Die;* and *A Stitch Before Dying.* As Katherine Spencer, she also writes the Cape Light series. A novice with needles, she finds many similarities between knitting and writing — inspiration, persistence, and good things happening by accident. She lives in Northport, New York. You can contact her at anne@annecanadeo.com or visit her on Facebook.

The employees of Thorndike Press hope you have enjoyed this Large Print book. All our Thorndike, Wheeler, and Kennebec Large Print titles are designed for easy reading, and all our books are made to last. Other Thorndike Press Large Print books are available at your library, through selected bookstores, or directly from us.

For information about titles, please call:
(800) 223-1244
or visit our Web site at:
http://gale.cengage.com/thorndike
To share your comments, please write:
Publisher
Thorndike Press
10 Water St., Suite 310
Waterville, ME 04901